Praise for The Wayward Spy

The Wayward Spy by Roger Croft is not your James Bond–type of spy thriller. Croft is more the John Le Carre–type writer with a heavy mix of Graham Greene. International intrigue, twisted plots, and spy craft all make for an interesting read...Michael Vaux is a very likeable character that readers are pulling for from the start—and there is just enough humor to keep this book a fun read.

—*Portland Book Review*

Croft deserves credit for building his story line on an unusual foundation.

—*Publishers Weekly*

Our protagonist Michael Vaux is not a career intelligence officer—he's a retired journalist, independent-minded, and seemingly never without a drink in his hand...The plot is elaborate and takes the reader down countless blind alleys. But the reader would be hard-pressed to foresee the final outcome.

—*Pete Willows, Egyptian Gazette/Mail, Cairo*

The Wayward Spy takes the best of spy novels from the likes of Le Carre and kicks it up a notch...Wayward this spy might be, but I found I couldn't put the book down.

—*San Francisco Book Review*

At the heart of this espionage story is the brewing nuclear arms buildup that could disrupt the balance of power in the Mideast...Syria is preparing to complete a multibillion-dollar arms deal with Russia—and Michael Vaux's old college friend is Syria's top arms negotiator.

—*Rudd Review*

Croft's book is cynical and bleak but also thought provoking...The prose is intricate and deeply textured... In the end, [Vaux] is torn between betraying his friends or betraying his country.

—*John D. Trudel, author of God's House*

Fun read, like the great spy novels, but with added humor.

—*Cybergwen.com*

The descriptions and details in the novel are as sharp as daggers...The plot is full of winding curves.

—*Lisa Bower*

Operation Saladin

Sequel To 'The Wayward Spy.'

Roger Croft

To Adam McCrum
Lifelong friend and ally

Other Books By Roger Croft

Swindle!
Bent Triangle
The Wayward Spy

Cassio Books International

ISBN 10: 1482311690

EAN 13: 9781482311693

Author's Note

Saladin, perhaps the most famous of historic Arab leaders, is known for his great victories against the Crusaders in the twelfth century. He liberated Jerusalem after nine decades of occupation by the Franks and later saw off England's King Richard [the Lionheart] and his decimated band of English crusaders. After the military victories, Saladin withdrew to Damascus and worked for the unification of Syria, Mesopotamia, Palestine and Egypt. In 1193, he died in Damascus, too poor to pay for his own funeral, leaving his family to rule over Egypt and neighboring lands.

Cairo, June 2000

Michael Vaux sat at his desk in the small cubicle assigned him in the offices of the *Cairo News*, an English-language sister publication to his Damascus-based daily. He had been in Cairo for six months, and he looked upon his appointment as head of the newspaper's one-man bureau as a gift from heaven. Cairo was an ancient city that had become a tolerant all-things-to-all-men kind of place in contrast to old Damascus, as politically arid as its climate.

He handed three pages of typewritten copy to a tall, slim girl whose jet-black hair was trussed up into a ponytail. She had full red lips and distinctive aquiline nose and reminded Vaux of the ubiquitous effigies of Queen Nefertiti. The three pages of type represented his column for the day, the sources for which were largely garnered from the local English-language press, BBC World and Voice of America. Occasionally, he managed to produce a passable facsimile of an exclusive report if he was lucky enough to have had a drink—usually a few drinks—the

previous evening with old and clubby Abdul Balthazar, chief
press officer at the presidential palace, who, as he constantly
made the Cairo press corps well aware, was once or twice a
month granted a cosy but exclusive interview with Egypt's aging, maddeningly uncommunicative leader President Mubarak.

Layla, in tight black jeans and high heels, took the copy and
walked swiftly to the cramped teleprinter room, where she
faxed Vaux's efforts to a grateful foreign editor in Damascus.
His work was over for the day, and he planned a quick walk
to the Café Riche, where he would meet up with the usual
crowd of expat journalists to 'shoot the shit,' as the saying
went, while downing a cold Stella beer or, for those like Vaux
who had finished for the day, something stronger. His phone
tinkled.

'Darling, can we meet?'

'I was just leaving for the Riche.'

'This is important, darling. Very important.'

'Why don't we meet there?'

'It's the biggest scoop of your life.'

Vaux sighed. 'I doubt that. But what are you talking about?'

'Assad's had a heart attack. He's dead.'

Vaux held the handset while he stood up to peer over the
steel partition to see whether the dramatic news had reached the
somewhat somnolent newsmen whose hidden presence within
their own cubicles served to muffle any phone conversations they
could be having with their precious 'contacts.' So far, the quiet of
the newsroom indicated that Veronica's terse message had indeed
been exclusive. But he wasn't working for a Cairo newspaper;
his masters were in Damascus, where the old man had died. He
would have to write a 'reaction' story, obviously, and just as he was
thinking about the sort of approach he would take—the reaction
of the man on the Cairo street?—a human figure loomed in the
narrow gap that formed the entry into his cubicle.

It was Fred Thompson, the *News*'s editor in chief, a fellow Brit who was near desperation (Vaux could tell from the familiar hangdog face and the ruffled thick hair) at not having seen any news that could qualify as tomorrow's front-page headline story. Vaux liked him. He was an old-school newspaperman who could write pithy editorials or cover a downtown fire as well and as elegantly as anyone. He was thick set, six feet tall, and his hair was turning gray. He'd been in Cairo for thirty years, and he spoke and read Arabic. This enabled him to read the Arab media, and many of his paper's best stories and feature articles were duly scalped from the *Al Ahram* or *El Gomhuria*, Cairo's leading Arabic newspapers.

'Working on a big scoop?' It was his habitual opening gambit, a kind of collegial greeting among fellow hacks.

'If I had one, why would I give it to you?' Vaux nodded to the one chair that stood in the corner. Thompson grabbed it, lifted it, and sat to face Vaux. The chair groaned and rocked as Thompson tried to make himself comfortable.

'I see a pregnant, somewhat awestruck look on that handsome face. What are you hiding from me?'

'Are you ready for this?'

'I detect you are going to give me some earth-shattering news or, more likely, report on some petty gossip about our expatriate community,' said Thompson. 'Which is it?'

He put on his stern, schoolmasterly look while he waited for the reply.

Vaux said, 'Assad's dead. Heart attack this morning.'

Thompson's mouth dropped. 'Michael, is this a silly prank?' Thompson got up and almost threw the wooden chair back in its familiar corner.

'Straight from the Syrian embassy, Fred.'

Thompson rushed into the newsroom, shouted orders for one and all to drop everything they were doing, and attend an editorial meeting in his office—now.

Vaux was happy. He'd given old Fred tomorrow's headline and a shot of much-needed adrenaline.

***

Outside, a wave of hot, humid air hit him as he walked the few dusty blocks to the Café Riche on nearby Talaat Harb Street, home base of poets, spies, politicians, and writers. Vaux nodded to Magdi, the portly white-haired proprietor who throughout the long day sat as sentinel at the cash desk near the entrance. Vaux made for a corner table at the end of the long, rectangular oak-paneled room where he could observe every customer and note the arrival of any newcomers. He felt the light movement of air as the ceiling fans worked slowly to dissipate the heat and the clouds of pungent tobacco smoke. There were few familiar faces. Filfil, the old Nubian waiter who had worked here since the 1940s, rushed to serve plates of cannelloni and lamb kebabs, along with local beers and whiskey. But the few clientele suggested the news of Assad's death had made the rounds and that everyone was busy broadcasting the big story in print or on the air—the surprise demise of a feared and sometimes loathed strongman and the reaction in Cairo. Before he had left the office, Vaux received a call from one of Balthazar's minions, who dictated an official announcement from the presidential palace.

> *President Hosni Mubarak has called a special Cabinet meeting Sunday to discuss the situation in Syria after the death of Hafez Assad. The president said it was too early to determine whether he would attend the funeral. President Mubarak has called for three days of official mourning.*

Vaux had thought it odd that Mubarak had put off any decision to attend the funeral. But relations between Syria and Egypt had always been erratic—going back to Syria's rupture with the legendary leader Gamal Abdul-Nasser, whose pan-Arab dream of a unified Egyptian-Syrian federal state had died at birth. This was in the early 60s and Damascus ultimately rejected the idea because it could only see itself as relegated to junior partnership. And then there was Anwar Sadat's peace deal with Israel, bitterly opposed by the Syrians who still demanded the return of the Israeli-occupied Golan Heights before any peace treaty could even be contemplated. So, Vaux guessed, they weren't the closest of allies, but Mubarak and Assad did have something in common: they were both Arab autocrats of long standing.

At that fleeting thought, Veronica loomed over the pink pages of the three-day-old *Financial Times*, which Vaux had found discarded on the adjoining banquette. Her deep-brown almond eyes lit up as she greeted him.

'Hi! What a day.'

'You made it, after all. Nobody's here, so I guess they're all busy as hell for a change.'

A tall, young waiter in a long blue robe with gold trim quickly came to the table to take her order. She asked for a large bottle of Nubia mineral water and wondered why Vaux was nursing a bottle of Stella rather than sipping his usual whisky. Veronica then related how the news had come in from Damascus via their secure telephone network and how various embassy staffers predicted the way events would likely unfold—the implications of what, after all, was an inevitable regime change. But the alarmists were outnumbered, and the more likely scenario of a smooth transfer of power to Assad's London-based eye doctor son, Bashar al-Asssad, seemed to be the consensus. The optimists, including Veronica, aka Alena, looked forward to a new 'reformist' regime, perhaps even the abandonment of the Baath Party's absolutist doctrines for a more democratic administration. But the undeniable truth was that nobody could predict the future with any real certainty.

Veronica Belmont, her given name when they had first met, was now officially second secretary at the Syrian embassy, a big old house in the Dokki district, a pleasant suburb on the west bank of the Nile where some forty other foreign legations had chosen to set up shop. There she was known as Alena Suleiman. Vaux had met her when she was working at the Gower Street premises of Department B3, a sub-subgroup of MI6's Mideast desk at Century House. Their relationship flourished and survived the trauma of her later defection to the 'Syrian side.' This, at any rate, was how Vaux persuaded himself to look at the course of events that marked his debut into what he called, usually derisively, 'the spy game.'

Vaux was to remember that hot day in June for a very long time. Not because he felt the slightest pang of emotion at the news of Assad's demise—it was, after all, a natural death of a fairly old man just about to turn seventy—but for how the new regime would wreck his own modest plans for the future and severely rend the complex fabric of his relationship with Veronica.

***

Some weeks later, Vaux looked forward to a routine day in the office. He arrived at the gray, gloomy building on Ramsis Street at his usual time, about 10:00 a.m. He grabbed a copy of that day's *Egyptian Gazette* from the newspaper rack that stood just inside the main newsroom. He would scan that venerable newspaper, for any news and/or good ideas that he could borrow for his column. He observed that, as usual, the day's editorial was neutral about developments in Damascus but urged the younger Assad, now installed as the new Syrian leader, to push for real reforms now, while his face was fresh and he enjoyed what seemed the genuine popularity that often comes with a change in regime. So far, Assad had done little—apart from delivering a few speeches that promised to liberate the economy from the unnecessary restraints imposed during various states of emergency.

His phone tinkled.

'Michael, we have to talk. Could you meet me for lunch? Somewhere quiet. It's urgent, darling.'

It was Veronica. Vaux sensed a nervous tension in her voice and an eagerness to discuss whatever was troubling her. Vaux didn't hesitate. He knew what she did for a living and that it carried with it unknown dangers and, particularly, unforeseeable journeys to various parts of the globe and, of course, to Syria, where she could easily be grounded if she lost a round in the never-ending political infighting that characterized all intelligence establishments. He knew from his checkered experience with MI6 in the early 90s just how ruthless and arbitrary decisions from the top echelons could be.

They met in the gloomy, ornate belle epoque dining room of the Windsor Hotel, close to the Corniche El Nil, the wide boulevard that runs alongside the Nile as it flows through the city. It was an ideal place for quiet conversation, and Vaux knew old Imad Mustafa, the maître d', from the lonely evenings when they would drink together in the art deco second-floor bar—before Veronica came and rescued him and brought him to Damascus to reunite with Ahmed Kadri, his old college friend. Imad had greeted them in the lobby and then guided them to a corner table close to the tall, heavily curtained window.

'Well, what's up, darling?'

'It's about Ahmed, Michael. He's disappeared.'

'What do you mean, "disappeared?"'

'Look, from what I gather, it's this. You remember Ahmed's two sworn enemies—the two bureaucrats, or whatever they were, who had got him fired from a big job in the civil service, then exiled to Morocco?'

'It was self-exile. He was biding his time and got lucky when the intelligence people were forced to act on my sworn statement that they were, in fact, undercover agents for the Brits. It was complete fiction, but both were forewarned and both got out of the country before they could be arrested and subjected to whatever Assad's people do to traitors. One can only imagine.'

Veronica said, 'Here's the bad news. One of those guys, Khateb, flew with his wife and daughter to London from Paris, where he worked at Sciences Po as an academic, and met up with Assad's wife who was still in London at that time, preparing for the big move back to Damascus. This was just days after old Assad's death. The point is, Asma, the younger Assad's wife, knew Khateb's wife through her daughter, who had attended the same private school in London as Asma's daughter. So Khateb got a hearing and convinced Asma that Kadri had framed him and that he had always been and was still totally loyal to the Assad regime. All he wanted was to return to his homeland and serve her husband, the new leader, dutifully and loyally.'

Vaux recalled the phony charges made by Kadri and why he had helped him convince Damascus that the two men were traitors. It was an episode in his life that he truly wanted to forget and, until now, almost had.

What prompted him to conspire with Ahmed that idyllic summer when his host had invited him to stay at the opulent cliffside villa was simply that he felt he owed Ahmed one; Kadri had fled to Tangier, and Vaux, now a rehabilitated undercover workhorse for B3, had been dispatched (in the guise of an innocent tourist) to that subtropical would-be paradise. Their friendship went back to their university days but had ossified with the years that had passed. Now the unbounded talents and machinations of Section B3 had brought them together again. Vaux's task: to surreptitiously tape every conversation the two old friends had with one another. B3 chief Sir Walter Mason saw Vaux as the only man in the Western world in whom Kadri would confide. And Kadri possessed a mountain of invaluable information about Syria's rumored nuclear program, the country's military readiness, its economic state of health, and many other morsels of intelligence that B3 would love to acquire. Sir Walter saw Kadri, recently at the apex of the Syrian power elite and now out in the cold, as a bitter and disillusioned man—and bitter men who nurse grudges can be big and inexhaustible talkers. Sir Walter was looking forward to bulking up his Mideast files. Vaux was duly equipped with the latest mobile eavesdropping device developed by MI6's technical boffins and dispatched to Morocco.

Historically, Hafez Assad, a Shia Alawite, had been tolerant of other sects and tribes within the Syrian mosaic. But now the hard-liners were on the ascendant, and in an Arabian night of long knives, they fired all the Sunnis, with the exception of a few of Assad's favorites, from all positions of power. Their loyalty, they claimed, couldn't be trusted. Ahmed Kadri was a nonpracticing Sunni and was disliked by self-made Khateb as a pushy, English-educated economist who had too many friends and contacts in the West.

But Kadri's wily, old, and loyal factotum, Abdullah, eventually unmasked Vaux's deception and disloyalty to his host in Tangier. And to make amends for his treachery toward a furious host, he had agreed to back up Kadri's accusations against the two men—Ibrahim Khateb and Abdul Khundkar, the two

Assad aides responsible for his fall from grace and dismissal.
Kadri called his contacts in Damascus and claimed that the two
men were undercover agents for the UK's Secret Intelligence
Service and that he could back up these charges with a soon-
to-be faxed affidavit signed by a former senior MI6 agent, now
retired. For several tense days, the wires hummed between
Tangier and Damascus, and Vaux held his breath. He wasn't
proud of what he had done. But it was a gesture of atonement
for what he had come around to thinking was an inexcusably
disloyal offense against Ahmed, whose friendship he treasured.
Meanwhile, the damage had been done: Vaux had passed on
the miniature CDs that had recorded their conversations to an
undercover Tangier-based agent, who had promptly sent them
via diplomatic courier to the British embassy in Rabat and then
on to Sir Walter in London.

So now, from what Veronica/Alena had told him, the big
plan to get Ahmed back in the good graces of the regime had
totally failed. He had been exposed. The fiction that he coau-
thored with Ahmed had been proved to be just that. Where
would the next shoe drop?

***

He looked at Alena as she thanked Imad for the glass of wine
he had just poured. Imad picked up the bottle of her favorite
Obelisk Rosetta Rose and put it into a silver ice bucket. Then
he poured a large measure of Cutty Sark into Vaux's cut-glass
tumbler. He knew Vaux hated all wines, and over many late-
night whisky shots together, they had agreed that some strange
genetic mutation had rendered him incapable of distinguishing
any wine—red or white, vintage or plonk—from vinegar.

Out of nowhere, Vaux now felt that familiar frisson, a
tender love for the beautiful, vulnerable woman at his side,

intensified perhaps by the desire to protect her from the erratic and possibly brutal conduct of her employers. Syria's intelligence agency for whom she worked surely knew of the nexus that linked her to Kadri and through Kadri to him. Kadri's resurrected influence in Damascus had sealed the two men's close friendship. A job as subeditor on the leading English-language newspaper was offered, and in the early 90s, he joined Ahmed and Alena in Damascus. Years later, he was offered the Cairo post, which he was happy to accept. Almost coincidentally, the General Security Directorate had promoted Alena to deputy station chief in Cairo.

'So where does all this leave us?' asked Vaux. The world had suddenly changed. His sponsor in Damascus was now persona non grata. Worse than that. He had probably been arrested. He had reportedly disappeared. Vaux knew what that meant in Syria's totalitarian regime—torture to extract every morsel of what they defined as relevant information, then perhaps a 'private' execution.

'I have a plan, darling. I don't want to discuss it here. Let's enjoy lunch, and this evening, you'll come to my place and we'll map out a strategy.' She looked into his eyes in that soft, beckoning 'I totally love you' sort of way, and Vaux raised his glass to her and finished off the Cutty Sark.

2

Alena Hussein lived in Gazira, a quiet quarter where straggly trees that lined the streets struggled to survive Cairo's torrid summer. From the sixth floor of the 1930s apartment block, she enjoyed a view of the murky Nile and, beyond the river, the imposing Egyptian Antiquities Museum, home to Tutankhamen, Ramses, and priceless Phareonic antiques. It was a comfortable and roomy apartment, with a large living room, two adequate bedrooms, a large Western-type bathroom, and a small kitchen. Off the kitchen was a sort of box room where the daily cook or maid could rest on a decorous chaise longue. It was a furnished flat, and the bulky armchairs and couch and the heavy oak dining table didn't reflect her more contemporary tastes, as she constantly reminded Vaux whenever he came over or stayed the night.

Her father was a Palestinian refugee who had trained to be a doctor. At the Charing Cross teaching hospital in London, he met an English nurse who became his future wife. In early

1990, just two years out of King's College, Alena walked into the
Knightsbridge offices of the Palestinian Liberation Organization
(PLO) and, as a Palestinian who had just lost a young brother to
Israeli bullets during a student demonstration on the West Bank,
volunteered her services to the cause. She was what spooks call
a 'walk-in,' a willing and able individual who wanted to help the
host agency however she could. Within two weeks, she was called
for an interview. In a small, hot room, she met Dr. Kamal Zubada,
who told her that, after background checks, they were willing to
give her employment for a trial period of six months. But the
position would not be with the PLO. She had been accepted as a
probationary officer within Syria's General Security Directorate
(GSD), and if she accepted, she was to be ready to be flown out
to Damascus within ten days for a short training and familiariza-
tion course. She would be serving the greater Arab cause just as
effectively within the Syrian intelligence outfit as with the PLO.
She would be expected to do economic research (she had graduated in economics) to assess the potential of target countries,
including, of course, Israel. Alena felt triumphant and readily accepted their offer.

Her first undercover job for the GSD was named Operation
Infidel. It was an elaborate but finally successful scheme to secure the recruitment of Alena by Britain's security services. The
GSD's chief of station in London (he was nominally the Syrian
embassy's cultural attaché) asked her to apply for a job in the
City at a bank known for its connections to MI6 through its
network of branch offices around the globe. She was quickly
passed on to the recruitment staff at the UK's Secret Intelligence
Service, who was informed of the likely availability of a young,
promising Arab-speaking graduate. Alena happily accepted the
offer of employment by SIS, whose sage guardians offered the
new, enthusiastic recruit to Sir Walter Mason's B3 subsection,
where the staff establishment had, as he had always complained,

a gaping hole that should be filled as soon as a likely candidate came along.

Thus the double agent game began.

By the time Operation Helvetia was conceived, Sir Walter had persuaded himself that Alena could be used most effectively in a low-key honey trap operation that would speed the recruitment of Michael Vaux as a key temporary operative in B3's plan to procure the secret Russia-Syria arms deal that SIS staffers had confirmed was in the works. For Vaux, her name would be Veronica Belmont, and her profile would describe her as a PhD in ancient history, busy researching Roman archives for an obscure think tank in London. She would meet an unsuspecting Vaux—a lonely divorcé, in Sir Walter's view—in his local pub, and the seduction would get underway. At no time did Vaux suspect she was an employee of MI6, and the first time he realized she was involved in the spy game was when, in Geneva, she had confronted him with a Mauser HSc pointed at his chest.

Vaux's love for her, he had always admitted, clouded his judgment at the time of what they called their Geneva affair; while playing the lead role in Operation Helvetia, he became confused about his own motivations. He bungled his attempt to procure the full details of the arms deal when he fell into the well-prepared trap Ahmed and Alena had set for him. As he was secretly photographing the papers outlining the arms pact, Kadri suddenly appeared on the scene with Alena at his side, the Mauser in her hand. He was asked politely to hand over his microminiature spy camera. Then his habitual Cutty Sark was drugged, and he was transported to the Russian legation on Lake Geneva. There, Alena confessed to Vaux that she was, in fact, a plant within MI6, a vital part of a plan and strategy to garner information and intelligence on the UK and, by extension, US policies in the Middle East, particularly those affecting Israel and its neighbors.

Simply put, she was a mole within the quiet and hallowed corridors of MI6, and Vaux tried to see the situation in Manichean black and white, in terms of moral certitude. But he had failed—and that was the first fatal step toward this exile's life in Cairo. *It is written*, as his Arab friends would tell him. He had become as fatalistic as the Arabs around him. His love for Alena and his affection for Ahmed were different sides of the same coin. He had long come to terms with this.

***

They went to bed as soon as he had arrived with the usual bottle of Obelisk Rosetta. He put it in the small fridge, took off his clothes, dumped them on the tiled floor in the bathroom, and joined her in the bedroom. She was warm and comforting. She was like when he had first met her: voracious, enthusiastic, sensual, like a teenager who had just discovered the joys of lovemaking. She knew, he thought afterward, what she was about to tell him could shatter their relationship. She feared it could cause the end of the affair. They could break up now. But betrayal and deception had its costs, and she was prepared to face them.

They lay entwined together in the warm afterglow of their lovemaking. She suddenly threw the sheets back and went into the bathroom. Vaux lit a Camel, got up, and asked her to pass him his clothes; then he heard the shower and the vocal, melodious humming above the roar and splashes of the water. He had noticed before that certain trait in happy females—not least his mother. If Veronica felt happy, then he would have to put it down to their recent coupling. For there was nothing to be happy about in the wake of Ahmed's 'disappearance,' and nothing in the immediate future could by any means enhance anyone's sense of happiness. He went to the fridge and grabbed a bottle of Stella Export, a staple of hers—spirits were against her religion, she had told him—and then opened the wine. He poured the dark-pink wine into a flute glass and put it back in the fridge. She went straight through to the bedroom and soon emerged in a white stressed-silk shirt and blue jeans. Her still-wet auburn hair was cut short in a boyish style, with silvery highlights. Vaux headed for the bathroom and had a quick shower. Now they sat opposite each other in the two overstuffed chintz-covered armchairs.

Vaux took a deep drag from another Camel. 'So what do I do now?' he asked. 'If Ahmed has become persona non grata, I'm hardly going to be greeted as a hero if and when I go back. In fact, since he got me the newspaper job in the first place, I fully expect to be fired within a very short space of time. Do you have another opinion, Alena?' He had always preferred to call her by her real name, but by early habit, he often used the pseudonym conferred on her by her wily bosses at B3.

She took a sip of the chilled Egyptian wine. She winced, as she always did with the first sharp taste. 'I have a plan, Michael. But let's lay out the scenario. Yes, you are right to assume you're about to be fired. But they may recall you first, to make sure you're within their grasp. They've always been puzzled about you two. They gave you the benefit of the doubt because the old man—Assad's father—believed you were responsible for fingering two of his henchmen as traitors. So now the tables have turned. They'll get you there and pump you for information about your background, your friendship with Ahmed, what you were actually doing in Geneva and later Tangier—whether your friendship was based on some homosexual relationship you had when you were both young students at Bristol University.

'That sort of thing. Those people just don't believe two men with completely different racial and cultural backgrounds and upbringings can really be friends, are capable of love and respect for each other. In your parlance, darling, you'll be put through the third degree. You can expect a period of isolation and perhaps the agonies of various forms of coercion. I don't have to paint the full picture, do I?

'So let's say there's no way you will agree to go back and see your old bosses in Damascus. Your newspaper career in Syria is over. Ahmed is not around to support you, speak up for you. He's gone—and God knows where.'

'But what about you? Would you go back?' asked Vaux.

'Michael, I'm totally loyal to the regime. You know that. I couldn't just walk away now. And there's not a shred of evidence that would indicate they doubt my loyalty. Yes, they know of our affair. My colleagues at the GSD are competent spooks, and I'm sure they know that you're here right now.' She got up and went to the big window that looked out to the forecourt and the road beyond. A small Fiat was parked near the porticoed entrance to the apartment, and she could see two men in shirtsleeves and open collars, blue-gray tobacco smoke creeping out of the car's slightly open windows.

She pulled the chintz curtain so that only a chink of pale light indicated anyone was at home. Vaux was used to this, but he wondered why, if they so trusted her, there was this constant surveillance. Or had they been told to follow *him*, given his known relationship with Ahmed Kadri? But the fact that he had noticed the tail some six months ago suggested perhaps that it had nothing to do with Kadri's sudden change in status.

Alena said, 'They're out there because they have nothing better to do. As an employee of a Syrian outfit closely tied to the Assad regime, as a foreign-based reporter or columnist for a semiofficial newspaper, you would come under automatic surveillance. They don't trust anyone who successfully gets out of Syria to work in a foreign milieu— even if it is an Arab milieu. They fear you might get some urge to break free, skip the country, and embarrass the newspaper and the bureaucrats who gave you permission to leave in the first place. They're scared of what you could tell the world about the inner workings of the regime and all the rest of it. And as a GSD operative myself, I can't blame them.'

Vaux wondered now whether, in a crunch, she would try to protect him. Did her loyalty to Syria and the new Assad regime take precedence over their relationship? There had always been that element of ambivalence. In Cold War terms, it was like a British journalist falling in love with a tough, loyal KGB field agent. Until today, he had thought it could work. Her colleagues at the GSD obviously knew about their affair, but up to now, it hadn't seemed to have any consequences. Her posting to Cairo eighteen months ago was a promotion—and, despite his romantic imagination, probably had nothing to do with his own posting here at the same time. Or did it? Was she here to watch him or delegate that menial task to her junior officers?

She said, 'You may hate me for what I'm going to tell you—'

Vaux's brief stint at the spooks' training camp in Aldershot suddenly kicked in. He stood up, went to the heavy oak sideboard, and opened a drawer. He got out a piece of paper and a ballpoint pen. On the notepaper he wrote:

> *Have you checked this place*
> *for bugs, listening devices, etc.?*
> *I love you, by the way.*

Alena read the note and nodded her head several times in rapid succession. She kissed the paper and blew a kiss toward him. Then she mimed a request for the pen in Vaux's hand. She wrote:

As my story unfolds, you will be reassured on
that score. Please be patient and understanding,
darling. I love you more than you suspect!

***

Alena Hussein then began a long explication of her relatively short career. She told Vaux that just three weeks after
walking into the PLO offices in London and later being hired
by Syria's intelligence service, she was told to apply for a job in
the City—a financial job.

'I was puzzled, but that's what they told me to do. I got
a job interview with HSBC at Canary Wharf. It went well, I
thought. Don't forget, I'd just graduated with an economics
degree. Ten days later, I was summoned back to HSBC, and so
I asked my Syrian handlers what to do. They told me to carry
on as if I wanted the bank job badly. At the next interview at
Canary Wharf, I met three gentlemen who, by instinct, I felt
were not bankers. As you know, I'm noted for my feminine
intuition. Their questions sort of gave them away. They were
political questions, some really loaded questions, and I suppose they were trying to find out whether I was politically
savvy. Then they asked whether, given my Palestinian background, I was an "unreconstructed" Arab nationalist.' She
mimed the quotation marks with her fingers. 'I told them
I had been born here, had gone to school and college in
London, and I loved England.

'Their question, by the way, was tinged with a little humor.
Anyway, they took my phone number and told me that they
would get in touch within a few days. I was living in a bed-sitter
in Earl's Court at the time, and the one phone shared by about
six lodgers was in the hallway downstairs. They left a number to
call, and my landlady gave me the message.

'The upshot of this diplomatic dance was that I was beckoned to Gower Street, where, as you well know, B3 hangs out. There, I met old Sir Walter and his small team of colleagues—Craw, whom you'll remember, and that Major Short military type. To cut a long story short, they offered me a job working for B3, which, they said, was a subsection of another MI6 subgroup of the main Mideast desk that operated then out at Century House—before their move to that monstrosity Babylon-on-Thames. I never did learn what the first subsection did. But B3, a very small outfit of so-called Middle East specialists, tended to concentrate on short-term strategies and what they called "contingency planning." In other words, your Operation Helvetia–type of deal, a short but sweet maneuver to collect the sort of hypersecret intelligence the UK could add to its arsenal of secret soft weapons against all contingencies.

'They offered me a job. In retrospect, I think they saw my knowledge of Arabic as my key qualification. But I was young and bright—if I do say so myself—and here endeth the first chapter. Michael, get me another drink, dearest.'

Vaux got up. She had said she had a plan but had now embarked on a longish autobiography, most details of which she had already told him. But he was prepared to be patient. He was the current loser in this game, and he'd listen to what she had to say. But he knew that as far as he was concerned, his life had suddenly changed. He wouldn't go back to Damascus, a city without Ahmed, devoid of Ahmed's cheery companionship, his constant visits, their late evenings together exploring the souks and the late-night bars and the occasional visits to 'houses of ill repute,' as Kadri often called those places where 'companions' became erotic partners for at least a few hours. He handed Alena the wine glass, now heavily coated with condensation.

She looked at him enigmatically, a curl to her lips, as if she expected a word of encouragement from her lover. Did he want her to go on? He answered without any need to ask him.

'Go on,' he said with a sigh. 'It's a fascinating story—and presumably a preamble to the plan you spoke of at lunch.'

'You've probably figured it out by now, Michael.'

'Not really, not fully...' He was impatient for the denouement.

'My handlers at the GSD were ecstatic. Their plan to send me into the British lion's den had worked like a dream. Operation Infidel had got off to a triumphant start. I was summoned to meet my Syrian case officer at a small pub in Hampstead, where I was introduced to Amin Hakki, whom you met in Geneva.'

'I remember him. He later defected to the US. But in Geneva, he appeared to be Ahmed's overseer.'

'So he briefed me about the immediate task ahead. You know the rest. I was able to blow wide-open Sir Walter's pet scheme of sending you to Geneva after they discovered that you and Ahmed had been close college friends. You were recommended for the job by that venerable old talent spotter Arthur Davis, who, typically, met you in a pub.'

'The same pub where I met you,' said Vaux, a tinge of nostalgia in his voice.

'Yes. And of course that was all deliberate, as you later learned.'

'A classic honey trap,' said Vaux, now with the timbre of regret.

'So the Syrian intelligence service now had a double agent at the very heart of the team they knew specialized in specific assignments affecting the Arab region. They were ecstatic—they couldn't believe their luck.

'Of course, Sir Walter and that silly man Craw also thought they had struck it lucky. Arthur Davis discovered you were bent on buying a home in the area where you were brought up, and he made sure a succession of fake buyers kept coming up with higher and higher bids for the property. He wanted to make you "hungry," as he put it. Anyway, I take it your need for more and more cash to fulfill your dream played into the incentives they had laid out for you before you accepted the Geneva job.

'There was a complete background check. They couldn't believe what they found in their dusty old files—probably opened when you started out in journalism as a toiler for *Time* magazine in various foreign parts. Lots of *Time* people do stuff for the CIA, but apparently, your hands were clean. Sir Walt and his team thought you'd come around, especially with your growing cash needs, but I was added to the mix to bring you totally in from the cold.'

She laughed a little nervously, and Vaux didn't know whether this had been prompted by a wish to apologize for the ruse or whether she was genuinely amused by the sequence of events that had drawn him into the viper's nest of deceit and conspiracy that would send him to Geneva to betray his long-lost friend.

Alena continued. 'The Geneva conference was a gift for both the Russians and the Syrians to get behind closed doors and hammer out that multibillion-dollar arms treaty. Your friend Ahmed knew how to close a deal, all right, despite pretty harsh financing terms demanded by Russia. Meanwhile, I hardly need to tell you, we caught you red-handed trying to copy details of the arms pact right there in Ahmed's hotel suite.'

'Yes,' said Vaux. 'Clearly, thanks to you, who knew our basic strategy in Geneva and reported on my every move to Kadri and his cohorts. And then you wanted me to believe that you were instrumental in turning my bumbling fiasco into a

plus for me and the Syrians. You promised that Sir Walter would
be delighted with Kadri's phony small arms deal—chicken feed
concocted for me to show my MI6 bosses. We could all three of
us look like winners.'

'Of course, darling! But I'm not taking all the credit for
saving the situation and turning it around for you. Ahmed
was desolated by your barefaced treachery. He literally cried
when I told him about Sir Walter's plan to use you, a redis-
covered old college friend, as the means by which MI6 would
filch the arms deal and chalk up a wonderful intelligence coup
for their side. He couldn't believe you could do this to him.
When he saw that my way was the best way for all of us, he
calmed down and even chuckled at the thought of recruiting
you for our own political purposes. I think he got a kick out
of it, and he certainly relished those "education" sessions with
Hakki when he saw that you were beginning to understand
our side of the arguments embroiling the region! He fought
Hakki, by the way, who opposed our plan to co-opt you—
rather than send you via a Russian freighter from Marseille
to Syria's main port of Latakia, where Hakki wanted to stage
a big show trial and display the great coup for our side in the
propaganda wars.'

Vaux was now wishing that Alena didn't have this claimed
semireligious antipathy toward hard liquor. He felt in dire need
of a good scotch. Instead, he got up and took another Stella
Export out of the fridge and poured the golden, sparkling contents into his glass. He didn't ask her if she wanted another glass
of wine, because something very disturbing, perhaps crucial, to
this revelatory confessional was surfacing in his mind.

'What about that young hitchhiker you met in Cornwall?
You sent her to her death! I remember you telling me that in
Cairo while I waited for the exit visa for Syria. And earlier,
I heard that you had been eliminated by a Special Branch

antiterrorist squad in that ghastly car crash after they found out that you were a GSD mole and responsible for the whole Helvetia shambles. You boasted you owed your life to the fact that you used that girl to drive your rented car back to Newquay, the last trip of her short life—'

'This is easily explained. It may sound fantastic, but it served our goals, as well as the Brits and the Yanks. In that rare concurrence of interests among the various national security services, we all wanted that CIA creep eliminated. You remember what I told you. I poisoned him with a quick-acting drug concocted in our labs by some lugubrious scientist. It could be transmitted by a scratch with a sharp instrument, so the silly dagger he always used as a sex tool made it easy for me. The bowie, an American dagger, excited him when he pointed it at a girl's neck. So during the boring foreplay, I scratched him lightly on the arm—by "accident," of course—and the poison did the rest.

'So, you ask, why would the CIA acquiesce in the "expedient demise" of one of their own? Simple. MI6 discovered he was passing vital intelligence—names of field agents, safe houses, new codes—to a KGB/FSB sleeper cell in the Belsize Park area of London. The Russians were paying him off with long weekends in Amsterdam and Copenhagen, both cities famous for their male brothels. He was queer as a coot, and he liked young hustlers. When he took off for these sex games, he told his wife he would be away on highly confidential business for the glory and security of the good old USA.

'The Brits informed the Yanks, they had a parley, and it was agreed that since the assassination was to occur on British territory, MI6 could do the dirty work. Coincidentally, it suited my people, because we figured the only reason this guy had arranged a meeting with the now fleeing Hakki was to exchange the details of the US-Syrian arms deal for either cash or a brand-new US passport, or both. My mission was to kill the American and grab the treasured bloody arms deal to prevent it from falling into the hands of the Brits. But, of course, as we found out later, much to the annoyance of my Syrian case officer, our US playboy had faxed, in code, the main details of the treaty to CIA's London center from the small hotel before I even got there.'

Vaux exhaled a big cloud of blue-gray cigarette smoke. 'You seem to have been an expert in the techniques of honey traps.'

She ignored the remark. 'So the car crash was a complete fabrication. Yes, Special Forces was used to monitor my actions on that day. They were a sort of protection platoon if anything went badly wrong. The poison took instantly, but had it failed, we would have had a mess on our hands. So, Michael, you can rest assured that no innocent young girl from New Zealand was involved in any shape or form. This fairy tale about a horrific road crash was simply a cover so that the local police could show that the suspected killer of an American in a local guesthouse had died in the getaway car. That piece of my story was totally false, as, of course, was the original report of a car crunched on the coastal highway to a flat, burned strip of steel by a 20-ton truck. The county police chief, all too ready to cover his arse, backed up the official version, and the local press agreed to report the fictitious nonstory after receiving a substantial subvention to help keep their local rag in the black.'

Vaux shook his head in disbelief. 'None of that squares with what Greene told me in Cairo. He said the GSD had sent you to kill the CIA agent and then grab the photocopies of the arms deal Hakki had handed over in return for his guarantee of asylum in the US, plus a passport and spending money. Hakki had now exposed you and MI6 wanted you out of the way because you were a traitor, a mole who had sabotaged their carefully planned Helvetia scam. Unbeknownst to you, Special Forces were tailing you with the express purpose of eliminating you on the way back to your hotel in Newquay. A spectacular road accident would be difficult to fabricate in such a small seaside community, and I don't believe a word of your story. I think that young girl died so you could make a getaway. Then, as you later told me, you rushed to the safe house in Camden Town, where the GSD debriefed you and took you to Luton Airport for a night flight to Damascus. The GSD figured you'd escaped the assassination attempt by Special Forces and whisked you back to Syria incognito for a complete debriefing and some promotion, perhaps to bigger and better things.'

Tears welled up in her eyes, and she looked toward the windows as a mute signal that the conversation was over.

He looked over his glass at her. She was ruffling her hair now that it was dry.

'Besides, to ask me to believe that MI6 and the CIA were in cahoots with the Syrians is a big stretch, Alena.'

Vaux decided to press home what he thought was the true version of this story.

'This CIA man was in his early forties, I believe. You say you killed him in the small b&b near Newquay as you were both preparing for sex. It was an ongoing liaison, initiated as all honey traps are, by sexual seduction. I should know. But you also say that both the CIA and MI6 wanted him out of the way because he was handing over vital intelligence to the Russkies. And the KGB/FSB rewarded him with sex junkets in cities where he could pick up boys without anyone he might know noticing. None of this adds up, Alena. You admit you seduced him, he succumbed, and here he was meeting you again in Cornwall for a romantic or sexual tryst. How the hell could he have been gay?'

She wanted to end this conversation. She said, 'I don't know the answer to that. Perhaps he was bisexual. In fact, he must have been—he was married, after all. And had two kids—two boys. At first, Craw and his crew wanted to use Chris Greene. Remember him? He was then in his mid-twenties, a handsome and likable guy.'

'Yes, of course I remember him. He met up with me when I was sitting on my arse in Cairo waiting for a visa to visit Ahmed in Damascus. It was the day you suddenly appeared on the scene again. And all those months, I had believed you were dead. How could I forget that particular day?'

Vaux persisted. 'So devious old Craw thought he'd test Greene's devotion to duty by proposing he go to bed with this CIA creep?'

Alena dabbed her eyes with a tissue. She tried to lighten the tone. 'It would have saved me a lot of aggravation. They thought Greene might have been willing to sacrifice his virginity, or whatever, for the greater cause. But he refused to make the ultimate sacrifice for queen and country. So I was the default candidate for the seduction gambit. They figured he swung both ways, so the honey trap would work with me just as well as some male.'

'And, of course, you do have a boyish figure.'

Alena brushed off the attempted witticism with a quick turn of her head toward the windows. Vaux got up to peer through the chink in the curtains. It was dark now, and a gentle breeze from the desert ruffled the palm fronds and the elegant stand of eucalyptus over the road swayed with the wind. He saw the Fiat. The watchers weren't being very professional; they had the map light on and were both reading newspapers. Occasionally, one or the other would raise his head and look at the building's entrance and then up to the strip of light that emanated from Alena's window. He turned to see her emerge from the kitchen with a full glass of wine. She didn't ask him if he wanted another beer but lit a Camel from his opened packet on the rattan coffee table and offered him the cigarette. He took it and sat down again.

'You know what's so bloody tragic about all this?'

'Don't be overdramatic, Michael.'

'I would say it's hard to exaggerate the drama. There was I, pretty bloody ignorant of the great Palestinian-Israeli impasse, pretty uninterested—if you want to know the truth—in the messy Middle East, especially after a long time in North America. I should have been more interested in the Palestinian question, I suppose, but it's not the only story in the world, and my whole career has been devoted to writing about subjects that could directly affect Mr. Average Joe, to making the guy in the street aware of how big events and political agendas can seriously affect his life and the future of his kids.'

'Nothing's more important in this part of the world than the Israeli-Arab conflict,' said Alena.

He threw up his hands in fake despair and then pointed toward the windows. 'And are they tailing you or me? If it's you they're watching, I think we'd better start discussing this plan of yours, don't you?'

She smiled and shook her head. 'I told you, they always keep tabs on Syrian nationals working abroad. You're a Brit, but you're working for a Syrian newspaper, and you can bet your life you are on their radar screen.'

'And why are you so confident your place is clean?'

'We don't eavesdrop on our own, darling. That would be a betrayal of trust. But to make sure our ill wishers haven't bugged the place while they pose as a team of house painters or plumbers, I get our men to check every week. So we're perfectly safe.'

'So what now?'

'Michael, what I have to tell you will not be easy—for me
or for you. I intercepted a cable today, sent by our Interior
Ministry to the ambassador. They're calling for your immediate return to Damascus, and they have requested the Egyptians
cancel your resident's permit. I don't think you should go home
tonight, nor do I think you should stay with me—for obvious
reasons.'

Vaux's rejection of her version of the tragic events in
Cornwall—the death of an innocent caught in the crossfire of
belligerents in a clandestine war—had seemed to annoy her.
She didn't want him to stay the night, nor return to his own
apartment. After several minutes of mutual silence, Alena got
up and sat beside him and smoothed his damp, ruffled hair. He
moved away.

'This is your way of saying good-bye?'

'A temporary absence, darling. Please don't be upset. I'll
work out something with my people. But it will take time. Call
me tomorrow morning—'

'Stop being so bloody calm, Alena. What was that speech
you made tonight all about? How bloody dedicated you are to
your masters in Damascus—the same people who are now per-
secuting dear old Ahmed? Torturing him, perhaps? You said so
yourself. I came here thinking your brilliant and fertile mind
could have worked something out, thinking you had some influence on the events that affect all three of us so profoundly. But
I see I was wrong. 'You're all right, Jack,' as they say in England,
so to hell with the rest of us!'

He heard her shouts as he grabbed his linen jacket. 'No! No!
No!' He flung open the heavy door and heard it slam against the
wall as he searched for the fire escape. There were ten apart-
ments on each floor, and he remembered seeing an exit close
to the elevator. He skipped down the concrete staircase to
the ground floor. Then he pushed at the bar of the emergency

door, and a blast of hot, humid air hit him as he ran through the tenants' car park and out into the street. He didn't bother to check if the Fiat was still sitting in the front driveway. A taxi stood at a nearby corner, and he asked the driver to take him north to the island suburb of Zamalek.

3

Fred Thompson, in baggy cotton pajamas and a silk polka-dot dressing gown, was not his usual calm self. He had been woken by heavy banging on his door. He looked over at his sleeping wife and then at the luminous alarm clock. It was 2:15 a.m., and he wondered what the hell was going on. Vaux stood before him, his face sweating and his hair still disheveled after the shower at Alena's place. He seemed short of breath, and Thompson beckoned him into the small lobby.

'I'm in a bit of a jam, Fred. Can we talk?'

'Of course, old man. Let's go into the dining room.' He led the way, opened a frosted-glass double door, and sat at the head of a long travertine table. He signaled Vaux to sit opposite him at the other end.

'Shoot, as they used to say in Hollywood.' Vaux detected a slight impatience in Thompson's attitude and tone, but he couldn't blame the man, having disturbed him in the early hours.

'This may sound odd, Fred, but I have no one else to turn to.'

'Get on with it, old man. What the hell's going on?'

'I had a flaming row tonight with Alena.'

Thompson now looked more relaxed. He liked Alena, and she often came round with Vaux for dinner and the odd cocktail party. He and Margaret, his wife of thirty years, had been to her place in Dokki. But he knew Alena's official position at the Syrian embassy was a cover, and he often wondered whether Vaux was getting hopelessly entangled in his relationships with Syria—the newspaper he worked for, his close friend Ahmed, and his lover Alena. He knew he was being very British about all this. But that's who he was—as he told his wife when she berated him for his concerns for Michael and his future.

'A domestic tiff? Dear me, Michael. You interrupt my beauty sleep because of a mere contretemps with beautiful, young Alena. I'm surprised you're not both falling out all the time. The age difference always bothered me, you know.'

Thompson wished he hadn't said that but guessed the sleeping pill he always took lowered his guard.

'It's not just any old row, Fred. I need some serious help.'

Vaux then told Fred Thompson the whole story: Ahmed Kadri's sudden disappearance and likely arrest, Syria's Interior Ministry demanding his return to Damascus, and the imminent cancellation of his residence permit in Egypt. To punctuate Vaux's report, Thompson got up and poured two large shots of scotch from the drink trolley and slid a small plate of nuts and raisins up the table toward him. He listened intently to what Vaux told him, and he noticed that Vaux omitted to mention anything about Alena's real job. He couldn't let him know that he was perfectly aware that she was the local deputy station chief of Syria's GSD.

Thompson leaned back on the fragile antique Windsor chair his wife had recently bought at the old Khan al-Khalili souk. Like Vaux, he hadn't given up cigarettes and was stubbing out his fifth Cleopatra when he realized Vaux had finished talking and was waiting for some sort of reaction from him.

'Don't like the sound of all this, Michael. I'm thinking of *you*, now—not Alena, not Kadri. You've reached a point when you've got to act quickly and save your own skin. Okay? They obviously want you back there for a full inquisition. And that's the last thing you want. Ahmed's got enemies in Damascus, and the new regime has apparently chosen to believe this other man's story. You yourself admit that you aided and abetted Ahmed Kadri in the ruse that cost this chap's career. In retrospect, don't you think Kadri was being overly vengeful?'

'Ahmed was hurt. He was loyal to the regime, and he was suddenly sent packing—not on any substantiated charges, but on the basis that a couple of Alawite colleagues didn't like the cut of his jib, if you will. He's a Sunni, and it was one of those periodic purges of the Sunnis. These two characters who were instrumental in his firing are primitive types. They hated him for his Western education, his Western suits, his taste for jazz and booze, and even, I suppose, his Western friends—all the things I liked about him.'

'I don't think our friends in Damascus would understand the jib analogy—much too English and nautical. But I see what you're getting at.'

Thompson got up and placed his empty glass on the drink trolley. He had heard enough, and he wanted to get back to bed and sleep on it.

'Look, there's a couch in the living room. Put your head down, and I'll sort this all out somehow.'

***

Vaux waited outside the coffee shop in the main hall of Ramses Station, Cairo's cavernous main railway terminal. It was 10:00 a.m.——too early for him to appreciate the piped, repetitive Arabic music that rose above the tumultuous din of trains arriving and departing and the shouts and excited chatter of people about to embark on long journeys to Egypt's southern reaches and beyond. In a few brief words, Thompson had given him instructions to meet a Mr. Adams, who would be able to assist him in the days ahead. Thompson then left his apartment for the *Cairo News* offices, and Vaux was left to make small talk with Margaret over several cups of café crème and a few dry croissants. She was Irish and looked slightly worn and tired, no doubt the cost of spending one's life with a Brit whose first love was journalism and whose second passion was living far from the drizzle and dark days of the England he loved to hate. Vaux had no idea who Mr. Adams was, but he was encouraged by the Englishness of the name. At his most pessimistic, he thought Adams could be a travel agent, someone who worked for American Express or Thomas Cook. Or he could be some old crony of Thompson's, a Mr. Fixit who handled the messes and crises expats often got into.

In a low, hushed voice, Thompson had also told Vaux that Adams would be wearing gray worsted trousers, a blue blazer with a college insignia on the breast pocket, and a straw panama. He would be seated at one of the tables near the long bar, and he would be reading the latest Paris edition of the *Herald Tribune*.

Vaux spotted him through the smudged grime of the windows. He pushed open the double doors, walked over to the long bar, and ordered a black coffee. Adams was engrossed in the newspaper, but Vaux noted the gold-braided college coat of arms and the panama, which hung from the back of the rattan chair. He sat down beside the man, who faked surprise, and then they both shook hands vigorously, just like old friends. He was a tall, slim man in his mid-forties, with a bald head and horn-rimmed glasses. Adams folded the big broadsheet into a more manageable package and launched into what his department called an 'emergency exit plan.'

An open window just above their heads let in wafts of diesel-scented humid air, and the thundering noise from the revved-up engine of the train waiting on Platform 1, adjacent to the coffee shop, muffled Adams's voice. Even so, he mumbled his words so that only Vaux could possibly hear him.

'Look, I know your problem—let's leave it at that. I can tell you that the local police were waiting in your apartment last night, so you did the right thing to avoid them. It was nothing sinister. Your residency permit has been revoked, and they were just doing their job. But our people have been working on this, and if you know what's best for you, you'll do as instructed. Our contacts confirm that your Syrian employers want you back in Damascus pronto—and somehow we don't think it's to offer you the top job on the *Damascus Times*. So we want you to get the next train to Alexandria, about an hour from now. It takes about three hours. Travel first class, old boy; then you won't be hassled by Arab bums or inquisitive railway inspectors. When you get to Alex, you will be met by one of the consulate people. They already know you for some reason. Just do what they say, and you'll be okay.'

Vaux's reaction to Adams's 'instructions' was a mixture of resentment and relief. These people, whoever they were, had arranged a safe exit at the cost of his giving up his cherished sovereignty. But he had no choice. He guessed Adams was from the embassy and delegated to do this sort of thing quite often. But the thought of landing up in the British consulate in Alexandria was almost as bad as sweating it out here in Cairo. He hadn't had any dealings with British diplomats since he suddenly and arbitrarily left MI6 that late summer in 1992 when he decided on the life-changing move to

Damascus, where he hoped to live out his life with Ahmed and
Alena. His sudden resignation was greeted with outrage, and
his former boss at Department B3, Sir Walter Mason, put out a
warrant for his arrest. But then, he figured he was never going
back. Now he felt he was delivering himself once again into the
hands of MI6 and the cold creative geniuses who hatched those
labyrinthine schemes and gothic plots that so often ended in
failure or fiasco.

'Are you still with me, old man?' asked Adams, somewhat
put off by Vaux's air of distraction.

'Sorry. Yes, of course.'

'Now, do you have money—enough to buy the rail ticket?'

'Yes, yes. I think so.'

Adams sighed. 'This is no time to be vague, Mr. Vaux. Do
you or don't you?' He looked around the restaurant to see if
anyone was taking an undue interest. At the next table sat a
woman covered from head to toe in a black abaya, with her
teenage son clad in blue jeans and a T-shirt. There were a few
solitary old men nursing their mint teas or coffee, but nobody,
in Adams's eyes, who looked like a dedicated watcher. He
quickly produced ten Egyptian twenty-pound notes from his
trouser pocket.

'Here, take this. The fare's about forty pounds, last time I
checked.' Then Adams fished in the inside pocket of his blazer.
He produced a rather tattered UK passport.

'I was told to give this to you. You may find it useful in the
days ahead. It's advisable to get rid of Michael Vaux, if you know
what I mean.'

Vaux smiled at this incongruous attempt at humor. But
Adams, who now watched Vaux closely, saw the smile evaporate
quickly. His face went 'white as a sheet,' he told his bemused
colleagues back in Garden City.

Vaux had looked at the name on the front cover of the worn hardcover passport. Once again, he was Derek Westropp, the alias given to him by MI6 when he agreed to do what he thought was a one-off operation in Geneva. A chill passed through him. He felt he had seen his own ghost.

4

As the lush green lands of the Nile delta flashed past his window, Vaux racked his brain trying to recall when he had last seen the old passport that he had used for what, in his own mental archives, he had filed away as the Geneva Caper. He knew he'd had it when he flew back to London, and he supposed he'd put it in a drawer in the house he had just bought on Willow Drive near Watford. He had stayed there about six months while the builders and the masons and the plumbers had fixed up the place to his specifications. He remembered that he had never bought all the furniture he needed—just the basics, like a bed, a kitchen table and chairs, and a bistro set for the terrace he had finally built. He couldn't recall a chest of drawers, so perhaps the old passport had been put on some mantelshelf to gather dust. After he had decided never to come back to England, he supposed the B3 team would have searched the unoccupied house for any telltale evidence that he had ever worked for them.

So it didn't take a genius to realize that somehow MI6 had now got into the game again. Perhaps they had been waiting for this moment. Perhaps they had even engineered it with the aid of Fred Thompson, whom he had never suspected of having contacts within the Secret Intelligence Service, but who had held his hand and led him into their clutches again. Was he falling into the fateful, dead-end trap of paranoia to believe that perhaps they had even anticipated the personal crisis he now faced? Would they detain him, ship him back to the UK, and then swallow him up in a sub-rosa trial and a lengthy prison sentence? Long-term residency at Wormwood Scrubs, where most of Britain's Cold War spies had been incarcerated, would be the final epitaph. He had no career, no prospects, and he had lost the love of his life and a male soul mate whose absence would cruelly intensify his isolation and solitude.

And so Michael Vaux, pretty much already at the end of his tether, wondered whether he should simply get off the train in Alexandria, meet whoever was sent to take him in, then run with all the strength he could muster to—where? He could easily get lost in the labyrinth of old streets and alleyways of Alexandria—but what then? He had no luggage, no clean shirts or underwear or socks, he needed a shower, and he had very little cash despite what he had told Adams. Vaux's innate fastidiousness supplied the answer: he'd bide his time. He would take note of what was planned for him, demand some new shirts and underwear, and generally smarten up. He would be less conspicuous to travel agents and airline employees if he looked passably respectable.

He looked through the train's grimy windows. Some sixty miles out of Cairo, the panorama changed abruptly, with snapshot images of half-finished and abandoned apartment buildings, small dilapidated dwellings, mud-caked fields dotted with tall, leaning palm trees where donkeys and a few sheep

grazed on sparse vegetation, and a periodic flash of the ubiquitous minarets that reassured the fellahin that all was not lost.
He hoped Alexandria would offer a more uplifting scene, its
famous Corniche perhaps acting as an eternal reminder of the
port city's long, romantic history.

The Cairo-Alexandria express train pulled into Misr Station
only five minutes late. He jumped down from the first-class
carriage and strode toward the main hall. He had been told the
person who would meet him and take care of his needs would
recognize him, so he quickly surveyed the group of people who
were waiting for their friends and relatives or business associ-
ates. He didn't recognize anyone, but maybe they were going by
a photograph, or maybe they were trusting to luck—a slightly
overweight man, somewhat disheveled, and with no baggage.
As he pushed through the cluster of people at the barrier, he
felt a hand on his shoulder. He swung round to see a man in
white shirt and blue jeans. He had thick black hair and spoke
with what used to be called a public school accent.

'Mr. Vaux, I presume,' said the man, and Vaux thought you
didn't get more English than that.

Vaux smiled, shook the man's outstretched hand, and
decided to let him do all the talking.

'There's a taxi waiting outside, and we'll go straight to a
place where you can wash and brush up.'

They piled into the backseat of a black-and-yellow taxi that
looked about as old and worn as Vaux now felt. The young man
beside him was in his mid-twenties, with a fresh, youthful complexion and an enthusiasm he remembered he once had in his
early days as a journalist. He had already told the driver where
to go, and Vaux sat back, somewhat ashamed to be traveling with
no baggage and clothes he hadn't taken off in forty-eight hours.

'No names, no pack drill until we get there, old boy. You'll
like it, by the way, so don't look so worried.'

'I'm hungry and tired. And I haven't a clue who you are or where you're taking me. So if I look worried, I can't think why,' said Vaux with a wan smile.

The taxi driver, who wore a tight-fitting white skullcap, occasionally checked them out in the rearview mirror.

Suddenly, he said, 'Very close, missir.'

He drove fast when they had the rare occasion to close a wide gap in the heavy traffic that clogged the roads at intersections. Vaux caught occasional glimpses of the famous Corniche and the blue Mediterranean beyond, and he thought of Alena. They had spent many weekends here and loved the city, often comically trying to relive the elusive romance of *The Alexandria Quartet*, the classic novel about love-obsessed men and women who lived here in the 1930s and the war years. Those memories and the jerky motion of the old taxi made him nauseous. Finally, they pulled up in front of a shabby building where a Barclays Bank occupied the main floor. Vaux wondered why a big bank like Barclays couldn't afford to patch up the peeling stucco that scarred the 1930s building. The man who had met him indicated that this was the final destination, and they both slid out of the slippery, plastic-covered backseat. The driver looked disappointed to see them go and mumbled, '*As-salama'laikoum*' (Peace be with you).

The man in blue jeans walked swiftly to what appeared to be an apartment lobby next to the bank. An old man in a shabby brown djellaba and red fez sat at a rickety table just behind the big glass-and-wrought-iron doors, a sort of sentinel who watched the people who came and went. He nodded to the man, and Vaux followed him to an old caged elevator. It slowly took them up to the fourth and top floor. They got out on a flat roof where clothes and bedsheets hung from lines strung from various walls and posts.

The man had a key to the corner apartment. He closed the door behind them and indicated Vaux should move into the adjacent living room. It was a big room and looked out on to the busy, traffic-clogged street. The motor horns of impatient drivers were amplified by the open french windows. A cool breeze from the Med acted as a natural air conditioner.

'I'm Ted Brown from the consulate, by the way. This place is yours for a few days, so make yourself at home. Just a few house rules. Don't try and use the phone; it hasn't worked in months. There's all sorts of food in the fridge and booze in the bar behind you.'

Vaux saw a wooden cabinet and a slide-out shelf on which a white plastic ice bucket was placed. There were no tongs.

'You'll have some new clothes delivered this evening, and tomorrow I'll accompany you to our tailor for a new suit and maybe a sports jacket. Got to spruce you up a bit, old man.'

'And then I presume a long interrogation?'

'I know nothing about that side of things. Just the general plan to talk to you, ask you for some relevant information, and then get you out of Egypt—safe and sound.'

'And what about my basic freedoms? Can I go out and explore the town?' Vaux was starting to feel a bit put-upon or perhaps the first pangs of claustrophobia.

'I have to tell you that's verboten, okay? It's in your own interest. You can bet your life the Syrian agents here will be on the lookout for you, not to mention Egypt's own Mukhabarat, who are always out to impress lesser Arabs of their brilliance in security matters. So we want you to stay put, here within this building. It's above the bank, you know, and the tenants are quiet.'

Vaux was not surprised. He was incarcerated. But he was also on a path to getting out of a place that held no future for him. So he would bide his time and, more immediately, have a shower and see what was offered in the fridge.

Brown then went over to check the drink cabinet.

'You'll find clean sheets on the bed, by the way, and I don't think you'll need for anything. One last thing, old boy. Can I have your passport?'

Later, Vaux couldn't figure out why he had initially said he didn't have a passport. He supposed it was a knee-jerk reaction to preserve whatever was left of his personal freedom.

But Brown had insisted, simply saying, 'Adams gave it to you this morning, didn't he?'

'But it's not my real name,' said Vaux lamely as he handed it over.

'No, I understand that. A *nom de guerre*, shall we say?'

When the door slammed behind Brown, old instincts took over, and Vaux checked closely for any listening devices that his hosts might have installed in the safe house. But he found nothing except the food in the fridge: flat breads, precooked kofta, what looked like a lamb stew with carrots and zucchini in a plastic container, a barbecued chicken, a few plastic cartons of brown rice and hummus, and three cold kebabs. The drinks were limited to a bottle of Grant's whisky, a flask of gin, and six cans of Luxor Classic lager. Vaux had noticed a bottle of Arak Rayan on the kitchen table, half-full. It was a Syrian brand of arak, and Ahmed's favorite. He peeled off his clothes, took a tepid shower, and then went to bed.

***

In the small, stuffy offices at Department B3's center of operations, Alan Craw, still slim despite his middle years, with thinner blond-gray hair and a fastidiousness about himself unchanged since his Oxford days, had opened the dog-eared file marked MICHAEL VAUX/DEREK WESTROPP. The manila folder hadn't seen the light of day for a good eight years—until two days ago, when Sir Nigel Adair, head of B3, Sir Walter Mason's successor, told Craw to reacquaint himself with the dossier. Craw now waited to be summoned.

He heard a gentle tap on his door. Anne Armitage-Hallard, who had replaced Sir Walter's old secretary and gatekeeper Ms. Dimbleby, put her head around the half-open door and told Craw that Sir Nigel was waiting for him. Craw beamed at the sight of Anne, who often provided the early-morning tonic he needed to get through another day with a man who had, after all, beaten him to the top job at B3 despite Craw's long years of service to old Sir Walter. 'Sir Walt,' as B3 staffers fondly knew him, had retired two years ago after several deferments.

'You look marvelous, Anne, as always, of course. No parties or late nights recently?' he asked in a characteristic effort at small talk and perhaps a little blatant flirtation.

'Thank you, Alan,' said Anne, ignoring the personal question and then withdrawing behind the door.

Craw sighed at the ephemeral beauty of youth. She was about twenty, Craw guessed, and dazzlingly attractive to a male such as himself who had survived twenty-five years of marriage to a rich and domineering woman who was now obsessed with various cosmetic stratagems to look as young and fresh as a girl like Anne.

Sir Nigel sat at what Craw would always think of as Sir Walter's big rosewood desk. He was a big, heavy man (unlike Sir Walter) with a dominant personality (ditto) who often made unilateral decisions without the valuable input of Alan Craw, his deputy, or any other staffer at B3. He'd come from MI5, the domestic intelligence agency, viewed by seasoned MI6 types like Craw as akin to a grammar school compared to their superior 'public' school. All of which was complete poppycock, as far as Sir Nigel was concerned, and in any case, he had convinced himself that the likes of Craw and his other minions had been shunted to B3 from MI6 proper at Century House because, in some vague way, they had failed to 'measure up.'

Sir Nigel was sipping coffee from an antique willow-pattern mug—he had thrown out the Styrofoam cups that Sir Walter tolerated—and nibbling at a chocolate digestive when Craw came in.

'Got to get that damn window cleaned up, Craw. You can't see anything for the pigeon droppings. Get housekeeping on to that, will you? I've waited twenty-four months for a whole face-lift for these drab offices, and nothing's happened yet.'

'Budget cuts, sir. Mr. Blair's determined to prove he's as good a penny-pincher as any Tory.'

'I suppose so,' said Sir Nigel resignedly. 'Now, what's the latest on the Vaux situation?'

Craw opened the folder and took out a recently penned annotation.

'Well, sir, he's come in from the cold—'

Sir Nigel nearly choked on his digestive. His head shook rapidly, and his arm waved in the air like a metronome. 'None of that silly talk, Craw. I can't stand these writers who coin a phrase that catches on with everyone—including us. We must be professional. Just tell me like it is. No flowery phrases.'

Craw noted the mood. 'Very well, sir. Everything so far has gone according to plan. We got him to Alex, and right now, he's probably sipping an ice-cold beer.'

This time Sir Nigel met Craw's darting eyes with a smile. 'Yes, I remember that film well. *Ice Cold in Alex*, starring my old favorite, Trevor Howard.'

'Actually, sir, it was John Mills,' said Craw. 'Co-starred, of course, with that incomparable English beauty, Sylvia Syms.'

Sir Nigel pulled himself back to the present. 'Well, get on with it, man. I haven't got all day. Lunch with the politicos. In the Iolanthe Room at the Savoy. No budget cuts there.'

'Where, I believe, Winston Churchill sometimes held his Cabinet meetings before taking a nap upstairs,' said Craw, the amateur historian.

Sir Nigel ignored the diversion.

'Anyway, Vaux will be put in a holding pattern until I get there early next week. With what we're going to throw at him, I think he'll be the man for Operation Ebla. But we expect a lot of aggravation before we get to that point.'

'Very well, Craw. What about his old passport? Are you taking it with you?'

'I sent it on ahead by diplomatic courier. We wanted him to lose his real identity as soon as he left Cairo.'

'Good. Who are you taking with you?'

'Chris Greene, sir. He was complaining recently that he hadn't been out in the field for a long time. So he's the natural choice.'

'Yes, a good man too. Young and ambitious and no fool,' said Sir Nigel, who by standing and pushing back his chair signaled that the interview was over.

Craw wondered whether that admiring description of Greene was a dig at him. He smiled at Anne, who sat at the small desk outside Sir Nigel's office. She smiled in return, and Craw immediately felt better.

5

Vaux awoke to the amplified cries of the muezzin from the nearby minaret as the faithful were called to prayer. Honking car horns signaled the start of the early-morning rush hour. Minutes later, he heard the double lock on his front door turn and then the squeak that always accompanied the slow opening. Fatima, the woman who came in every morning to prepare his breakfast, quietly shuffled to the kitchen, warmed some milk for his café au lait, put a fresh croissant on the tray, and gently knocked on his bedroom door. She was a short, heavy woman who wore a long gray dress and a head scarf. She always smiled a greeting but said little because she didn't speak English. Despite several years in Damascus, Vaux's Arabic was embarrassingly deficient—the result of working on an English-language newspaper and having Arab friends who spoke excellent English. But he managed to communicate with her with the help of Vaux's odd word and their mutual gestures.

It had become routine now. She put the tray on his bedside table, nodded a greeting, and smiled. He returned the smile and said *chukran*. This was his fourth day at the safe house, and she was one of three humans he would meet all day—the others were Ted Brown and his driver, a retired sergeant in the UK's Special Forces whose poker face and stern demeanor reminded Vaux of his National Service days.

He felt as if he were under house arrest, but nothing that smacked of any legal maneuverings or lawyer talk had, he thanked God, reared its ugly head yet. Brown was always cheerful, in contrast to his military companion-driver, and had done what he'd said he would do: he'd brought in six cotton shirts of various colors, several pairs of underwear, and socks—and a real live Greek tailor who measured Vaux for a lightweight suit. Fatima polished his shoes every morning even though up to now he had not been allowed to step outside in the street. This he yearned to do, but once again, his request was met with solid resistance.

'No, old man, not yet,' declared Brown with a confident smile. 'It's for your own protection. You're an illegal alien now, and if a policeman or a security type asks you for an ID, you'd be done for.'

'Why don't you give me back my Westropp passport?'

'It hasn't been stamped with an entry visa by any consulate, Egyptian border guard, or airport customs man. You'd be in trouble right there.'

Vaux resigned himself to his uncertain fate. So far, everything had been very civilized. But his isolation had intensified his longing for Alena and his regrets. He shouldn't have walked out on her like that. Meanwhile, Brown unloaded a few more paperbacks for Vaux to read. And the ex-army man was bent over a small television set that they had brought in that morning.

He pressed the plug into an electric connection that hung precariously from the wall, and suddenly, the bluish screen lit up. A few twists of the dial brought up a silent newsreader whose Arabic came out loud and clear once Sarge had twisted a few more dials.

'Well done, Sarge,' said Brown. 'There you are, Vaux—all the conveniences of the modern world. You ask and we supply. Anything else before we go?'

'I'll be Britain's greatest expert on the murder mysteries of P. D. James before long—if you can't think of any other author, Ted. I like William Boyd, if you can find any of his stuff. And, of course, I'd appreciate some information of what you people plan for me. That's only natural. I can't stay here for the rest of my life. Or can I?'

'The consulate's library is somewhat limited, but I'll see what I can do. On the other matter, we have some good news. Tomorrow, a couple of guys from London will descend on us, and you'll be able to get some clue about what's intended for you.'

'Lawyers, I presume.'

'No, not really,' said Brown. He nodded to Sarge, a signal that he should leave and go down to the consulate's Land Rover, parked outside the building.

'Look, I can tell you this. There'll be two big wigs from the department for which, I believe, you did some work some years ago. They want to talk to you and clear up a few details about what you've been doing since you served queen and country. That's all. A little debriefing, I suppose.'

'And then the reckoning,' murmured Vaux.

Brown ignored the remark. 'Then we've got to work on your exit strategy—that should be fun. Meanwhile, enjoy the books and the TV. You can get CNN International somewhere on the dial.'

***

Craw had pulled rank and stretched out his long legs
in the first-class cabin, isolated by formal government request, while Greene had a window seat in business class.
They had booked through a private travel agency, and Craw
had demanded to fly British Airways, ostensibly on patriotic
grounds (buy British!), but really on his eternal hope that
he might get lucky with one of the attractive female flight
attendants, most of whom lived close to Heathrow. Such a
location would facilitate any possible future liaison. Greene,
oblivious to the older man's predilections, had his nose in a
Middle East travel guide, a basic tool considering the tasks
and responsibilities allotted to the particular government department he worked for.

It was a four-hour trip, and the Boeing 737 landed smoothly
at Alexandria Airport, known locally as El Nousha. They were
met by Ted Brown, who used his diplomatic corps credentials
to ensure a quick and polite passage through passport control
and customs. An old but immaculate black Daimler Sovereign
waited for them just outside the main exit, and an Egyptian
chauffeur in a black cap and formal livery stood at attention as
he held the rear door for both men to sink into the soft luxury
of the wide backseat. Brown piled their bags into the car's trunk
and then sat up front with the chauffeur.

To forestall any plans the consulate might have had about
their accommodations, Craw quickly told Brown that they had
reserved rooms at the Cecil Hotel, the luxurious and storied
hotel of colonial and World War II memories.

'We assumed you'd be staying at the consulate, sir. We've
plenty of space, and you'll love the location. The Cecil's a bit
shabby in places, and it's quite noisy—just steps away from the
traffic chaos of the Corniche.'

'But, my dear fellow, that's why we came—just a couple of tourists. We don't want to stay in the stuffiness of the consulate, thank you. Besides, we have to work at arm's length, as I'm sure you are aware. No, Greene and I will set up shop in the Cecil, thank you very much. I've reserved a suite, and it's too late to change things. Plenty of time to meet you people and the consul himself. We don't have to be on top of one another. We have some delicate tasks ahead.'

'Very well, sir,' said Brown as he turned around to look at Greene, who raised his eyebrows in the silent mutual bewilderment shared by two younger men at the whims and fuss of older colleagues.

They drove in silence through choked, noisy streets to the old hotel. The suite was big, with two bedrooms and a living area. The ceilings were high, and paintings and tapestries hung from the walls. The furniture was a mixture of art deco and contemporary, and Craw felt he had chosen well. He claimed the bigger bedroom by quickly dumping his suitcase on the wide double bed and then went over to the tall french windows that looked out over the traffic-clogged Corniche and the azure blue of the Mediterranean beyond. In his smaller room, Greene slowly unpacked and then went through to the living room, where he was pleased to see a TV and a small minibar. He grabbed a bottle of Heineken and approached the heavy-curtained casement window to enjoy the same view.

***

On the second day of their stay in Alexandria, Craw told Greene to call Ted Brown and arrange their first meeting with Michael Vaux. Greene had been riffling through the VAUX file that Craw had carelessly left on the small Louis XV desk in their joint living room. The three-page summary of Operation

Helvetia intrigued him. He hadn't realized until now that mild blame for the fiasco had been placed squarely on his shoulders: the charges against him had been a lack of 'sedulousness' in carrying out his task to shadow Vaux wherever and whenever he left his Geneva hotel—a failing that, according to the type-written report, had resulted in Vaux's complete disappearance for a few days, when he ostensibly sought to partake of the mineral waters of Vevey 'as a cure, no doubt, for his suspected alcoholism,' noted the report in parentheses. This was a pa-tently unjust accusation, Greene thought, and he wondered who had written the report and who had provided such in-supportable allegations. He had never been given a chance to defend himself before this self-serving committee of inquiry, which had been behind closed doors and whose members, he knew, consisted of Department B3's principal directors—Sir Walter, Craw, and a Major Short, who was on secondment from military intelligence and whose cold codfish eyes sent a chill through Greene's slim body even today.

Greene had always claimed he had done his best on his as-signment to shadow Vaux during his stay in Geneva. But he had also been told to follow Ahmed Kadri every afternoon when he would leave the Russian consulate on the banks of Lake Geneva on his return journey to the Hotel des Bergues, farther south on that picturesque lakeshore. Sometimes, juggling the dif-ferent times for his surveillance duties, blind spots inevitably cropped up. But now he knew that the powers that be didn't agree, and he had failed, thus contributing to the total shambles of the operation and the damaging loss of Michael Vaux's loyalty to the overall cause.

He flipped through to the last few pages and saw a sum-mary of RECOMMENDATIONS to avoid a repeat perfor-mance of the failure of what, at the outset, seemed such a brilliantly conceived project. He looked for his name in the Ten

New Commandments but found only an innocuous comment that could have pertained to him: 'No field agent given surveillance duties shall be burdened with two targets. His sole purpose will always be to act as a "watcher" of the primary target.'

Greene let out an audible sigh just as Craw walked in from his bedroom. Dressed in a dark-gray suit, wearing his Worcester College tie with a white crisp shirt, he declared himself ready. He picked up the VAUX file and put it in his leather Velextra Diplomatico briefcase, a recent birthday gift from his wife given to him the day before she told him she wanted a divorce.

'Okay, Greene, the car will be here in ten minutes— just enough time for a quick one at Monty's Bar on the first floor. You do realize, don't you, that this hotel was General Montgomery's HQ in the North African campaign?'

Greene said he'd seen a picture in the hotel lobby of the great general getting into a jeep outside the Cecil.

Earlier, Craw had called Brown for the car despite the short distance to the safe house over Barclays. Once the first meeting with Vaux was over, they agreed to have lunch with the consul and a few of his colleagues.

***

'I always like to do this sort of thing around a table,' said Craw.

Vaux heard the clatter of the external roof elevator doors closing, then raucous laughter and loud voices. He had just pulled on the light cotton pants of his new suit and decided not to wear a jacket or tie. He sat at the table in the kitchen, sipping his third coffee, while Fatima made his bed. Then he heard the turn of the double lock and the continuing bonhomie among the expected visitors. He didn't know whom they would be but wasn't surprised to see an older and grayer Craw walk in first, arm outstretched for a solid handshake. Greene had changed little. He still looked relatively youthful, slim, and earnest.

'This is the only table we have, so perhaps we can all sit here,' replied Vaux, responding to Craw's alleged preferences.

'This is just fine,' said Craw.

They all sat down, and Craw looked over the rickety oil-skin-covered table at Brown, who had just pulled out a chair for himself.

'This is strictly a departmental meeting, old boy. Do you mind?'

'Oh, no, not at all,' said an apologetic Brown, who then left the kitchen to join Sarge, who was again bent over the silent, flickering TV.

In the kitchen, a silence descended. The muted sound of traffic could be heard through the small open sash window, then the clip-clop of a sturdy horse as a calèche made its way down a nearby side street toward the Corniche. A ship's bellowing siren blew over the low roofs from the harbor. The mood was somber. Vaux sat back, his arms folded, and waited to see what sort of attitude Craw would adopt. He knew he was pompous and arrogant, but sometimes a civilized streak emerged and he could be quite human. Greene was always affable, and in a strange way, Vaux thought he could rely on him as an ally if things got too tense. It was Greene who, eight years or so ago, had told him of Alena's 'expedient demise,' the euphemism for assassination employed by the high priests of the SIS. Vaux had always known that Greene spoke from the heart, so he had been misled, mis-informed, just as he had. This, as far as Vaux was concerned, at least put him in the category of honest broker.

'Well, Vaux, this is a fine old pickle you've got yourself into,' said Craw. He took some papers out of his briefcase and shuffled through them, as if to check a prepared speech.

Greene sucked on the neck of a bottle of Coke that Fatima had offered. His eyes darted over to Vaux, who met them with a shrug.

Craw continued. 'Let's see if we've got this straight, old boy. We understand that Kadri's in big trouble. He's your protector, to put it candidly—has been since you left us—and now you're on the lam because they want you back in Damascus to presumably quiz you about your connection or relationship with Kadri. Right so far?'

'That about sums it up,' said Vaux. 'But I'd suggest it's somewhat more complicated than that.'

'We're here to listen, old man. Spill all the beans. Greene here will lend a sympathetic ear.'

'Does that mean you won't?' asked Vaux. He hoped he sounded reasonably lighthearted.

Craw put on one of his no-nonsense faces. 'Please, Vaux, start the ball rolling.'

Vaux summarized his history over the last eight years: his decision to follow his old friend Ahmed Kadri to Syria and his relationship with Alena Hussein, who, as they knew, worked for the Syrian intelligence establishment; how Kadri secured a job for him and how the threesome lived in Damascus and enjoyed life together.

'Yes, yes, yes. We know all that, Vaux. But we're not here as nursemaids or psychiatrists. No more bad-luck stories. We're here to talk turkey, eh, Greene?'

Greene always felt dominated by Craw when he was used as a third man in delicate negotiations of one sort or another. But he liked to sometimes preempt his boss and say things that perhaps Craw would prefer to have been left for him to say.

'I think Vaux should know, sir, that there are no pending legal actions against him. I'm sure he's aware that Sir Walter ordered a warrant for his arrest after he quit Morocco for his

Syrian job. He may not know that our legal people found him innocent of any offense.'

Vaux was surprised at this news. He was always under the impression that if he returned to the UK, he'd be grabbed and charged.

'That's good to know. Thanks for telling me, Chris.'

Craw swept in. 'That's right, Vaux. The legal wallahs decided you had carried out your assignment. You had been hired as a temporary NOC, nonofficial cover officer, and your decision not to come back to us was not illegal in itself. It may have been doubtful from an ethical point of view—and certainly not very patriotic—but there are no charges pending against you.'

Greene piped in. 'You did everything you were meant to do. Those recordings of your conversations with Kadri were transcribed and duly dispatched to us at Gower Street. Sir Walter's files were replenished with invaluable intelligence, and he looked forward to your face-to-face report that would have concluded the operation. But, of course, when you didn't appear and instead stayed with Kadri, he was mad as hell. Hence the arrest warrant. It was just something the old man could do. He felt betrayed and helpless. He wanted to lash out. Do you understand that? He liked you as well—and that hurt.'

'Then why am I put in a safe house pending your inquiry and told to remain incommunicado, unable to organize anything that could point to some sort of future for myself?' said Vaux in disingenuous mode.

Craw was not going to rise to this bait. He gestured to Greene to take over.

'It's for your protection, Michael. I'm sure you can see that. The Egyptians, at times, may have rocky relations with the Syrians, but their intelligence people cooperate when they find themselves dealing with perceived enemy agents. The Syrians want you back to help them build their case against Kadri—and then they'll probably accuse you of being a sleeper agent working for the UK all along. They'd be half right.'

'What are you talking about?' asked Vaux, puzzled by Greene's claim.

'You *were* employed by us. That's all they need, believe me. That's enough to link MI6 with Kadri. And Alena could be the last shoe to drop,' said Greene.

Fatima knocked gently at the door and gestured with her arms and smiles that she could replenish the soft drinks and coffee if they wished. They nodded, and she served Greene with a clean glass along with the Coke and two more cups of milky coffee.

Vaux decided to take the lead now. 'So how do I get out of here? Warrant or no warrant, I want to return to England as soon as possible.'

'What about your relationship with Alena Hussein?' asked Craw.

'It's on ice,' said Vaux. 'That's all I can say.'

They sipped their drinks. Greene stretched his arms and smiled at Vaux, a gesture perhaps of encouragement. Craw got to his feet and began to walk around the kitchen like a zoo animal needing exercise. His hands were clasped behind his back.

'Look, Vaux, we have a proposition.'

6

Vaux looked out on to the long garden that stretched down to the riverbank. On its slow and sluggish way to the North Sea, the Stour meandered through this part of Suffolk, bordered by long reeds and thick clusters of rushes on the low banks and by weeping willows whose branches dropped to touch the surface of the water. Beyond the river was a big expanse of what the English called 'common land,' a historic legal concept that meant what it said. Thus the green acres of grass that fanned out from the other side of the river were taken over by gamboling dogs and their walkers, an occasional herd of cattle as a local farmer exercised his medieval rights, and on weekends, by families who had driven in from nearby towns to watch the majestic swans and frenetic ducks, residents of this territory since time immemorial.

It was a calm, rural scene, and once again, Vaux was reminded of the quiet beauty of the English countryside. In this Suffolk manor house, there were reproductions of

Constable's bucolic paintings of this part of the world, and a few Gainsborough portraits (also reproductions) to commemorate the great artist's restored residence in the area. Vaux had just poured himself a Cutty Sark, and when the phone rang, he was pondering a dinner at The Swan, a nearby hotel that served traditional English country fare like jugged hare and roast beef. He moved over to the desk and picked up the receiver.

'Hello?'

'Can we do the usual tonight?' It was Craw, and the question meant that Vaux should go to the public phone box, about three hundred yards down the country lane from the house.

'That'll be okay,' said Vaux, code for 'message received and understood' in Craw's obligatory military jargon. Ironic, Vaux always thought, since the man had been exempt from military service due to a childhood case of scarlet fever that the military medics feared had probably weakened his heart.

It was only a 'checking in' call, as Craw referred to the routine daily contact. Vaux had been installed in the house as an expedient following his successful exit from Alexandria. They had given him a new identity—a passport, three credit cards, and an international driving license—and it was a sad Vaux who witnessed the shredding of his Derek Westropp passport. He had wanted to keep it for nostalgic reasons, but Craw insisted on the complete obliteration of the past. Thus even his legit passport, issued to Michael Vaux and held at the embassy in Cairo, also had to go. He comforted himself for these losses with the recognition that his new alias was at least elegant: he was now 'Justin Horner,' and Horner thought it diplomatic to accept the terms offered by MI6 in exchange for his escape from Egypt, his freedom from any legal repercussions due to unforeseeable mishaps in the past, and the official car that took him into the depths of Suffolk.

In truth, of course, Vaux had no leverage. Hunted by Syria's GSD agents, aided and abetted erratically and more or less enthusiastically by Egypt's Mukhabarat, the basic fact that Department B3 had found yet another assignment for him reaffirmed Vaux's sometimes fleeting belief in a fate that periodically picked him up, dusted him off, and relaunched him into an acceptable and familiar world.

***

In the small, hot kitchen, where the only ventilation came from a narrow window that let in a zephyr of cool air waft in from the calm waters of the Mediterranean, Craw had outlined B3's latest planned enterprise, which, given Vaux's sudden availability, had taken on a new life. It was in danger of wilting on the vine, said Craw, and now it had a real chance of revival that could bear rich fruits. Vaux, mesmerized by Craw's unfailing ability to mix mysterious metaphors, listened with mild interest, his mind sometimes wavering from thoughts of Alena and Ahmed to the relief he felt in hearing that England considered him a free man.

Chris Greene had been given the task of organizing Vaux's getaway. With a brand-new identity, a new Tom Selleck mustache, dyed black hair, and to smooth the way, a few friendly handouts to favored immigration officials at the port of Alexandria, Vaux was sent on his way by Greek freighter to Athens, and thence by cheery and hospitable British Airways to London. A tall young man in chauffeur's livery brandishing a white cardboard sign marked HORNER met him at Heathrow. The young man offered to carry the scuffed consulate-supplied suitcase to Sir Walter Mason's Rolls Royce Silver Seraph, parked at the curb in front of arrivals. The driver had been told not to engage in any friendly chatter—just to get the party to his destination.

The driver put the bag down in the foyer, and Vaux began to explore the old house. It looked Elizabethan, though he was no expert on architectural history. The gabled facade of the building, the low beamed ceilings, the big inglenook fireplace—all suggested an ancient manor house. There was a spacious lounge that opened on to a glass-ceilinged conservatory, stuffed with exotic plants, shrubs, and bulbs. French windows gave way to a wrought iron balcony overlooking the long garden. No other human stirred in the house, and he sat down to find out what was inside the regular envelope that the driver had given him before he left to drive back to London.

Dear Mr. Horner,

Welcome to the River House. I hope you enjoy your stay. As you have no doubt noticed, the place is empty, pending a sale probably in the spring. This is not a 'safe house' as such (the telephones are not secure). It was inherited by my wife, Sybil, when her beloved sister died three months ago. Mrs. Appleby will be in soon to turn down your bed and prepare a snack, if required. You are very close to The Swan, just up the lane and over the river. Good pub food and ale. I am now retired, as you probably know. Look forward to having a drink (or two) with you sometime to talk about old times. Please destroy this note by flushing it down the toilet. The basement loo is closest to the foyer.

Thank you,
Walter Mason

In that very English way, old Sir Walt was sending the clear message that all was forgiven for past failings or transgressions.

***

'Let's cut to the chase,' said Alan Craw, as if blame for the extended period of inaction had been squarely put on Vaux.

Craw had arrived at the manor house early one morning, along with Chris Greene, both attired in casual country clothes, as if two friends had dropped in on Justin Horner to enjoy a restful weekend. Craw had driven his silver Aston Martin Vantage from Knightsbridge, picking Greene up from his apartment in Chalk Farm. Not having given Greene any warning of the weekend assignment, Craw waited impatiently as Greene threw some clothes into a canvas holdall. The way Craw drove—fast and erratic—it took only two hours to get up to Suffolk. On the way, he outlined the general strategy of Operation Ebla, Vaux's key role, and the very early stages of the mission.

'Why Ebla?' Greene asked.

'It's an ancient Syrian town, southwest of Aleppo. Goes back to 2500 BC. Excavations all over the place. They've also discovered ancient documents that confirm it was a major political and commercial center. The old ruins, including a magnificent acropolis, have been carefully restored. It's an historic treasure—which is why the Syrians have chosen the location for their major uranium-enrichment site and the center of their total nuclear weapons program. Such irreplaceable cultural assets, they believe, could never be obliterated or destroyed by Western or Israeli aggression. The West would never live it down. All this, Greene, is top secret, and we're at an early stage. I could be talking poppycock. That's what our excursion is all about. Vaux has to be in the know, as it were, before we can proceed further.'

With this enigmatic caveat, Craw drove the rest of the way in silence. Despite some twelve years at Department B3, Greene felt like an acolyte again, the junior who would be told only what Craw decided to impart. Even so, he looked forward to a couple of days in the country and the company of Michael Vaux.

Mrs. Appleby had made coffee for the three men, who sat in the conservatory. She put some chocolate digestive biscuits on a big oval plate and then left for the kitchen. The french windows were open. It was a warm late-August morning, and the squawks and hoots from the wild inhabitants of the river punctuated the conversation. Craw got up to close the inside doors so that their conversation couldn't be overheard in the house. He knew how village gossip could sabotage a delicate operation as much as hidden bugs beamed to the enemy.

Vaux said, 'I've been waiting here for this briefing for ten long days. So I agree, let's get on with it.'

'Entirely out of my control, old boy. Someone once said— I believe it was Le Carre—that the covert intelligence game is a waiting game, or something to that effect. Anyway, I want Greene to start off with an overall summary. Where we are and where we want to go.' He looked at Greene, who decided to relate what he knew about Operation Ebla—before it had been given that name.

'As we discussed in Alex, Michael—'

Craw intervened. 'Don't you think we had better get used to calling him Justin, Greene? We're going out to dinner tonight, and we must assert Vaux's new identity among the villagers.'

Vaux didn't point out that the sort of five-star restaurant in the surrounding areas that Craw would no doubt select after painstaking study were unlikely to be frequented by the sort of people Craw meant by 'villagers.'

'Yes, of course,' agreed Greene. He smiled at Vaux, an acknowledgment that they both had to share the whims and excesses of a tedious colleague.

He continued. 'As we told you in Alex, a Syrian nuclear scientist contacted us recently. To be brief, he wants out of Syria. He wants us to grant him asylum and bring over his wife and two daughters. He's been working on Assad's nuclear program and possesses all the documented facts the West would love to get our collective hands on. These include details of Syria's ambitions in the nuclear area as well as its hush-hush program for the development of WMDs, weapons of mass destruction. These include chemical and biological weapons. We believe they are already producing sarin nerve gas; tabun, a particularly lethal nerve agent; and mustard gas of various types—all of which are outlawed by the Chemical Weapons Convention of 1993 and which Syria has refused to sign.'

'Don't get too technical, Greene. Not yet, anyway. The point is, Vaux—sorry, Horner. The point is this chap's a Sunni. I'm sure, having lived in Damascus, you are fully aware of the religious tensions in the country between the majority Sunnis and the Shia Alawites who govern. The late, departed Assad was, of course, an Alawite, as is his son. Then there's the Christians and Kurds—what a melting pot!'

Vaux said, 'You can probably add the Druze to the pot. But what's the status of this defector? Is he here now or waiting patiently in Syria for some sort of rescue operation?'

'Who said anything about a rescue operation?' said Craw

'I assumed—'

'Don't assume anything, dear boy,' said Craw, who now thought it appropriate to take over from Greene's introductory briefing.

'We have a problem. This scientist—no names yet—is so trusted by Syrian officials that he often attends international conferences. So there's an easy way to get him out of there once the opportunity presents itself. The stumbling block is his wife and the two girls. Even though he's a Sunni, he's trusted by the Alawite clan—which, as you know, is not unusual. In the old man's Syria, Sunnis and Alawites got along together. Your old friend Ahmed Kadri is a Sunni, after all. And Assad had a sprinkling of all the sects and tribes, including Christians, in his official cabinet as well as in the government apparatus at large. His son hasn't changed that. To add to the complications is the fact that this man's wife is a Christian, and the two daughters, both in their early teens, have been taught both religions so that they can decide whether to be Muslims or Christians when they come of age—or that's how I understand it.'

Vaux felt a pang of sadness at the mention of Ahmed. He still didn't know what had happened to him. He couldn't contact Alena, who would surely know by now. So he thought this could be an appropriate time to ask about the two people who had dominated his life in recent years.

'Speaking of Ahmed, I wondered whether you had any news—your people in Syria, for instance.'

Craw drained the last dregs of his coffee and looked a little peeved. He nodded to Greene as if it was a subject that, as far as he was concerned, was closed.

'No news on that score, I'm afraid,' said Greene. 'As far as Hussein is concerned, she's still in Cairo, and the back channels indicate she's in no trouble, despite the shock of your sudden disappearance. They called her back to Damascus for a couple of days, no doubt in an effort to find out whether she helped you do a runner, but she seems to have convinced them that she had nothing to do with your "desertion" from the newspaper— which, we understand, is how they view our little operation to get you out of there. So she's in the clear, as I suppose she should be. She had no idea that we would come into the picture so quickly or that Thompson had an inside line to us. So she's still held in high regard by our Syrian friends. But as far as Ahmed Kadri, no news, I'm afraid.'

Craw stood up and walked over to the open french windows.

'Lovely view, positively bucolic. We were lucky to have found this place. Better than some shabby and grimy old safe house in the outskirts of London, eh, Vaux? Of course, it's thanks to Sir Walter whose recently deceased sister-in-law used to live here. There are a few disadvantages, of course. I should mention that, on Monday morning, the telephone people will be here to check up on a malfunction, or whatever. When they've gone, you will find a brand-new red telephone that will be totally secure. So you won't have to traipse up to the public call box anymore.'

Craw picked up a straw trilby he'd placed on the coffee table and walked down the few steps to the garden and decided to head for the riverbank, where four white wrought iron chairs were placed around a marble-topped table. He took off his hat, sat down, and admired the view. Greene flipped through a folder that he'd brought with him and looked at Vaux with friendly eyes. They had both survived yet another pompous session with the boss.

'You should know, Michael, this Syrian scientist, his code name's Saladin. So I don't have to tell you that, in any communication with us, that's the name to use. Your role in all this, of course, will mean that you'll eventually know his real name. But more on that later.'

Mrs. Appleby, a portly lady in her early sixties with white hair tied back into a bun, opened the door and asked Vaux whether they would all be having lunch. Vaux looked at Greene for some direction, and Greene said he thought that would be very nice. Mrs. Appleby then suggested she show the bedrooms she'd selected for the two weekend guests.

Looking back to Greene as she slowly climbed the old oak staircase, she said, 'This way, you'll have first choice, sir.' Greene was shown the Yellow Room, then the Blue Room, and finally, the Green Room. He was superstitious, so he thought it was probably a good omen to choose a room whose name closely resembled his. Before Mrs. Appleby left him to test the bed, he hadn't been able to resist asking her what room Mr. Horner had chosen.

'Oh, that's what Mrs. Abel called the "master bedroom," sir. She was married to an American, you see. There are two bathrooms on this floor, by the way, sir. And if they're both busy, you can use the one upstairs in the attic.'

***

The evening had gone well. Craw, as expected, selected an expensive restaurant from the local yellow pages. It was in a small village about thirty miles away. They commandeered an old Jaguar XJ that sat in a garage behind the house. It hadn't been driven, according to Sir Walter, since his sister-in-law died but was still in good shape. Greene, who had been chosen by Craw as the designated driver, took the wheel and drove them to The Duck Place. In an expansive mood, Craw allowed Greene one bottle of Double Diamond. But Greene didn't feel as celebratory as Craw, who was ecstatic when the sommelier assured him that he could indeed offer a bottle of his favorite Echezeux Grand Cru from the cellar. Craw had ordered no shoptalk during dinner, but he took great delight in putting up the volume when he thought it appropriate to use Vaux's alias.

'Could you get Mr. Horner another Cutty Sark, Waiter?' he shouted above the hubbub of the restaurant's loud and lively clientele. 'He doesn't like wine, so I've got to drink this whole lot myself!'

Craw paid in cash and kept the receipt. Greene drove back as carefully as if he'd had a lot more than one beer. The three secret agents retired at about midnight. But Vaux couldn't sleep. Driving back from The Duck Place, Craw had been unusually expansive and informative—not surprising, Vaux thought, considering his alcohol intake. So many facts and figures were swirling around inside Vaux's cranium, he could not shut them all off. In the master bedroom, he tossed and turned and finally gave up. He got up out of his bed and sat down at the mahogany writing table that stood in front of the leaded windows. He took a sheet from a pad of notepaper and a ball-point pen from an old stained mug stuffed with pens and pencils, rubber bands, and paper clips.

He began to write:

Operation Ebla:

Facts of the situation—to date.

1) A Syrian nuclear scientist code-named Saladin wants to defect to Britain. He is high up in the ranks of the Syrian government agency that overlooks the development of its nuclear program—the Atomic Energy Commission of Syria. He travels worldwide, and his latest foray abroad was to attend a big meeting of the International Atomic Energy Association (IAEA) in Vienna.

2) The Brits were contacted by a double agent (code name Gertrude, after renowned Arabist Gertrude Bell, Craw informed us) who works for Syria's GSD, Syria's major intelligence outfit. Gertrude was in Vienna on surveillance work— euphemism for watching Syrian delegates for any wobbly loyalties. There, she made certain promises and guarantees to Saladin, who realized the price of admission to theWest was a hefty dossier on Syria's nuclear programs—civil and military, plus comprehensive facts and figures on Syria's armed forces.

3) Saladin had no problems with this. The stumbling block is his family. His wife and two daughters live in Damascus. The girls (in their early teens) attend a private school for Syrian foreign service officials, and the wife is a Christian (Eastern Orthodox) whose full-time job is being a wife and mother. Understandably, Saladin insists there can be no deal unless we can secure their exit. It's all or nothing, as Craw put it.

4) Saladin will be in London within a week or so. His mission: to brief the Syrian legation on Syria's ongoing nuclear program as well as the country's overall military / air power programs, including a modernization drive spurred, it seems, by renewed Russian assistance, technologically and financially. B3 wants to use this opportunity to debrief Saladin in an informal way through the medium of yours truly. He will be recommended a short stay in this area (he says he is free to travel in the UK for leisure or health reasons).

5) Saladin will have no idea that Justin Horner has any connection with the clandestine world of intelligence. He will meet me at this big and comfortable house, and we will become two men, hopefully friends, who find themselves in Suffolk on a short rest cure, a diversionary holiday to refuel our energy banks to once again go out and confront the working world.

6) *Craw is hoping that, among other things, this new 'friendship' will in some way develop into a plausible and practicable plan to get the family out of Syria. Craw says (gloomily) that without the whole family, this 'dazzling' intelligence coup could 'die on the vine' (his metaphor!).*

7) *Finally, Craw and his chief believe my familiarity with Damascus / Syria / Cairo will help ignite the sort of 'intimacy' between two men that could lubricate Operation Ebla in the twin tasks of securing the precious WMD dossier and the successful evacuation from Syria of the family Saladin.*

8) *But how?*

Vaux drew a deep breath and put down the pen. He felt he had to collect his thoughts to counter the vagueness and opacity that had so far imbued the preliminary plans for Operation Ebla. He often found that writing a summary of any situation that confronted him helped to clear the air and think straight. He wasn't sure whether this time that antidote to a confused mind had worked. He looked through the window at the dark night. There was no moon. But he could make out the murky, sluggish river and even a few wide-awake ducks swimming in line close to the bank. The night canopy sparkled with masses of bright stars and planets he should have been able to name but couldn't.

He knew his notes had to be for his eyes only, so he took the sheet of paper to bed with him, stuffing it under his pillow. In the morning, he'd follow Sir Walter's earlier instructions and flush it down the toilet. As sleep came at last, Vaux wondered fleetingly whether this clever, ambivalent 'Gertrude' had ever come across Alena, still out there in the field, diligently working in the interests of Syria and, as she always insisted, the greater Arab cause.

***

Mrs. Appleby fussed around the dining room table, placing various items of cutlery, plates, and cups and saucers. She had put several entrée dishes on the long mahogany sideboard, and eight fried eggs lay gently quaking on a heated chafing dish. The three men ate silently, and Craw asked for more toast.

'Excellent restaurant last night, eh, Horner?'

'Absolutely.'

Craw waited until Mrs. Appleby had returned to the kitchen. He looked around the room to make sure no uninvited party had arrived while he was concentrating on breakfast.

'Greene will give you the number where you can call me on the secure line. Greene will also keep you abreast of events. He'll be your handler while I get busy to rope Saladin into our orbit. It should only be a matter of a few weeks, so relax and enjoy the great English countryside,' said Craw.

Then, as a casual afterthought, he said, 'Oh, and by the way, Sir Nigel asked me to remind you that you had signed the Official Secrets Act some years ago. It's as relevant now as it was then.'

Then he asked Greene to fetch his Valextra briefcase and take his overnight leather suitcase to the Aston Martin. Greene and Vaux exchanged sympathetic looks, and feeling a frisson of lightheartedness at the early resumption of his now familiar lonely existence, Vaux asked Craw why he always named the brand of his admittedly very smart briefcase.

Craw looked baffled. 'Because, my dear Justin, they cost around five thousand pounds apiece.'

Greene dumped the bag on the parquet floor and then left with the other case. Craw opened the briefcase, searched inside with his slender, manicured hands, and produced a Webley .38, a piece familiar to Vaux since his national service days.

'Christ, I thought these were collectors' items,' said Vaux.

'Just an insurance policy, Vaux. They still work—six bullets in the chamber. Keep it out of sight, old boy.'

Vaux put the gun in the pocket of his dressing gown. They both got up, shook hands, and Craw left. In the driveway, Vaux watched Craw speak to Greene and gesture for him to move out of the driver's seat, shaking his head at the impetuousness of youth. The car screeched forward and threw up a cloud of gravel as Vaux waved to them.

Mrs. Appleby hovered with a shiny Melitta cafetière of fresh coffee as Vaux sat down at the table again. He told her the guests had left, and she said she would like to have said good-bye to the gentlemen. She had no idea that they were in such a rush.

7

Three days after what the idle gossips at MI6 would later call Craw's 'dirty weekend' in Suffolk (the more prurient toilers at Century House suspected Craw harbored homoerotic fantasies about young, handsome Greene), three 'tourists' who had never met before had an 8:00 p.m. rendezvous at a shabby, ill-lit pub off the Edgware Road. Their host was Mr. Jacob Wolfson, who had briefed himself on their respective identities. He also knew their career histories: short, but all three showing not one single failure in their chosen vocation.

The four men seemed like a group of old friends, talking and laughing and drinking their pints of bitter, though a more careful and diligent listener would have noticed traces of accents from across the English channel, perhaps Germany or Scandinavia and certainly France. They talked and laughed loudly, patted one another on the back, and finally, left together, nodding good-bye to other customers and wishing them a nice evening.

The host quickly took them to a Mercedes Benz S Class saloon parked nearby on murky New Quebec Street. They all piled in. But he did not start the engine. He handed each man a small card with an address. They were all to stay at different hotels, small two-star places, explained the host, where a low profile would be easy to maintain. In the morning, an envelope would be left at the front desk of each hotel in which a left luggage locker ticket would be found. The location and number of the locker would be on the electronic receipt, and in those lockers, the three men would find the tools of their trade, plus their new passports.

In a low voice, Mr. Wolfson then told them the location of their target and that they could take their time and wait for the easiest opportunity to complete their task. There were plenty of small hotels and b&bs in the destination area, and the only hostelry out of bounds was called The Swan. He gave no reason for this exception. The three men speculated in silent unison that it had something to do with price. In the canvas holdalls waiting to be claimed by them at the left luggage location at Liverpool Street station, they would also find the info they needed: the name of the target, a photo of him entering the Syrian embassy in Belgrave Square, the man's temporary address, likely daily habits (country walks?), restaurants and/or pubs in the small village nearby. Trains ran from the Liverpool Street terminal to the area almost on an hourly basis. Finally, Wolfson asked to see the passports the men were carrying. He flipped the pages and checked the photos against their names: Bob Kirby, the English; Victoire Gaillard, from Paris; and Ernst Stockmann, the man from Essen. All was good. His people had done another excellent job.

***

Lady Sybil Mason called Mrs. Appleby quite frequently, but on this bright, sunny August morning, she had a special request to make—at least that's how she saw it, even if Mrs. Appleby considered it a direct order. She told her late sister's housekeeper that Mrs. Abel's last wishes were to convert the old riverside house to a sort of executives' retreat. Not a nursing home, no, not at all, she had replied to Mrs. Appleby's attempt to get down to brass tacks. There would be just a few guests to start with, and Mr. Justin Horner could be described as their first client. Again, she corrected Mrs. Appleby when the latter chose to ask about any future intake of 'patients.'

Another 'client' was due shortly. The local medical clinic had been notified, and the doctors collective had agreed that they would be happy to offer the usual National Health services to any clients who needed medical attention. Checkups would be offered, and the client's medications would be checked and monitored. But essentially, the residence would be a place of leisure—with good, healthy food, complete rest, and no pressure from the hassles of the outside world. Lady Sybil didn't elaborate on the topic of diet, but Mrs. Appleby resolved not to change a thing in her usual repertoire unless requested. Thus breakfasts would feature fruit, cereals, bacon and eggs, and sausages. She would prepare a light salad for lunch and a nice roast for dinner. Once a week, she would take delivery of wild salmon or some plaice fillets from the local fishmonger—and she was sure that's what Lady Sybil would want.

Vaux was sitting in the conservatory when Mrs. Appleby came in with the just-delivered *Daily Telegraph*. She seemed a little nervous, and Vaux felt she was looking at him more closely than usual, as if she were curious about his state of well-being or his health or peace of mind. He looked up at her and asked if there was anything bothering her or whether he could do anything to help out with her domestic chores.

'Oh, no, Mr. Horner, you mustn't exert yourself. You should just take it easy. I'll wipe the garden seats off in a minute;

they get very damp with the dew, you see. Then you can sit by the river for a spell. Now, please just rest, and I'll bring you in something to drink. Perhaps a milky coffee or a nice fresh-squeezed orange juice?'

Vaux couldn't fathom this sudden onslaught of concern for his well-being and looked her straight in the eye. 'Mrs. Appleby, what I'd really like is a bloody mary. I need a pick-me-up before I toddle into the village, if you don't mind.'

'Oh, Mr. Horner, are you quite sure? Aren't you supposed to rest and—what do they say these days?—dry out and that sort of thing. Your health is very important, you know, and you must look after yourself.'

Vaux downed a spicy bloody mary and then walked up the hill to the village. In the Bull & Bush, a quick call to Craw from the public phone box cleared up the mystery of Mrs. Appleby's sudden onrush of motherhood.

'That's the cover, dear boy. You're now residing in an executive retreat, a place to relax, cut down on the liquor, and eat a healthy diet—in your case, that wouldn't be such a bad idea, either. In any event, you will soon be joined by Saladin himself, and you will no doubt learn his real name when he checks in. Don't forget to keep the conversation general at first, and then try and extract some key information. Are you with me, Vaux?'

It was the usual vague but rosy conversation he always had these days with Craw. Perhaps he would learn more about the progress, if any, of Operation Ebla from Greene, who, according to Craw, would appear on the scene tomorrow. He would be staying at The Swan and would contact Vaux in due course.

***

Dr. Nessim Said, a slightly built man with cropped, grizzled hair, checked into the River House in the early afternoon. Mrs.

Appleby insisted he sign the brand-new leather-covered guest book, just below the forged signature of one Justin Horner. She felt compelled to commit this felony to reassure the new client that he wasn't alone in the house and need not fear isolation, which perhaps could intensify any stress and contribute to a further decline in his state of mental health. Besides, Mr. Horner was an understanding man, and she was sure he wouldn't object to the innocent subterfuge.

Dr. Said was shown to the Yellow Room, where he unpacked a single suitcase. He had never heard of this Mr. Horner, so perhaps what Craw had told him was true: it wasn't a so-called safe house, but a legitimate country retreat for exhausted businessmen. There was nothing he could do anyway but await events to unfold and learn more about the plans to extricate his wife and children from Syria as soon as possible. Then, he supposed, a thorough debriefing and the handover of the dossier that would expose Syria's nuclear weapons plans, its chemical weapons stockpiles, the order of battle of its armed forces in any future war with Israel, and the country's long- and short-range missile capabilities, readiness of air defenses, and potential military manpower in a crisis situation. The whole bill of goods.

Vaux approached the Syrian warily. At dinner, they would discuss his experiences in Damascus and Cairo, where he had worked as a correspondent for the *Damascus Times*. Said was intrigued by Vaux's life story, his career as a journalist for several well-known publications, his stormy marriage and 'recent divorce,' and now his doctor-ordered rest cure before contemplating his eventual retirement. But Said revealed little about himself in the early days of their acquaintance, often retiring to his room for long hours.

Vaux met Chris Greene every day at The Swan, where he had installed himself in one of the few guest rooms.

'How's it going, Mike—sorry, Justin?' was his usual greeting.

Vaux's usual reply: 'It's coming along, I guess.'

'A few messages from Craw, old boy. Numero uno, as promised, we've opened an account for you at Coutts & Co., the queen's bank.'

'In that case, I'm sure the money will be quite safe,' said Vaux.

'Your stipend will be paid on a monthly basis, just so you know. Numero duo, Craw wonders whether a fleeting visit by him could get the ball rolling.'

'I don't really know. He's opening up gradually. Sometimes I feel he's about to tell his own life story any moment, but then he clams up. I think he feels I'm curious, and of course, I've been very open about myself.'

'Except for the obvious, I hope,' Greene said lightheartedly. 'Give Craw a call on the secure line when old Said isn't about. You know how he likes progress reports.'

They decided on a pre-lunch drink at the hotel's bar-restaurant. It was a spacious set of rooms, and Vaux could see the river and the old mansion house on the opposite bank. He observed a solitary Nessim (they were now on first-name terms) sitting on a deck chair, reading a book under the big willow. On the common, dog walkers unleashed excited canines that frenetically chased balls and one another.

They sat down at a table by the big windows and contemplated the view in silence. Suddenly, Vaux said he couldn't see much point in Craw coming down. It could even upset Said, who seemed nervous as well as shy. He needed time to work on him and open him up.

'But look, you're here and you're the handler. I notice you are staying incommunicado. Why add a rambunctious Craw to the mix?'

'He's the case officer, Vaux. You have to get used to the way we work.'

Vaux sighed. 'Give me a few more days.'

They ordered The Swan's special of the day—a club sandwich and two bottles of Bass Pale Ale. When they parted, they shook hands out of habit.

'Any news from Cairo?' asked Vaux.

'Alena, you mean?'

'Yes.'

'Only that she's still in Cairo. But she's been traveling a lot, it seems. To home base in Damascus as well as to Tartus on the Med. And even into Lebanon.'

'Strange,' said Vaux.

***

That evening, Said relaxed a little more. Mrs. Appleby had cooked roast lamb at his request and had bought a packet of couscous, which she steamed with the vegetables, according to his written instructions. They sat in the conservatory and began a long conversation on world affairs.

'Clinton seems to be putting a real effort into the Mideast problem. The Camp David negotiations are probably the biggest step any American president has taken since Carter's Camp David treaty that ended the Israeli-Egyptian conflict,' said Vaux, rather too pompously. But he had his reasons.

'The Israelis haven't got their heart in any deal, Justin. They will sign agreements, then claim the Palestinians aren't living up to their promises and break the whole thing off. Or else some random terrorist act will sabotage the whole process. Goodwill can evaporate in a matter of hours when there's blood on the street or a blown-up bus full of dead children. The Israelis still think time is on their side, but demographically, they couldn't be more wrong,' said Said.

'What about the other Arab countries? Syria must be hoping for some settlement or deal to get back the Golan Heights.'

'Syria's a special case. The regime is hard, brutal, and cruel. You know, because you lived there, that the minority Alawites control everything. One of these days, the lid will blow off that country—and I think the new Assad regime may be the precursor to a very bloody civil war. The Sunnis don't want to take it anymore, and with the possibility of Sunnis in the military not supporting the regime in a Sunni-Shia showdown, you're looking at potential mayhem, a blood bath.'

'Perhaps Bashar al-Assad will fulfill his promise to bring in sweeping reforms, more democracy—'

'Highly unlikely. There's a lot of talk about all that, but his father's Old Guard is still very much in power, and the family wealth is too tied up in the status quo to bring on any real changes.'

'You're a businessman, I take it,' Vaux said ingenuously.

'I'm a scientist, Mr. Horner. I'm employed by the Syrian government, and I love my work. However, sometimes I feel I should go in a new direction, perhaps work on other scientific projects. But it's totally impossible. The Syrian power elite wouldn't hear of it. They let unskilled workers emigrate to places like Australia or Canada, but not their treasured scientists or engineers. When I say this, I am thinking above all for my daughters. I would like them to have a freer life, a better life, a more fulfilling life.'

Said now looked forlorn, lost. Vaux asked if there was anything he could do to help—if so, he would. But Said shook his head, said good night, and went upstairs to his room. Vaux felt some breakthrough had been achieved, and now he needed guidance from Craw as to how to proceed. He got up and went to the casement window that looked out on to the sweep of the driveway and the country lane beyond. He got behind the heavy curtain and pulled it aside gradually. The white Ford Taurus was still there. He had seen the same car the previous evening, and his mind went back to that last night with Alena when she had dismissed the GSD watchers as having nothing better to do.

He couldn't sleep. Visions of Alena kept crowding his thoughts. His love for her hadn't faltered, and she remained the only woman he desired to be with. Then Ahmed's ghostly figure stumbled into his consciousness. What a blissful period it had been, the unlikely love triangle that had seemed so durable, so beckoning, when he finally rejected any idea of returning to England to potter around his precious home in unproductive retirement. But now all three of them seemed to be irrevocably torn apart, spinning away from each other to meet their lonely fates.

8

Sir Nigel Adair looked out to the dank inner well of the grim building that housed Department B3, the sub-subgroup of MI6's Middle and Near East desk. His secretary, Anne, had opened the sash window an inch to help clear the damp mustiness that seemed to gather malodorous strength overnight. Sir Nigel had summoned Craw for a comprehensive progress report on Operation Ebla. He heard a light tapping on his door. He turned around to observe his deputy's entrance.

'Good morning, Sir Nigel,' Craw said quietly.

'I'll be the judge of that later, Craw. Meanwhile, what's happening?'

'About, sir?'

'Operation Ebla, of course! Where are we on this?'

'We're making progress, sir.'

Sir Nigel had sat down at his desk and looked infinitely patient, his chin now resting on his steepled hands.

'Go on, Craw.'

'Well, as I informed you late last week, our Dr. Said, code name Saladin, is now settled in the Suffolk residence. Vaux reports to Greene every morning, and it seems the two men—Said and Vaux—are getting on well together.'

'That's hardly unexpected, is it? Wasn't that the whole idea of using Vaux for this project?'

'Yes, exactly. Anyway, I've told Greene that Vaux must start to put some pressure on our defector, in the hope, of course, that we'll learn something about where he could have stashed the key dossier. I still think that as a matter of insurance, our best fallback position is to discover the exact location of the package, which, of course, he's using as leverage to get his family to come across.'

'I think you're slightly off-kilter here, Craw. First, let me tell you about two key developments. First, the code wallahs at Cheltenham have been reading several intercepts between Tel Aviv and Israel's embassy here. The cables indicate something big is in the works. There's some exercise going on—they call it Operation Jael—and they say it is coming to a successful conclusion. There are no specifics, but we have to remain vigilant. I looked up the name. Jael was an ancient biblical heroine who murdered her chief enemy by hammering a tent peg through his head while he was sleeping. Can't think how that fits in with today's world. In any case, MI5 seems pretty convinced that there's been a leak and that Mossad now knows that Dr. Said is selling us this vital intelligence about Syria's armed might, as it were, and it could be that they plan to beat us to it.'

'I doubt very much that our good doctor would want to settle in Israel,' said Craw.

'That's as may be. They could buy him off with bloody gold and cash, though, couldn't they?'

Sir Nigel got up, walked to the grime-covered window, and observed the busy offices opposite. Lawyers, accountants, clerks, young secretaries, tea merchants, scrap dealers—the essence of London's commercial world.

'See these people, Craw? Hustle and bustle, the real world, real lives. Not our shadowy existence, this life of "plot and counter-plot, ruse and treachery, cross and double-cross, true agent, false agent, double agent..." That's a quote—what Churchill thought of us poor minions in the spy game.'

He turned around, hands behind his back. Craw was making notes in a small black book, scratching away with his ancient Conway Stewart fountain pen.

'Anyway, now you know. We may have to deal with competitors here. If the Israelis get hold of this, they'll only pass on to us what they see fit, plus the usual chicken feed. And besides, this is our baby, and we mean to keep it.

'Now I come to my second point. We have learned through agent "Gertrude" that arrangements are well advanced for the escape of the Said family—the wife and two kids. She's done a brilliant job for us—"Gertrude", I mean—and our worries on that score are considerably diminished. This has to be conveyed to Said through Vaux or Greene.'

'Greene, sir. Dr. Said has no idea that Vaux is working with us.'

'Good, excellent. All right, Craw.'

Craw approached the brightly varnished door, installed in the 1920s, the upper half of which was a thick, translucent frosted glass. But he had an afterthought.

'What about the Syrians, sir? Any repercussions about Said's absence?'

'Absolutely not. He's a privileged scientific apparatchik. They give their regime people a lot of leeway. Their loyalty is unquestioned—until it's too late.'

Reassured, Craw walked out of the office; smiled weakly at Anne, who was clicking away at the computer keyboard; and suddenly felt a surge of wistful nostalgia for the familiar clatter produced by old Miss Dimbleby's Imperial typewriter, the constant mood music in Sir Walter Mason's days.

***

That evening, Vaux observed a change of mood, almost a different man. Dr. Said made a few Arabic jokes, and even when Vaux didn't get them, he laughed along with him. Obviously, his now regular morning meeting with Greene had gone well. Vaux couldn't think of any other reason for the change in the man, from dour, doleful pessimist to sunny, middle-aged academic who now saw the world through perhaps a more realistic and happy perspective.

'I think your stay here is paying dividends, Nessim. It's as if a weight has been taken off your shoulders,' said Vaux, hoping to launch a more intimate conversation, a connection, some rapport, with the man that perhaps the boys at B3 would view with satisfaction.

They sat down in the conservatory, while Mrs. Appleby served coffee and brought Vaux a chilled Courvoisier.

'No more than one, now, Mr. Horner. Doctor's orders,' she said sternly. Vaux couldn't recall any recent consultations with any doctor. Perhaps she was in on the cover story.

After she'd left the room, Said opened up. 'Something has changed in my life—and as an observant man, you have noticed, my friend. I can't go into the details, but suffice it to say that my beloved wife will be over here shortly, with our two adorable daughters. It hasn't been easy, you see, to get exit visas in our country. So, of course, I am looking forward to a wonderful reunion.'

'In London, you mean?'

'Yes, of course. I shall leave here in a day or so, and one of my regrets is that I shall leave you here alone. You have been a good fellow guest, and I view you as my friend. I thank you for your companionship.'

'I won't pretend that I shan't miss you,' Vaux replied, trying to think of a nice segue into more confidential and strategic matters of state. He said, 'But I thought you were here for some meetings and then returning to your duties in Syria.'

'It's slightly more complicated, Mr. Horner.'

'Please call me Justin, Doctor.'

'Yes, indeed. You are a good friend, and you well know how we Arabs value friendship.'

Said stood up, drank the last dregs of his black coffee, and moved as though to head toward the staircase and so to bed. Vaux cursed silently. They were just broaching sensitive areas, but Said had brought everything to a halt.

Said suddenly turned to face Vaux. 'Justin, would you mind to please come to my room? I need to show you something.'

They heard the bang of the front door as Mrs. Appleby headed home to her husband with foil-wrapped roast lamb and boiled potatoes to replace the couscous the gentlemen liked.

Vaux was all too willing to ascend the stairs to the Yellow Room, his mind racing through all the possibilities. Family photographs? A photo album? Perhaps a camera whose intricacies would be explained so that, in the morning, Vaux could take his picture, the river and garden as the background.

'Please sit, Justin.' Said went to the large window and looked out on to the river. He began to talk, slowly and quietly, never turning around to face Vaux.

'As you have observed, my friend, I have been somewhat lighthearted these past few hours. The good news about the imminent reunion with my wife and daughters is, of course, the reason. But nothing is certain yet. Like most Arabs, I am a fatalist. Perhaps no one deserves absolute happiness, let alone bliss. God willing—*insh'allah*, as we say. None of us know what tomorrow will bring.'

Vaux had no reply to this native fatalism. The Arabs, in any case, believed that 'it is written,' that men's lives are pre-ordained. He would like to have lit up a Camel, but he knew the bedrooms were non-smoking areas. Now he wanted Said to ramble on; he was sure something useful would be learned.

When Said turned around, his eyes were glistening as they focused closely on Vaux. 'I will tell you something, my friend. I have a premonition. There is something about this place. I don't know, perhaps I feel exposed, more exposed to the outside world than usual. In Syria, you see, we are very privileged, we scientists. The security people protect us, perhaps too much. Here, in the English countryside, it's more natural, but at the same time, I feel a sort of vulnerability.'

Vaux moved as if preparing to make some comment.

'No, no, my friend. You will hear me out. Then you can speak, if you don't mind.'

'Go on,' said Vaux, adjusting himself in the unsteady straight-backed cane chair.

'I have not been frank with you, Justin. When you have seen me go out in the mornings, it is not for a constitutional, a country walk. No, it's because I have a date with one of your British government people. He is staying here in the area, and we usually meet at Wimpy's in the High Street.

'I am negotiating to come over here permanently, you see. You may think I'm a traitor, but my family comes first. I have told you I have little faith in the future of my country. Assad is like his father. We have a saying in Arabic: "The apple does not fall far from the tree." The regime is totally corrupt. Assad and his family, his cronies, even distant relations are feathering their own nests, stashing massive fortunes away in Switzerland and elsewhere. And meanwhile, the average citizen is very poor. There is no reason for this except greed. We are living under a "kleptocracy", as I think you in the democratic West call such avaricious regimes. I am a nuclear scientist, Justin. I have had offers from many countries to come and work for them. And now I have decided that it's the right time to accept an offer from the United Kingdom.'

Said raised his arm to prevent Vaux from making some remark.

'Please. You can have your say when I have finished. Now I come to the critical point. In a stout file, I have stashed every plan and policy position taken by Damascus relating to the development of nuclear power and nuclear weapons, including plans to build a large enrichment plant at Ebla to produce enough uranium to build these ghastly weapons. And that's not all. I have contacts in the military, mainly fellow Sunnis and a few Christians too, and we have assembled a full dossier on Syria's military capabilities, its inventories of chemical weapons—a comprehensive profile of Syria's preparedness for war.

'Now I come to the crux and the conclusion. Sorry if my English is flowery or stilted. Remember that I learned from exiled old English schoolmasters who'd been abroad for thirty years! Their vocabulary was probably out of date and hardly contemporary.

'Justin, Mr. Horner, sir, I am vouchsafing the location of the dossier to you, my friend. You are intelligent, a man of the world, a well-traveled man. It is imperative that someone who is trustworthy and a disinterested friend should know where Syria's military secrets and war game plans are to be found. You and I met by happenstance. And we Arabs put more store in that than prearranged relationships, manipulated by third parties whose interests often don't coincide with ours. This, understand, is why I trust you.'

He sat down at the small escritoire in the corner of the room and began to transfer numbers and data from a small black diary to a piece of notepaper.

'Here, take this, the location and number of the safe-deposit box. Don't worry, I'm not totally stupid. As long as I am alive, they will only open the box for me—and they have a photo ID, of course. But if anything happens to me, then you are sanctioned to open the box and retrieve its contents. You will, of course, have to produce a death certificate. Please honor me with your sworn promise that you will betray our secret to no one—no government official, no bank officer, not even my family, unless and until they are in need of the dossier and the information therein contained to ensure their safe exile in this country.'

They shook hands, Said's tight grip prolonged, like a drowning man clutching at a tree limb in a raging river.

Vaux heard himself say, 'I promise to fulfill your wishes, Doctor, should any action be required of me, which I doubt. Everything will work out, I'm quite sure of that.'

It was almost an automatic response to Said's desperate request, but a very human response. What bothered Vaux now was the hard-to-suppress feeling of triumph at the prospect of pulling off one of the greatest intelligence coups in recent times. He had the goods on Syria, a country he was now beginning to loathe, a nation that held Ahmed captive and that, in his mind, had seduced Alena, a very human Palestinian who had fought relentlessly to free her country from Israeli occupation, into working for what had become one of the most repressive regimes in the Mideast. Said continued to speak to him, and he made an effort to concentrate.

'To be quite clear, the documents are my family's ticket to freedom. You must understand this, my friend. If I fall or I am pushed under a bus, they will still have the means to procure valid passports and citizenship of your country.'

Vaux still wondered what had brought on this full confessional from a man who seemed to be on the brink of securing his freedom.

'But why should anything happen to you at this stage?'

'I told you, did I not? I feel exposed, vulnerable. The Syrian intelligence people from the embassy called the other day. No problem. It's no secret that I accepted a friend's invitation to spend a few days in the country. But if they ever got wind of my intentions, the negotiations that are still not completed... Well, who knows what they would do?'

Vaux felt like reassuring this nervous would-be immigrant. But he was on dangerous ground here, and he had to remind himself that he was a retired journalist named Justin Horner taking a dry-out rest cure. He recalled the mystery Ford Taurus that he had seen parked down the lane on several successive nights. He had meant to check with Greene. But he guessed it was their own watchers doing their duty.

9

The previous night's odd drama had an insidious effect on Vaux. Dr. Said's fears and concerns about his own safety had somehow affected his usual fairly positive view on the progress of Operation Ebla. He felt anxious now and wondered whether everything was really going so smoothly. His vague assignment had miraculously paid off—beyond Sir Nigel and Craw's wildest dreams. Nobody was more surprised than he at the sudden success of their choice of him as the catalyst in a convoluted plot to acquire Syria's top military secrets. Before leaving the house for another meeting with Chris Greene, he fished the Webley out of his travel bag and put it in the inside pocket of his corduroy jacket. It was a salute to superstition or paranoia, he supposed, but he knew he felt better with its easier access.

'Just left Saladin, Mike. He seems uneasy today. Perhaps he doesn't want to leave the rest house. Or perhaps he's become very fond of you,' said Greene as they sat down in the bar at The Swan.

'When's he leaving?' asked Vaux.

'Tomorrow, I think. Craw's coming down too and wants to stay here for some reason. Progress reports, appreciation of the situation, and all that military jargon he uses, even though he's never worn a uniform.'

Vaux studied Greene: the ready laugh, the still-youthful face, straight nose, blue eyes, ears stuck out a little, thick blondish hair. A twinge of envy sneaked its way into his soul as he contemplated a young man just on the cusp of middle age but not quite there yet. Then his thoughts turned blacker: Would he tell Greene what had happened with Said, or should he leave it? Should he savor the gift that had been—to use Said's own word—vouchsafed to him, and like a chess player, attempt to foresee the imminent moves of the antagonists in this drama before deciding on the final maneuver? While Greene prattled on about Craw and office politics, Vaux decided to say nothing about his coup. After all, all would probably go well. Said's wife and daughters might arrive soon, and then the good doctor would hand over the dossier as promised. He would have played what Craw had called a sort of 'guardian' role in the operation. When it was all over, he'd be left to work out his future life.

***

As he approached the River House, he saw the flashing blue lights of an ambulance and two local police cars in the street outside the house. In the driveway, another ambulance, rear doors open, had parked just outside the front entrance. He ran the last hundred yards to the house but was stopped from entering by a constable.

'Excuse me, I'm staying here,' he told the man.

'Nobody can go in just now, sir,' said the policeman, a tall, very slim young man who barred Vaux's entrance with his long arm.

'What's happened?' asked Vaux.

Then he looked down at the slate steps that led up to the open double doors of the porch. A red puddle of blood glistened in the sunlight, with more blood smudges trailing across to the hallway. Vaux heard Mrs. Appleby's raised voice and loud cries, and Vaux pushed past the officer, who tried but failed to grab him by the sleeve.

Mrs. Appleby cried out, 'Oh, Mr. Horner, sir. The doctor's been shot—right outside the 'ouse! It's dreadful, it is. I heard nothing except a scratching noise. It was Dr. Said trying to get my attention, I suppose. I never heard a shot.'

'And who are you, sir?' asked a man who stood by Mrs. Appleby while he tried, with the aid of a plump blonde female officer, to get her to sit down on one of the chairs in the hallway. He wore a tweed jacket, dark-blue pants, and brown suede brogues.

'My name's Horner. I'm staying here. What in hell's happened?'

'A man's been shot, sir. This lady here made the emergency call within seconds of the incident. Our medics are doing their best. I'm Inspector Curry.'

Curry nodded toward the conservatory. Through the open glass doors, Vaux saw four men bending over Said, whose short salt-and-pepper hair was caked in blood. A stream of red-and-white matter oozed from the socket of one eye. Half his neck had been shot away. One by one, they all stood up, shaking their heads. A woman dressed in gray scrubs draped a white sheet over the body.

A heavy man in a white smock that covered a light-blue suit came toward them. 'Sorry, Jim. Nothing we could do. Shot at point-blank range through the eye. Managed to crawl across the floor to the conservatory, but died soon after getting there, I would say. Another shot to his throat. Both were fatal.'

'You did your best, Doc. Time?' asked Curry.

'I'd say about forty minutes ago. Broad daylight, just as he was entering the house, obviously.'

'Thank you, Doc. This is Mr. Horner, who's also staying here.'

A female constable had her arm around Mrs. Appleby as she led her into the dining room. She was still sobbing and looked over at Vaux as she left the hall.

Dr. Said had now been put on a stretcher, and Vaux looked down at the covered body and at the grim-faced medics as they passed on the way to the waiting ambulance.

'Do you mind waiting in the dining room, sir? There's a few questions I'd like to ask you.'

'Not at all,' said Vaux. 'Could I use the phone, by any chance?'

'To call whom? You don't need any solicitors just yet, sir.'

Vaux smiled at the inspector's attempt to lighten the atmosphere.

'Just a friend who's staying at The Swan. He also knew Dr. Said well,' said Vaux.

'You can keep him informed, sir. But we don't need anyone here who's not directly involved in the crime scene. It'll be bad enough when the local press gets ahold of this through the bush telegraph. I'm sure you understand.'

The red secure phone had been placed in a drawer at the bottom of a tall bookcase in the hallway. The regular white telephone sat on a foldout shelf next to a drink cabinet by the door of the dining room. He knew Inspector Curry's eyes were following him, so he decided to call Greene on the regular phone and tell him to get over to the house. The phone in Greene's room rang for what seemed an eternity. He left an urgent message at the front desk.

Mrs. Appleby had recovered enough to suggest a cup of tea. They heard the ambulance slowly take off, and the backup ambulance left soon after. Then they heard a car door slam and the heavy footfalls of someone coming through the flagged hallway. Curry got up, opened the door, and beckoned to a short, wiry man who, despite the warm day, wore a trench coat and trilby. Another constable who had materialized from nowhere closed the door behind the man.

'This is Chief Inspector Fairclough, Mr. Horner,' said Curry.

Vaux got up from the table and shook Chief Inspector Fairclough's small hands. No words were exchanged.

'What have we got, Curry?' Fairclough asked abruptly.

'Victim is a man in his fifties. According to his passport—procured from Mrs. Appleby, the housekeeper here—he is a Syrian national, sir. On a sort of sabbatical, as it were. This is a semiofficial executives' retreat, I gather. Is that right, Mr. Horner?'

Vaux had to maintain the cover story, even if its purpose had suddenly evaporated. The subject who had promised to provide Department B3 with a big intelligence victory had suddenly been eliminated. But by whom? Somehow he had to pass a message on to Craw, his case officer, via Said's handler Greene. He had been instructed by Craw in one of the briefing sessions that if anything 'untoward' happened to Dr. Said, Vaux should simply use the code word 'ex-Saladin' to activate 'emergency plans.' Craw had been thinking more in terms of Said's sudden disappearance, his recurring fear that Said would undergo a change of heart and decide simply to return quietly to the Syrian embassy and then back home.

'Mr. Horner?'

'Oh, yes, sorry. Yes, I came here to enjoy a short respite from the workaday world and so, I believe, did Dr. Said. But is anything being done to pursue the presumed assassin?'

'Assassin, you say!' said Fairclough. 'That's a bit rich, isn't it? We're looking for a hit-and-run killer or killers who were probably after Dr. Said's wallet. Simple as that, eh, Curry? And a full alert has been sent out to all appropriate agencies for the apprehension of the likely perpetrators. Trouble is, so far, we have no description of the car that was presumably used for the getaway. But right of this moment, sir, we think the probable motive has to be simple robbery. Is that right, Curry?'

'That's our first interpretation, sir, yes. As we speak, I have several officers making the rounds of nearby houses to discover whether anyone saw or heard the car.'

'Maybe you are right, and it was just a run-of-the-mill hold-up. But in that case, wouldn't he have been mugged, knocked to the ground, kicked in the head for his cash, rather than shot in cold blood?' asked Vaux.

'We have to cover all possibilities, Mr. Horner. Now, Curry, have we found a wallet?'

'No, sir. But many people don't carry wallets these days. He had cash in his trouser pocket, about fifty pounds. He carried his passport in his inside jacket pocket,' said Curry.

Fairclough looked disappointed at the collapse of his robbery theory. 'So, despite the violence, they may have got away with nothing. And you, Mr. Horner, could we see your ID, please? A driver's license or passport will do.'

'My passport's in the bedroom upstairs. May I go and get it?'

'Please do,' said Curry.

Fairclough stood up and looked around the dining room. He waited for Vaux to leave.

'There's something odd here, Curry. This chap Horner's right. Why a brutal shooting when a knock on the head would have sufficed? If, that is, they were just common-or-garden thieves. It looks more like some sort of contract killing, doesn't it? You'll have to dig into this chap's background. And, meanwhile, inform the Syrian embassy people in London that one of their citizens has bought it. We don't get many of these exotic birds, do we? Plenty of Jamaicans, Pakis, and Africans—but very few Arabs turn up as murder victims.'

Mrs. Appleby, still sniffling and eyes streaming, brought in a big tray of cups and saucers and placed a pot of tea on a thick woolen coaster in the center of the table. She put down a plate of biscuits grabbed from an old Fortnum & Mason tin that sat on the kitchen's welsh dresser. Fairclough quickly retrieved his favorite, a chocolate macadamia.

'Any witnesses?' he asked.

'No, sir. Only Mrs. Appleby here. After the fact, as it were. We have a written statement in which she says she is "pretty sure" she heard a car drive away at great speed just after getting to the door and finding Mr. Said.'

'But no description of the car?'

'No, sir.'

As Vaux, Justin Horner's passport in hand, passed through the hall, he heard the phone tinkle. It wasn't a very loud bell, and he didn't think the police officers in the dining room could have heard it. He picked up the receiver and was relieved by the sound of Greene's voice. Vaux cut off the young man.

'Get over here now, Chris. Ex-Saladin. Call Craw now, before you come over.'

'But I haven't got a secure phone. Can't call him from here. He'd have my guts for garters.'

'For Christ's sake, come on over and we'll work it out.'

As Vaux entered the dining room, he heard Curry tell his boss that the forensics team had done their work on the porch but were examining the driveway and road for tire marks and any other evidence that could help identify the getaway car. Pathology would get back to them on probable time of death as soon as they could.

Then Vaux remembered the watchers in the car. 'On several occasions, I saw a white Ford Taurus parked just up the road. I wouldn't have thought anything of it except that it was there more or less every day.'

'Really, Mr. Horner? That's interesting,' said Curry while Fairclough scribbled on a small notepad.

'Get on to the car rental companies, Curry. I know Avis has a fleet of Taurus models. This could be a useful lead. Thank you, Mr. Horner.'

***

While Chief Inspector Fairclough enjoyed his cup of tea and biscuits and chatted with Curry about a speech he had to make at a local chamber of commerce meeting that evening, three men walked up the escalators to the departure level at Stansted Airport, about thirty-five miles northeast of London. They were not late for their flights, just anxious to get airborne. Ernst Stockmann had an Air Berlin flight to Dusseldorf in sixty minutes; Victoire Gaillard's KLM flight to Marseilles would depart in forty minutes; and Bob Kirby had apparently planned a short vacation on the Riviera. His easyJet flight to Nice was scheduled to leave at 7:00 p.m.

Kirby, the English driver, had left the rented Ford Taurus at the Avis drop-off, and they hauled the four canvas holdalls toward the airport entrance. Just before they got to the main doors, a man they recognized quickly came up to them, shook hands with all three men, and patted their backs and shoulders to celebrate a momentary reunion. As they resumed their walk to the sliding entry doors, the friend picked up the heaviest bag and was soon lost in the streams of people arriving and leaving the airport.

One week after the killing of Dr. Nessim Said, an emergency meeting was called at the cramped offices of Department B3. Sir Nigel Adair ordered Alan Craw, his deputy, to quash all civilian police inquiries into the murder of Dr. Nessim Said, and Suffolk's chief constable hastily agreed, relieved that the mystery killing had been taken out of his hands. He told Chief Inspector Fairclough, the officer in charge of the investigation, that the top intelligence people in the UK had ordered a complete shutdown of any local police investigation into the shooting of this Dr. Nessim Said and a total ban on any intramural conversations or personal observations about witnesses, including Mr. Justin Horner, then guest at the rest house, and Mrs. Appleby, the housekeeper and former employee of Lady Sybil Mason's sister, now deceased.

Suffolk's top cop issued a gag order: 'Everyone should wipe the slate and forget what happened that morning at the River House due to grave national security concerns. MI5 and Special Forces are taking over the murder probe, and there's an end to it. Period, full stop.' The coroner and first responder medical teams were likewise bound by time-honored oaths of secrecy and confidentiality. What the chief constable had no control over, however, were stories appearing spasmodically in the local and national press that suggested a top-level cover-up of a mysterious shooting in the depths of rural Suffolk, the victim a middle-aged male whose identity had yet to be revealed.

Sir Nigel called for more chairs to be brought into his office, requested that Anne order coffee and biscuits from the small café on the ground floor, and wondered why Sir Walter Mason, his predecessor, had tolerated the post–World War II domestic arrangements he had to put up with. Yet, still, he preferred his small sanctum to the hustle and bustle of MI6's grandiose command center—even with their canteens, their big conference theaters, and their nicely furnished committee rooms that boasted all the latest high-tech gear, including desktop computers, those mysteriously named modems, and the clunky so-called mobile phones, which seemed to get lighter and more portable every year.

Facing him, with jackets off, ties loosened, and it seemed to Sir Nigel, looking rather sheepish, all three of them, were Alan Craw, Chris Greene, and Michael Vaux aka Justin Horner.

'I won't beat about the bush, gentlemen, but this is a tragedy. Not just the passing of Dr. Said, but our complete failure in this matter. A veritable cock-up, a total collapse of Operation Ebla, what will be perceived by our MI6 colleagues as perhaps a good enough reason to disband our section altogether. This was just the sort of venture we are supposed to excel in, gentlemen. It's our raison d'être, if you will. Unless we succeed in these specialist tasks allotted to us, then we'll lose our jobs, easy as that.'

Craw looked down at his highly polished oxfords, eyebrows raised a little. He knew that Sir Nigel had tenure, and he knew that civil service rules rendered him—and probably Greene—secure for the rest of their careers in public service. He couldn't say the same for Vaux, of course. However, his job was to listen, and it was no surprise to observe an angry boss. He suddenly realized he had been asked a question.

'Well, Craw?'

'Oh, sorry, sir. What was that again?'

Sir Nigel gave out a theatrical sigh. He slowly and plainly said, 'I asked you whether your own inquiries into this calamity have yet produced any results that we could at least find mildly encouraging.'

'Not at this point, sir.'

Sir Nigel shook his head, resigned perhaps to the unsurprising lack of progress. He now looked at Vaux. He thought his appearance somewhat haggard and wondered why—given that he had spent at least three weeks in a beautiful part of the country, waited on hand and foot by old Mrs. Appleby, whom Lady Mason swore by as a good and loyal servant inherited from her beloved late sister.

'Vaux, in your conversations with Said, did he ever give you any indication whatsoever—an unintended hint, perhaps, any careless reference at all—as to the location of this vital dossier he had promised us as the quid pro quo for asylum?'

Vaux's mind seized up. 'No, sir.'

***

While Department B3's inquest into the disaster continued that morning, the listeners at GCHQ in Cheltenham detected a marked increase in telephonic communications between the Syrian embassy at 5 Belgrave Square and the headquarters of

Syria's General Security Directorate in Damascus. GSD demanded an immediate rundown of the facts relating to the
murder of one of the country's foremost nuclear scientists and
the arrangements that had been made to protect Dr. Said. Why
had routine security measures not been taken? In particular,
why had Dr. Said, a national treasure, been allowed to travel
within the United Kingdom alone and unguarded? More to the
point, why had GSD London station not seen fit to set up a
team of discreet watchers to follow the scientist and look out
for his own protection wherever he went.

Manaf Fouladkar, the GSD's London station chief, known
officially as the second secretary at the Syrian mission, called an
emergency meeting with his two deputies, whose covers were
provided by the embassy's cultural attaché. Foulkadkar was
overweight, balding, and his sweaty face wore a constant frown.
This morning was no exception. Before he began to speak, his
two assistants heard the distinct clicks as he progressed through
his thirty-three prayer beads.

Now, letting the ivory rosary dangle from his left hand, he
looked up at his two colleagues with a stern face. '*Ibn el shar-
moota*! This is a calamity of the first order. Here we have HQ
playing what the Americans call Monday morning quarterback
and demanding to know why we didn't put out a watching team
to make sure old Said came to no trouble. Now he's been shot,
and they want some answers. I don't have to tell you he was a
key man in our drive to develop our nuclear program. So, dear
colleagues, what's our story?'

The sad news was that neither he nor his colleagues could
explain what had happened. There had been no directives about
any need for constant surveillance of this scientist who had traveled outside Syria countless times to international gatherings of
one sort or another. His total loyalty to the Syrian regime was
unquestioned, and there had never been any reason to suspect

he had enemies who would plot his murder. The consensus, voiced by Fouladkar with a tissue wipe to his forehead, was that it could have been a simple act of violence perpetrated in the course of attempted theft. Fouladkar directed veteran agent Abdul Halim to check the police reports for updates on the investigation and the postmortem results and told the young probationer Rafik Shihabi to monitor the English press. Both were to report to him the next morning.

***

On Gower Street, theories and hypotheses had also flown up and around, only to be shot down like pheasants at one of Sir Nigel's exclusive weekend shoots. Sir Nigel, who did not much care for the Arabs and thought his promotion to head of Department B3 had had something to do with the universal impression at Century House that he held the 350 million inhabitants of the Middle East in mild contempt, leaned toward the conclusion that the deed had been done by the Syrians, Said's own people.

Predictably, Alan Craw, Sir Nigel's deputy, agreed. 'They're a perfidious lot, so it wouldn't surprise me at all,' he said.

'Greene, we haven't heard from you yet. What's your theory?' asked Sir Nigel.

'I'm leaning toward a random act, sir. Otherwise, nothing makes any sense,' Greene said, with a glance at Vaux, who he knew had also seen and talked to Dr. Said just hours before he was gunned down. 'For one thing, he appeared, if anything, to be very relaxed when I met up with him at Wimpy's for our usual morning debriefing.'

Craw raised his eyebrows at this elevation from morning coffee and a chat to a serious stage of discovery in professional tradecraft.

'He was looking forward to returning to London the next day, as Vaux will verify. And he seemed to think that good news regarding his wife and kids was imminent. Then, he said, the whole business would be over, although he also said he would be happy to work for the UK's nuclear industry—a statement he no doubt thought I would report back on. He was probably wondering what exactly he was going to do once he'd established British citizenship and all that.'

Sir Nigel pushed back on his aging swivel chair and picked up a chocolate éclair that sat alone on the plate of biscuits Anne had brought in earlier.

'So you think it was a violent robbery, is that it?'

'I think the odds favor that theory, yes, sir.'

'Vaux, how about you?'

For no reason he could ever think of, no spark that he could recall that had been struck that morning within the four walls of Sir Nigel's cramped and fetid office, Vaux heard himself simply say, 'Operation Sphinx.'

Sir Nigel sat up straight, choked as a bite of the éclair went down the wrong way, and took a swig of the lukewarm coffee.

After a few more coughs and silently waving his arms at the three men as if pleading for patience, he cleared his throat and asked Vaux what the hell he was talking about.

'Well, sir, when I was based in Paris, doing a stint at the *Herald Tribune*, there was an infamous assassination, the sort of thing that makes sensational headlines for a few days and then the world forgets and gets on with life.'

'Yes, go on, Vaux. We're all ears.'

'I'd have to check the dates and details, but it has to have been in 1980, because I was there just for that year. Operation Sphinx was the name given to the operation that resulted in the murder of an Egyptian nuclear scientist. I'll have to look up the archives to refresh my memory—I forget his name. Anyway, nobody could prove anything. The scientist, who, I remember, was also a professor at Alexandria University, was shot in his room at the Méridien Hotel.

'And, as a newspaperman, I remember some of the more sordid and juicy bits. His mistress, who apparently was a high-class hooker, was, on the same day, pushed under a bus on the Boulevard Saint-Germain, right opposite Les Deux Maggots of Hemingway fame. That's how I remember it.'

'Yes, yes, Vaux, but get to the point. Who was responsible for the killing?'

'No one knew. But Mossad was the number one suspect. The Israelis neither confirmed nor denied it, but the Operation Sphinx label came out eventually. At that time, the Israelis were dead set on thwarting any nuclear ambitions the Arabs may harbor. They were against any country in the Mideast having nuclear weapons, except themselves. And I guess that's still true.'

Sir Nigel's usually hangdog face lifted, his eyes brightened. 'This could be a repeat performance, then. Good thinking, Vaux. Now, I want you to do some research. Take Greene with you. Look up our newspaper archives. Comb them for any other incidents of a similar nature in recent years. Greene, I want you first to go to the registry at Thames House and get everything we have on Mossad's activities in the UK. It may be all computerized by now. If so, I'm sorry for you. But you've got to learn some time how to navigate these newfangled data banks, or whatever they're called these days.'

II

In general, spymasters are the ultimate control freaks. If each and every agent did their job according to instructions, acted conscientiously (never through greed or personal advancement), and always in the interest of the nation, then all should go well and smoothly. There would be plenty of credit to go around. But on this particular day, Sir Nigel Adair found it difficult to believe that *anything* was under control. At breakfast at his Knightsbridge mansion flat, Lady Mary, his devoted wife, served his usual cereal with skim milk and Swiss yogurt when he heard the phone ring in the hallway. Sir Nigel audibly cursed as he got up, wiped his mouth with a crisp napkin, and left his wife to shuffle through the small kitchen to answer.

She called to him. 'I told them you were just sitting down to breakfast, but they insist it's urgent, dear.'

'Yes, Adair here. What is it?'

It was Craw, sounding alarmist as usual. He did wish the man weren't so high-strung. 'Sorry to bother you, sir. But I thought you ought to know. The *Mirror* has come out with a picture of Vaux as he was leaving the River House in Suffolk. The caption reads, "Mystery Man at River House of Murder."'

At first, Sir Nigel couldn't get his head around the possible implications of Vaux's exposure. 'That hardly concerns our investigation into who killed Said, does it?'

'Well, sir, yes, I think it's all part of the problem we're facing. If anything, the complexities multiply exponentially.'

'What does that mean in English?' Sir Nigel asked gruffly.

'As you know, I'm at the office by seven thirty most mornings, sir. And I saw that, during the night, the GCHQ boys reported that the Syrian embassy faxed the photo from the *Mirror* to the GSD intelligence center in Damascus. They're obviously looking into who this guy is. They know their nuclear scientist was gunned down in front of the house, so they're asking who this person is. If they match the pic with what's undoubtedly in their files, they'll come up with Vaux—and that could be problematic for our Mr. Justin Horner, what?'

'Well, I suppose it could. But who put them on to this? I mean, who took the original photo? Who's the culprit—a lowly newspaper photographer?'

Craw, who was never in the best of moods this early in the morning, ignored what he thought was a silly question. 'I think we'd better have a meeting on this as soon as you get here, sir. We don't want Vaux to lose his cover this soon in the game. And we certainly don't want to put Vaux under protection, with all that entails in costs and inconvenience.'

'Quite right, Craw. I'll be there at the usual time, provided my driver doesn't have to fight clogged streets and traffic jams. There's a sale on at Harrods, which always makes things worse around here.'

'Yes, sir.' Craw rang off and asked Anne, who had just arrived, to call Vaux immediately.

Anne said she didn't know where he was.

'But he must have left a contact number. It's an iron rule in this job,' protested Craw.

'I'll do my best to get hold of him,' said Anne.

***

Sir Nigel's culprit was a twenty-three-year-old budding reporter who happened to live in the small Suffolk village close to the River House. It was the sort of hamlet where everyone knew everybody. Mrs. Appleby, always gregarious and talkative, knew the young man's mother, and despite being told by that Chief Inspector Fairclough that she shouldn't talk about the tragic incident, she saw no harm in confiding in Mrs. Hastings. She thought it would go no further than her neighbor's ears.

But it did. John Hastings had tried to get hired as a junior reporter for two years after graduating from East Anglia University with a journalism degree. But he'd had no luck. So he decided to become a photojournalist as a step toward his ultimate ambition—to join the writing staff of a national daily. Equipment was expensive, so he borrowed five hundred pounds from his grandfather and bought a used Kodak-Nicon Professional DCS 315. He drove an old Riley Roadster around the county and took pictures he thought he could sell to the local press. Motorway car crashes involving multiple vehicles were always easy to sell to the national tabloids. Murders and sex crimes were also highly marketable. And so, after his mother passed on Mrs. Appleby's news flash, young Hastings saw the potential, leapt to his feet, and drove quickly to the site of the shooting. Fairclough's edict to all witnesses to shut their mouths had been ignored the instant Mrs. Appleby left for home. So Hastings spent many hours and several days at his chosen vantage point—just behind a big plane tree that faced Sir Walter's sister-in-law's Elizabethan pile.

And so it was that the *Daily Mirror*, an aggressive combatant in London's tabloid wars, procured a sharp image of Vaux getting into a waiting taxi as Mrs. Appleby embraced him with a warm farewell. Vaux's face had been blown up, and although the printed result was somewhat spotty and blurred around the edges, there was no mistaking it was Vaux.

Rafik Shehabi, the young GSD agent who posed as an assistant cultural attaché, was an early riser, thanks to his eighteen-month-old son's nutritional needs and his young wife's preference to stay in bed until at least 8:00 a.m. Through the cramped Chelsea apartment's letter box every weekday morning thumped the *Mirror*, the *Sun*, and the *Times*. That morning, Hastings's picture loomed large on the *Mirror*'s front page, and the caption was equally bold. 'River House' caught his attention simply because he had read a coded report from an east coast subagent who had cribbed the local paper's scoop about the incident two days after Fairclough's gag order. Shehabi duly reported his own early-morning coup to his chief, Manaf Fouladkar, who faxed the picture and accompanying text over to their superiors in Damascus.

***

Michael Vaux phoned Anne to tell her he would not be in the office until midday at the earliest. He was in his old hunting grounds in Hertfordshire where he had once bought a house, a bijou bungalow with a magnificent view of the green belt, only to give it away to a needy friend before taking off for the Middle East. She hadn't heard this brief story before so was hesitant to tell Craw anything more than Mr. Vaux said he'd be late in coming in.

'Oh, God! On a day like today! Try and get hold of him again, would you? It's essential that I talk to him now—before he leaves the hotel to do whatever he's planning to do. Any more of those biscuits that Sir Nigel wolfed down yesterday?'

***

In the immediate aftermath of Said's murder, Vaux had given no thought to the piece of notepaper Said had entrusted to him on the evening before his death. He'd tucked it away somewhere late that night, and the devastating shock of the next day's events had blocked out any thoughts about Dr. Said's fail-safe move to ensure his family's freedom if 'anything should happen to him.' It was somewhere deep in Vaux's traumatized brain, but it hadn't surfaced.

So the weekend after Sir Nigel Adair's emergency meeting, Vaux decided to visit his old neighborhood in Hertfordshire, the place where he was brought up and where he had returned nearly ten years earlier. He left most of his meager belongings at the small hotel in Swiss Cottage, where Department B3, under the cover name of Acme Global Consultants, Ltd., had a permanent penthouse suite. He decided to stay at the Pig & Whistle, a local pub that rented out a couple of rooms to the odd weary traveler in need of a few drinks, some traditional English food, and a warm bed.

The former owner and his boyfriend had vanished, the mixed clientele with them. Now a portly, balding man appeared to be the landlord, aided and assisted by an elegant, slim bottle blonde, who, like her husband, was probably in her mid-fifties.

Vaux booked in for two nights, parked his rented Ford Mondeo behind the pub, and walked to Willow Drive, where his friend John Goodchild, the man he'd given his bungalow to, lived and where both men had grown up together. They were neighborhood tearaways who had drifted apart when they went on to different schools and had been out of contact for some thirty years before Vaux's return to the area.

Vaux banged the lion's head knocker on Goodchild's front door. He heard dogs barking, a scuffling, and a throat-clearing cough. Two small dogs jumped up at him, tails wagging and noses sniffing, as they greeted him as an old friend. John Goodchild, balder and heavier now, had aged. His puffy eyes widened in surprise, his hand went out, and Vaux pushed it aside for a mutual hug.

'Jesus Christ, Mike, why didn't you tell me you were coming? Come through.'

Vaux was seated at the old wooden kitchen table and offered a can of Heineken. Nobody else was around, and the dogs had scampered into the garden. Nothing much had changed in ten years. The boys had all grown up, and the eldest, Patrick, had given John a grandson. The peripatetic wife (she had three sisters scattered all over England) was away in Brighton with her eldest sister. Goodchild asked very few questions about Vaux's recent past and seemed reluctant to talk about the bungalow Vaux had given him by a deed of sale signed in Cairo and carried back to a Watford real estate solicitor by Chris Greene. Greene had been glad to do a favor for Vaux despite his disappointment at failing to persuade him not to follow Alena and Ahmed to Damascus.

Vaux, on his third can of beer, finally decided to broach the subject. 'Did you sell the house or what?' he asked.

'Your house? Oh, no, Mike. No, I decided to rent it out. Help with day-to-day expenses and all that. Also, if you want to know the truth, I thought it better that way if you ever came back, like. Know what I mean?'

In a way, Vaux was relieved. Maybe, after the fiasco of Operation Ebla, he'd need a home, and there was nothing he'd like more than to move back in and enjoy the bungalow he had renovated and whose long view of leafy meadows and rolling hills had always reminded him of England's 'green and pleasant land.'

'I don't understand what you mean, John. You mean I could rent it from you?'

'Oh, shit no, mate. You can have it back. It's yours, isn't it? I never took that stuff seriously. I know you better than you know yourself. We was at school together, don't forget. I knew you'd be back sometime, when the romance, or whatever it was that kept you away from here, ended. And besides, I've got this place. One house is enough for me.'

Vaux was speechless. 'Well, I don't know what to say.'

'There's just one fly in the ointment,' said Goodchild, his dark-rimmed eyes focused on the checkered oilcloth that covered the kitchen table. 'And that's that the people now renting are sitting there, and probably, we've no legal power to get them out. As far as I know, they've been paying the rent on the dot each month, and according to Patrick, who does the gardening and odd jobs for them, they've put a lot of effort into keeping the place well maintained and all that shit.'

'That's okay. I didn't come here to get the house back. I just wondered what you had done with it. I'd assumed you'd sold it, and I was curious about the price you may have fetched.'

'Oh, crikey, prices have soared since you left. I reckon the place could fetch at least three hundred and fifty thousand pounds today.' John Goodchild didn't know that Vaux had eventually paid £420,000, thanks, he now knew, to Arthur Davis, the veteran MI6 talent spotter who created a phantom would-be buyer to make competitive bids for the house to persuade Vaux that he would badly need the handsome payoff he was promised for his efforts toward the success of B3's ill-fated Operation Helvetia.

'Is Arthur Davis still around?'

'No, mate. Funniest thing, he died of a heart attack on his way over for a pint at the Pig & Whistle. Just like his father-in-law—donkey's years ago. He had a good innings, though.'

'And old Mrs. Parker?' Mrs. Parker had been Vaux's self-appointed housekeeper when he finally moved into the bungalow. She had lived on Willow Drive for sixty years, enjoyed a pint of Guinness ('doctor's orders') every morning at the Pig & Whistle, and befriended the man whose mother she remembered and who then seemed a lonely, helpless bachelor.

'Oh, she died soon after you decided not to come back from Egypt or wherever. Went in her sleep, she did. No suffering.'

***

That evening, a low, dark cloud of depression enveloped the weekend tourist. News of Mrs. P's death (she had always told him to call her Mrs. P) and of old Davis's collapse while on his way over to 'the Pig' from his big mock-Tudor house opposite the pub on Watford Lane added to the gloom of a wet September evening. And now, as he looked toward the pub's back terrace, he saw Alena, young, elegant, and beautiful, at their first meeting, their polite exchanges and gentle flirting. He ordered another double Cutty Sark because he wanted to smudge out the element of betrayal that had sowed its first seeds that night. She was a lie, a false image; she had been told to be there and talk to him if, by good luck, he approached her. And yet he still loved her. *If only*, he thought, *we could recreate our cherished moments, press the rewind button, relive the past.* The stout, affable landlord leaned over the bar and touched his arm. Closing time. And so Vaux once again

went up the narrow staircase to the front bedroom, looked
out the sash windows at The Cedars (Davis's house), and saw
the pines swaying in the stiff breeze that had blown in from
nowhere.

12

On this particular morning, Alan Craw looked drawn and older than his years. Vaux attributed this to the progress or difficulties Craw was experiencing in long and arduous negotiations over a satisfactory divorce settlement. Craw had married the daughter of a renowned merchant banker who had made his pile in the heady days of the 1960s, when financial regulations were loose and *who* you knew was often more important than *what* you knew. It was a time of big corporate mergers and acquisitions, a frenetic housing boom, and it had to be said, unprecedented prosperity and an emerging affluence that benefited all social classes.

Craw had just come down from Oxford, where he had been recruited by MI6 talent spotters and despite his social background (his father had earned a living as a London Transport bus driver) he found himself mixing in the highest echelons of society. He was pleasantly surprised at how many doors could be opened by a first-class degree in Politics, Philosophy, and

Economics. Several years at a good state grammar school followed by the dulcet days at Worcester College, Oxford, had tempered his moderately Cockney accent to a geographically neutral BBC newsreader's drawl. And so, at a cocktail party at the Ritz put on to celebrate her father's latest financial coup, Craw met June Cavendish, the beautiful and eligible daughter of James Cavendish, controlling shareholder of merchant bankers Cavendish, Rothschild, Ltd., the latter partner unrelated to *the* Rothschilds. Nothing was too good for his beloved daughter, and a big house in the leafy northwest London 'village' of Hampstead was his wedding gift to the handsome pair.

Vaux had to give Craw his due. In his younger years, he had been handsome as well as academically bright, yet beyond these two key attributes, there didn't seem to be much else. He liked the man but always felt he was essentially a ditherer and also a quiet schemer who put his own interests and advancement above anything else. Now his marriage had crumbled, midlife crises having overwhelmed both parties simultaneously, and the legal separation, because of the one-sidedness of the couple's wealth (there were no offspring), was proving hard and arduous.

Craw had called Vaux into his office. Anne brought in two cups of Nescafé, two skim milk mini-cartons, and a plate of chocolate digestives, then left. An open folder in front of him, he looked up over his half-moon glasses and gave a wan smile.

'Good weekend?'

It was Tuesday morning, and Vaux hadn't showed his face on the Monday following his weekend stay at the Pig & Whistle.

'Very good, thank you,' Vaux said coolly.

'Take a look at this,' said Craw, shoving the front page of the *Mirror* over his desk. Vaux turned the page around and recognized himself immediately.

'Shit,' he murmured.

'You can't go gallivanting around London Town and Hertfordshire now that they've outed you, can you, old boy? Be very careful and alert at all times. And from today on, I'm arranging a minder for you. He'll sleep at the hotel and stay with you at all times. Understood?'

Vaux knew that this sort of personnel crisis enabled Craw to pull rank and talk like a pompous idiot. But he did have a point. He nodded his head in agreement.

'Now, to business, Special Forces has sent us a preliminary report on their joint inquiry into the unfortunate death of Dr. Said. It appears that the Ford Taurus you had reported seeing on several occasions near the house was a rental. A man by the almost certainly false name of Kirby hired the car from Sudbury. The rental people say it was returned on the date of the shooting. Kirby was accompanied by two other men whose descriptions are here in the file. Nobody has been able to match this fellow Kirby with any of the personal details Avis took down. In other words, the driver's license was phony. Kirby paid in cash. The car was checked in at Stansted Airport at the drop-off, so nobody can tell us who the driver was or how many passengers there might have been.

'However, there's one break—if you can call it that. This chap Kirby took a KLM flight to Nice. UKSF has sent two good men to follow up that lead. They're going to check the big hotels and basically do a recce. But all they've got to go on is the physical description of the man who rented the car at the Avis office.'

'Nothing on the other two men?' asked Vaux.

'Zilch. My guess is that they were all traveling on false passports and IDs, anyway. So we're up against a brick wall, Vaux. A very elaborate and sophisticated brick wall.'

Vaux said, 'Is Greene in yet? I want to see if he's got any-where with the archives and registry. It might help us link this case to Mossad, you never know.'

'You seem to be obsessed by this Mossad theory. Why on earth would one of our allies send an anonymous hit team to undermine our own efforts to get the goods on Syria's nuclear program?'

Vaux said, 'They've got form, that's all. I told you about that killing in Paris, and I'm sure Greene must have unearthed similar cases going back over the years. The bottom line is that the Israelis really don't trust anyone to do any dirty work for them. So they've devised this program—they call it "targeted killings," really a eu-phemism for assassination. Anyone they deem a threat to their ex-istence, anyone they think is working with another government whose policies don't favor their long-term survival as a tiny Jewish island in a sea of antagonistic Arabs, are potential targets.'

'But Said was a scientist, a professional man, a family man. And he was about to spill the beans for us. If the Israelis did this, it was a bad miscalculation on their part, that's all I can say. Oh, and by the way, Greene has the morning off. I told him to go get a haircut. He's looking rough these days, and his appearance doesn't sit well with Sir Nigel. I can tell. He was quite testy to him the other day.'

Craw then closed the folder. 'You know I've moved in with him, don't you? Just for a few weeks until this bloody divorce comes through.'

'No, I didn't. Is his place big enough for two giants in the world of espionage?'

'Very funny, Vaux. But, yes, he has a two-bedroom suite in a rather elegant town house in Chalk Farm.'

***

In Nice that evening, two men sat down together at a small bistro table in a sidewalk café close to the Place Massena, just a short walk from the Promenade des Anglais that runs along the town's long crescent-shaped stretch of stony beach. They were dressed in casual outfits, bought that morning in a Gap store near Piccadilly. Captain Charles Stevens ordered a large Coke. His companion, Sergeant Brian Parry, was more adventurous; he preferred a large *pression*, or draft beer.

'This'll probably wind up as a total fiasco,' Stevens said gloomily.

'Don't say that, sir. We've only just got 'ere,' said the sergeant.

'We've nothing to go on. Just a physical description—fairly long black hair, an Errol Flynn moustache, blue jeans, and black leather bomber jacket. Not even a proper photograph, just an identikit job.'

'You know what I think?' said Parry. He waited for Stevens to shake his head, invite him to speak. 'He'll change his clothes, get a haircut, maybe even dye his hair blond. But he'll keep that egotistical moustache. Errol Flynn moustaches, besides the fact that Flynn's been dead donkey's years, are a sort of fetish, I'd say, not unconnected to the man's vision of himself—pride in his success with the girls, that sort of thing,' said the Sergeant.

'All I need right now is an amateur psychiatrist,' Stevens said dismissively.

'I'm not kidding. That's what I'm looking out for.'

The two men from UK Special Forces had first checked into a small Holiday Inn on Rue Victor Hugo, about midway between the SNCF railway station and the beaches. The tall, young blonde at reception was the first to be shown the iden-tikit mock-up of Kirby, but she shook her head. Then they be-gan the early-evening tour of the best five-star hotels in Nice before switching to the four and three stars. Nobody had ever seen anyone resembling the hunted man. Some of the more snooty establishments refused to confirm or deny any sighting and demanded to see an official warrant from the French police before anything could be divulged. In fact, MI5 had contacted the DGSE, France's external intelligence agency, before the two-man SF team had left for France, and the warrant had been waiting at the agency's representative office in Nice for twelve hours.

So Captain Stevens and Sergeant Parry were taking a brief break from the hunt. Suddenly, Parry jumped up, drank down the lukewarm beer, and ran off in the direction of the columned porticoes of the city's local government complex. He had seen a man with a pencil-thin moustache and about the same build as the suspect. He was heading toward the Promenade and the beach.

***

'Look here, Vaux, I don't want to have to go through all this. Just give me a précis, a summary of the salient points.'

Vaux sat next to Chris Greene, who had put a fat manila file on Sir Nigel Adair's desk. Craw was out of the office, visiting his solicitor and legal counsel. The long, drawn-out divorce negotiations were nearing completion.

'I'll let Greene take the fort, sir. He did most of the research.'

'Very well. Let's have it, Greene. The highlights first.'

'Well, sir, as Michael pointed out, perhaps the most notorious case of a suspected Mossad assassination was Operation Sphinx in 1980. The Israeli government never denied Mossad's participation, nor confirmed it. That's always been their position.'

'Go on,' said Sir Nigel, glancing through the newly washed window that looked out to the internal well of the building. Once again, he noticed that the accountants' offices opposite were seemingly in turmoil, with men and women milling about, handing each other papers and files, and sipping from Styrofoam cups. He was glad he ran a moderately quiet and uncrowded ship.

'Going a little further back, in 1962, one Heinz Krug, a West German rocket scientist who was working on Egypt's new missile systems, was abducted in Munich and presumably murdered. His body was never found. Interpol stepped in to aid the investigation, and the Swiss police arrested two Mossad agents.

'In the same year, five Egyptian workers employed by the Cairo government were blown up by a letter bomb. They were working at a government rocket factory. The Israelis called their 1962 assassination program Operation Damocles.

'So far, I've mentioned incidents involving what you could call the architects of Arab efforts to develop their own nuclear and missile systems. But there's a slew of Mossad killings involving Palestinian politicians, Hamas leaders and spokesmen, as well as PLO and Fatah officials, from foreign representatives to press officers and the like.'

'Any thoughts, Vaux?' Sir Nigel seemed somewhat dumbfounded by Greene's bloody litany of clandestine killings by a legitimate pro-Western government.

'The pattern is usually the same. While the Israelis admit with a nod and a wink that they are responsible for these murders, they argue that they are necessary to defend the right of Israel to exist. They cannot wait for the slow wheels of international justice to turn in their favor. And, as I said, they call these political assassinations "targeted killings." It's an astonishing and dangerous concept—preemptive strikes against sworn enemies who may do you harm in the future.'

Sir Nigel protested. 'But these killings are extrajudicial. No trial, just presumption of guilt. Guilt by association, I suppose. In Dr. Said's case, they knew he was working for the Syrian government, and they knew he was a key player in Syria's push toward nuclear arms and nuclear energy. So he was put on the death list, as it were, even though he was treating with us at the time and could have produced an intelligence coup of major proportions.'

This last peroration by Sir Nigel, head of MI6's Department B3, had the effect of jogging Vaux's stalled memory. The processes of recollection began to stream through his mind. He now remembered the note that Said had given him, and he knew he should act quickly. But Vaux was Vaux. He said nothing but resolved to hunt for the flimsy piece of paper as if his life depended on it.

Sir Nigel had asked Vaux a question.

'Sorry, sir. My mind was on something completely different.'

'For God's sake, Vaux, there's nothing more important than the matter we are discussing at the moment. I asked you whether you thought the Syrians themselves had a hand in this, having perhaps found out that Said was defecting and giving us a fat file of info relating to their military needs, capabilities, nuclear and conventional—all that stuff. Well? Who do you think are the number one suspects—the Syrians or the Israelis?'

'I'll have to use that old cliché, sir. "The jury's still out." I understand MI5 and Special Forces have set up a joint investigation and they're following up certain leads. Meanwhile, perhaps we are forgetting some humanitarian questions here.'

'Now, what are you talking about? By the way, I agree that it's too early yet to point any fingers.'

Greene jumped the gun on Vaux. 'I think Michael is probably referring to our promise to get Dr. Said's family over here—asylum and all that.'

Sir Nigel said, 'Yes, well, that's up to the powers that be at Century House. They're rabid at the moment at the loss of such a prize, letting it all slip through our fingers, as it were. I don't want to bother them on that point just yet.'

Vaux said, 'So the wife and two daughters are in a sort of limbo?'

'Well, I wouldn't call it that. We can't behave shabbily toward them—after all, there may be more prize defectors lining up to do a runner. And you can be sure that how we handle the outcome of this tragedy will be noted by enemies and friends alike. But rest assured, gentlemen, we have contacts in Syria, obviously, and we understand that the escape route and mechanisms have been established. They are just waiting for the green light, and meanwhile, we have to hope the Syrians don't suspect anything is in the works regarding the transfer of Said's widow and children to the UK.'

***

Sergeant Parry broke into a trot as he approached the café. Captain Stevens had switched to a glass of clouded, yellowish Ricard. Parry was out of breath and shaking his head.

'Thought I might have got lucky. Followed the guy to the Hotel Negresco, went into the lobby, and there he was with a wife and a small child. I listened to their conversation, and they were as Italian as spaghetti. Not our man.'

'How do you know our target's not Italian?'

'Nah, no hint of that. The Avis lady said our friend spoke more like a Cockney than anything else. Didn't you read the report?'

'I left it to you.'

'I think I'll have another *pression*,' said Parry in what he thought was a close-enough French accent.

***

Vaux took a taxi to Swiss Cottage. In an effort to get some exercise, he walked up five floors to the penthouse suite and was about to insert the plastic electronic key when he realized the door was slightly ajar. So far, the minder Craw had promised had not materialized. So he knew the open door could mean the minder had let himself in. On the other hand, that would have gone against 'official operating procedures,' and he doubted if the security man would act so carelessly. He instinctively pulled the Webley out of the shoulder holster (worn since acquiring it from housekeeping) and gently pushed open the door.

The place, always dimly lit, looked tidy, and the only noise he detected was the low hum of the air-conditioning. He walked slowly toward the bedroom, quietly pushed at the double doors, and everything, including the large king-size bed, looked in order. The bathroom had been cleaned, and fresh towels were hanging from the chrome bars above the oval-shaped bath. He went through to the living room, picked up the phone, and asked for the front desk. He complained about the open door and received profuse apologies. Blame was placed squarely on the hotel's maids and cleaners for the unfortunate oversight.

Then his search began. He rummaged through every pocket of every pair of pants he possessed (about six, including two serviceable suits), then sports jackets, one navy blue blazer, and a couple of casual coats, including his de rigueur trench coat. No success. He wondered if someone—the Syrians or the Israelis—had beaten him to it. Had they got access to the place and found Dr. Said's note? He knew he had put the handwritten note somewhere reasonably secure and hidden from searching eyes. But amid the drama of Said's sudden killing and the subsequent police investigation, the location of the note had simply gone out of his mind. He sat down in an overstuffed leather armchair that faced the large office desk close to the long windows.

The view was not unpleasant: a leafy street that led up to the quaint Ye Olde Swiss Cottage public house, designed in the last century as a veritable Alpine retreat. The irony didn't escape him. Here he was, staying in a hotel suite under a false name, his bills paid for by a fictitious company, looking out the window at an ersatz Alpine lodge. Then he shook himself from his reveries and tried hard to think about the sequence of events that had immediately followed the killing of Dr. Said.

He felt like having a drink but knew he needed to keep a clear head. The recall wheels turned deliberatively slow. He remembered putting the small piece of paper in a drawer—probably one of the drawers in that old worm-eaten chest at the River House. Then what? He knew he was an experienced packer. In and out of hotels his whole life, he was an expert in the mechanics and rituals of packing and unpacking, of entering and exiting homes or billets that had served as short-term shelters or longer-term but temporary places to crash. Then he thought of the suitcase, a battered but accommodating Samsonite, 'loaned' him by the caring housekeeping staff at the consulate in Alexandria for his quick exit from Egypt. He found it where he knew he had stored it—on the top of a large walnut wardrobe in the bedroom. He took it down, a cumbersome old traveling companion with a gold leaf CD imprinted on the inside lid. He delved into several flimsy internal side pockets. He found a small bottle of aspirin, a brochure for some hotel in Cannes, and yes, the note in question!

'Oh my God,' he muttered. 'Here it is.'

13

The low, intermittent buzz of the secure phone woke him up at 5:00 a.m. Vaux had been reading E. M. Forster's *Howards End* until he fell asleep, his bedside lamp still on and the paperback in his hands. He walked through to the living room to pick up the red phone on the old oak desk. B3's on-duty security officer told him in a stern military tone that his presence was required immediately and that Sir Nigel had called for a full-dress meeting at 6:30 a.m., sharp. An official car would be calling for him at 6:00 a.m., and meanwhile, he was to take every precaution in regard to his personal safety—a hint, no doubt, that the Webley could come in handy.

It was still dark outside, and Vaux heard raindrops tapping at the window. He felt sluggish and hungover despite not having a drink the previous evening. So he cursed audibly, walked through to the bathroom, and to save time, shaved in the shower. He thought of the previous evening's discovery and decided to tell no one until he had seen the contents of Dr. Said's safe-deposit box at the Bishopsgate branch of Lloyds bank. Events seemed to be evolving at a rapid pace, and Vaux instinctively became self-protective. Sole possession of the intelligence bonanza promised by the Said file offered an almost unassailable weapon in any future turf war that could hurt or benefit his immediate prospects. That's the way he was. It had always been him against the world, and throughout his journalistic career, he had played his cards close to his vest. He'd show his cards when he thought fortune favored him.

***

Sir Nigel presided. He looked as if he had got up at his usual time. His long leonine head of hair was brushed back over his ears with a gel-induced sheen. His toothbrush moustache was neatly trimmed, and he wore his tortoiseshell horn-rimmed glasses—usually a sign that he was in a very serious, business-like mood. Craw flitted around Sir Nigel's desk, putting various papers and files in place while Anne squeezed her way through with a tray of coffee cups and biscuits. Chris Greene sat next to Vaux on an uncomfortable high-back chair of 1930s vintage. Vaux crossed and uncrossed his legs, anxious to hear what had sparked this all-hands-on-deck confab.

Sir Nigel waited until Anne had closed the door. He took off his glasses and looked intensely at Vaux. There was what Vaux later considered a theatrically long silence, everybody waiting to hear what the chief had to say. Through the murky sash window, Vaux observed the wan light of dawn as it suffused the building's inner well.

'This matter concerns all of us very deeply, and for you, Vaux, I cannot overemphasize its seriousness.'

He opened the file that Craw had placed directly in front of him.

'Around 2 a.m. this morning, GCHQ picked up a coded message sent from Damascus GSD headquarters to the embassy here in London. It concerned the newspaper report and photos published in regard to the murder of Dr. Said in Suffolk. Not surprisingly, perhaps, they have now put two and two together, and they have recognized the so-called mystery man at the River House as one Michael Vaux, aka Justin Horner.

'Hardly surprising when you come to think about it, eh Vaux? After all, you lived and worked in Damascus for several years on that English-language paper; you were palsy-walsy with one Ahmed Kadri, a high-up Syrian government official; and last but not least, you disappeared from your Cairo posting rather than return to Damascus, where they wanted to interrogate you about Kadri after he had become persona non grata, as far as the Assad regime was concerned. Is that a fairly accurate summary of where we stand today, Craw?'

'An excellent summary, sir, if only a preamble of the immediate task ahead—our instructions for you, Vaux, et cetera.'

'Yes,' said Sir Nigel. 'Well, the bad news—the really bad news—is that according to this SIGINT flash, Damascus has, in today's parlance, put out a contract. They informed the GSD officials here—and we know who they are, obviously—that they are to do nothing and should await the team of fixers who will be sent here to do the job. Are you getting my drift, Vaux?'

Vaux *was* getting Sir Nigel's drift. 'I'm in their crosshairs, obviously,' he said.

Sir Nigel took a cream cracker from the chipped, faded Royal Doulton plate and then pushed it toward Craw's out-stretched hands. All four men were now nibbling while they awaited Sir Nigel's next pronouncement.

'But here's the important point. Within a few days, "Gertrude," code name for our agent who operates within

the high echelons of the Syrian intelligence network and
continues to do a fabulous job for us, will send us the
descriptions, real names, and noms de guerre, and hopefully
photos, et cetera, of what we can crudely call the hit team.
Craw, please outline our immediate strategy in regard to
this emergency.'

Craw said, 'We believe that the Syrians killed Said because
somehow they discovered his treasonous plan to swap their
topmost strategic secrets for his liberty, for his blessings
from the British government, and above all, for permission
to live here and bring his family over. We don't know how
Said's elaborate plans leaked, how they found out and why
they decided to kill him rather than persuade him to return
and work things out. He was a key nuclear scientist, as we
all know, and he had been relatively free to travel around the
world to international conferences and the like. Christ, they
even trusted him to disappear to our putative health farm in
Suffolk for a few days or weeks.

'Given what we now know, you, Vaux, have to take evasive
action.' He turned to look at Vaux, who was trying to digest
Craw's latest military jargon.

'What do you suggest I do?'

'We'll discuss that once our meeting with Sir Nigel is
concluded.'

Greene was now looking concerned. 'Does all this mean
that our theory about the Israelis pursuing the "targeted killing"
strategy is null and void?'

'Yes, I'm afraid so, Greene,' said Craw. 'Your research was
excellent, but we feel we were barking up the wrong tree with
that theory.'

Vaux said, 'It certainly seemed plausible, given Mossad's
track record. And frankly, with all due respect, Sir Nigel,
haven't we missed one crucial point in all this?'

Sir Nigel's eyes widened with moderate surprise. He made a gesture that invited Vaux to continue his line of reasoning.

Vaux replied with one word: 'Motive.'

Craw made some sound that suggested bewilderment at Vaux's failure to grasp the essentials. 'What about it?' he asked.

'Well, think for a minute. So they identified me as the man in front of the River House, hugging Mrs. Appleby good-bye. Therefore, we can assume they considered it highly likely that I was aiding and abetting Dr. Said's plan to defect. I understand that. But why would that cause them to exact the maximum penalty—murder me, if you will. I don't see the logic of that. It's one thing for the GSD to be mad at me for all my earlier entanglements with B3 and with their colleague Alena—and, yes, for my quick exit back to England after the fall from grace of my great friend Ahmed Kadri—'

Craw interrupted. 'You disappeared, old man. We got you out through Alexandria, and they never saw your face again. You basically cocked a snook at them and quit without saying good-bye, let alone arranging for some successor at the Cairo bureau of the *Damascus Times*.' Craw had adopted the position of prosecuting counsel for Vaux's former employers.

'And that's a motive for killing me?' asked Vaux, suppressing some exasperation at the way the conversation was going.

Sir Nigel intervened. 'Look, Vaux, who cares about their motivations? We know they're a bunch of thugs, anyway. It's payback time—revenge, if you like. They want to show us they can't be treated like that. And I'll tell you one more thing. Your former mistress has just had another promotion. She's back in Damascus at their main complex, and she's apparently thriving. How do you like that?'

Vaux felt a sensation that could only be called something between anguish and despair. He would probably never see Alena again, so deep was she entrenched with her masters. He said, 'But you see, this in a way only adds another twist to this byzantine affair.'

'What's that supposed to mean?' asked Craw as his puzzled face glanced toward Sir Nigel. It was as though he wanted to spare his boss any unpleasant theories that could weaken their resolve.

'Alena and Ahmed were very close. They were both fervent supporters of the Palestinian struggle to end the Israeli occupation and, of course, both devotees to the greater Arab cause. They were never lovers. When Alena performed services for her GSD bosses in Geneva, they became closer than ever. Ahmed admired her for the risks she was taking—working as a mole right here in these offices.'

'We all know that story,' said Sir Nigel, as if to make it clear that such treachery never happened on his watch.

Craw looked sheepish, and Greene, whose crush on Alena had come to florescence in Geneva, looked sad.

Craw began to speak softly, in a theatrical pretense of sympathy. 'We know all three of you people became entangled together, emotionally and, of course, in the case of you and Ahmed, platonically. And we all know that the triangle was shattered when, in June, they picked up Kadri for framing two highly placed Alawite officials, accusing them of being in the pay of MI6. But that was in the early 90s. You had no way of knowing, Vaux, that you were going to be treated badly if you had returned to Damascus. But you chose to flee, and we were obliged to come to your rescue.'

Vaux said, 'That's a slight distortion of history, Alan. Alena told me in no uncertain terms that they were furious at me for what they called my duplicity. Don't forget it was I who signed an affidavit that alleged that these two men were moles planted by MI6 and operating within the GSD. And it was my credibility that convinced their spymasters that Kadri's allegations were valid.'

'Enough gentlemen!' exclaimed Sir Nigel. 'Craw, please brief Vaux about our plans for his safety. Thank you all.' He got up, pushed back his swivel chair, and walked over to the sash window. His hands were clenched behind his back, and his thoughts concentrated on the necessary arrangements to be made for his big annual pheasant shoot. The season would open in a few weeks.

14

Sergeant Parry leaned against the mottled bark of a tall plane tree opposite the Hotel Splendide, a small, grubby hotel where rooms were often rented by the hour. He waited for Captain Stevens. The hotel was situated in a small square within the labyrinthine network of narrow cobbled streets in the ancient port area of Nice. In the center of the square stood a still-functioning fountain, a stone nymph out of whose rosebud mouth poured a gentle stream of water. In the small pool in which she knelt, coins of various sizes glittered in the mild morning sunlight. He had called Stevens on the walkie-talkie, and now he heard the clatter (Stevens liked steel-tipped heels) of his partner's determined strides.

'He's in that bloody hotel, sir. I'll swear it's 'im.'

'What makes you so sure this time?' asked the ever-skeptical captain. This was the fourth suspect in two days. Three previous parties had been followed on sighting—the pencil moustache betraying their potential real identity—but all had proven to be what the sergeant called 'damp squibs.'

'Exactly the right build, for one thing, a face closer to the identikit image than any of our previous suspects, and that good old Errol Flynn face fungus. Also, he talks with a London accent,' said Parry with unabashed enthusiasm.

'What's your plan of action, Sergeant?'

'Our usual mode of entry, sir.'

'Yes, but do we know the room number?'

'Yes, sir. I followed him into reception. He asked for the key. Then I booked a room on the same floor.'

'Well done, Brian. Do we need to call anyone for support? The local gendarmes, have they been informed?'

'Fuck no, sir. I don't trust the local police one iota.'

'Any communication with DGSE?'

'Not yet, sir.' Parry was getting agitated. The captain's insistence on doing everything by the book would only hold things up. 'We have to act swiftly, sir. Get the bastard and call the security boys later.'

They walked into the small lobby of the hotel. A middle-aged buxom blonde sat behind the front desk. She stood up, nodded to Parry and then to Stevens. She'd often seen male guests bring other men up to their rooms, but usually, there was a bigger age gap.

His small Sig Sauer 230 in his hand, Parry kicked open the door. Stevens was behind him. The suspect was lying on a faded and soiled bedspread. He had been sleeping. His crunched face betrayed total surprise and nascent fear. His hand instantly went to grab something under his pillow. But Parry jumped on him, threw the pillow to the ground, and saw the black Beretta 70. He swiped it to the floor, and Stevens quickly picked it up.

***

Following what Craw had termed Sir Nigel's crisis conference, Vaux was shuffled into an official Whitehall limo, destination unknown. He observed the streets they passed, the old postal codes on the ancient street plaques (SW1, NW2), and some of the familiar buildings and street markets. Camden Town rushed by, then Chalk Farm and Golders Green. The safe house was in a drab nineteenth-century terrace in Hendon, a dreary suburb of north London. The historic manor house in Suffolk seemed a long way away.

The driver, in official black livery with a black cap and the familiar cockade badge above the peak, ushered him into the house. It was chilly and dark.

'Three bedrooms upstairs, one big lounge downstairs, and a kitchen,' said the man. 'Make yourself at home, sir. Your personal luggage is being picked up at Swiss Cottage and should be here soon.'

A Mr. Jim Tripp would also be arriving—the implication being that he was to be Vaux's minder, a constant round-the-clock companion and guard. Vaux hoped to God he would get along with his enforced companion.

Vaux heard the door slam and then checked the lock. It was a brass Yale dead bolt. He turned the locking lever so that no one outside with a key could open the door, and then he went upstairs. The biggest of the three bedrooms was in the front of the house, and he went over to the windows and drew back the net curtains. Yes, it was a very dreary street, the opposite terraces exact replicas of his side of the street. A light drizzle added to the forlorn appearance of the small front gardens, some paved and others boasting postage-stamp lawns and bedraggled plants struggling to survive the polluted air thrown up by the constant traffic. Acacia Avenue was the road of choice for many motorists heading for the West End and the City. The bed had not been made up. He tested what looked like a brand-new mattress for its hardness (which he preferred) and was agreeably satisfied.

He maneuvered the uncovered pillows and lay down to await events.

A loud banging on the front door waked him. He got up and skipped down the narrow staircase. Through the multicolored diamond glass panels of the front door, he saw a tall, dark image. Before turning the locking lever, he asked who it was.

'Tripp, sir.'

Tripp was tall, lean, and about forty years old. He had a lined, narrow face, thin lips, and deep-brown eyes. And from his not unpleasant accent, Vaux guessed he was a Yorkshireman, born and bred.

'Settling in, are we?'

His first remark concerned Vaux for several reasons. It sounded patronizingly like a sergeant major question, and it implied a long stay at Acacia Avenue.

'Next time you ask me who I am, I'll answer with the following code name: Alpha. All right, sir?'

'Yes, of course. I'm Beta, if that will help. Now all we have to wait for is the lady who I was told would be doing the cooking and cleaning during what I hope is a short stay,' said Vaux.

'Don't you worry about that, sir. She'll be here shortly, and then we all of us can get acquainted.'

***

Mrs. Clark made an inaugural dinner of mashed potatoes, canned peas, and pork sausages. Vaux ate with Warrant Officer Jim Tripp, who he learned had been seconded to a secret service security squad from Special Forces. He had done stints with MI5 as well as MI6, and he had lived in this nondescript suburban dwelling before.

'Now, here's the usual routine, sir. Until we hear otherwise, you will stay here, and you will be looked after by Mrs. Clark.

She knows the house and all the local shops. If you want anything—cigarettes, drinks, booze, et cetera—just ask. Don't be shy. I'll be here at all times, and I see you have grabbed the front bedroom. That's all right. I'll have the back room that looks out on to the garden and the allotments at the rear,' said Tripp.

He then told Vaux about the secure phone (in the kitchen in the top drawer of the glasses and crockery cabinet) and inquired about Vaux's preparedness for anything that 'might happen.'

'If you mean am I armed, yes, I have a Webley.'

'Excellent, sir.'

Then, to Vaux's surprise and relief, Tripp suggested a pint at the local.

'I know the people there, and I also know that no human being can be cooped up in a place like this without some outside recreation. You'll be all right. We'll stay vigilant, and you'll wear a trilby you'll find in the hall wardrobe, plus these.' He proffered a pair of darkly tinted wire-framed glasses with plain lenses.

***

Late that evening, Vaux indulged his lifelong habit of putting pen to paper in order to assess the situation that now faced him.

The total mess:

1) Now semi-incarcerated in an MI6 safe house in North London for an indefinite period. Reason: my own safety following reports that Syria's spy agency, the General Security Directorate (GSD), is hatching a plot to kill me.

2) What is their motive for this drastic plan?

a) They figure I was instrumental in persuading Dr. Nessim Said to defect to the UK. Said has a bundle of information on his country's nuclear arms/power program, plus Syria's crucial order of battle in any future Mideast war. Also details on the health or otherwise of Assad's military/air force/missiles inventory.

b) They base their reasoning on the fact that they identified me as the man who was staying at the River House in Suffolk at the same time as Dr. Said. Top brass at B3 saw the River House as a convenient hideaway for presumed negotiations on Said's planned defection.

c) Add another ingredient: I had a love affair with Alena, one of their treasured agents, a double agent who successfully sabotaged Department B3's Operation Helvetia in Geneva. I was the star player in that fiasco, and they would have preferred me to sink into oblivion after MI6 (B3) discovered my liaison with Alena.

d) But following the dismissal of Ahmed Kadri from the new Assad regime, my fortuitous career in MI6 was resuscitated, and my appointed task was now to pump Dr. Nessim Said for all the information and intelligence we could get about Syria: its armaments drive, its secret codes, safe houses, likely double agents working within Britain's intelligence agencies. (Was Alena a lone wolf?)

e) What must have really got up their noses: my collusion with Kadri to frame the two senior officials, members of the elder Assad's cabinet, as double agents who worked for MI6. This was Kadri's revenge for their cooked-up charges against him—which led to his own dismissal and then his self-exile in Tangier in the early 90s.

f) Final reason to loathe my very being: the triangle of affection and love and loyalty that linked Ahmed Kadri, Alena Hussein, and me, a nexus forged by shared experiences, long absences, and a general compatibility. My love for Alena was perhaps the key to our reunion in Damascus (after Kadri was reinstated). Kadri facilitated everything: my job on the Damascus Times, my living arrangements, etc.

3) Puzzling questions:

a) Sir Nigel Adair, head of Department B3, asserts (from SIGINT data—intelligence acquired through intercepts of communications either coded or in plain text between Syria, its embassy in London, and GSD agents) that a hit team has already been selected and is presumably on its way to track me down.

b) Alena, now promoted to some high position in Damascus following her stint as deputy chief at GSD station in Cairo, has never tried to get in touch with me. Why? If she knows about the assassination plot (and it seems unlikely that she would be kept in ignorance), she would surely use her ample skills to somehow warn me of the dangers I face. True, it could be very difficult for her, but I have never known her to be at a loss in such circumstances. I know she loves me and must be under considerable strain. I am sure she must be aware, as a senior apparatchik in the Damascus intelligence scene, of these ominous developments, and I am equally sure she still loves me.

c) Little does Alena know that we have, according to Sir Nigel, an excellent agent planted within the top echelons of the GSD, code name Gertrude. She has been useful up to now and has confirmed the assassination plot. I gather she is also working on the evacuation of Said's widow and children from Syria— apparently due to a very British resolve to honor our promises to Said before he was killed.

d) Israeli intervention in the form of a 'targeted killing' of a key Syrian nuclear scientist fits into Israeli past plots and current strategies. In such killings, Mossad usually hires mercenaries. But Sir Nigel has dismissed these suspicions as unfounded. He and Craw are gunning for the Syrians.

e) So who killed Dr. Nessim Said? The Syrians or the Israelis? Both had motives: the Syrians could have suspected a traitor to their cause, a man who was willing to sell his nation's secrets for asylum and a nice life in England. MY QUESTION: How did they discover Said's plans?

The Israeli motive is clear-cut: eliminate any scientist/engineer who is helping to develop nuclear power or nuclear bombs/missiles, etc. for any Arab country, including Syria, its old enemy.

Vaux put his plastic ballpoint down on a slim glass tray designed for the old days of fountain pens and gold propelling pencils. Then it hit him. He had failed to mention that he possessed the ultimate holy grail in this whole affair: the documents that sat in a safe-deposit box at a Lloyds bank branch in the City. He'd write that crucial postscript tomorrow. It had been a long day.

15

Vaux got lucky. The central registry, housed in the labyrinthine dungeon where MI5 stored the voluminous archives of Britain's intelligence agencies, had not yet computerized the year of Alena Hussein's exposure as a double agent for Syria. The slow and painstaking process of digitizing the old dog-eared files and official memoranda of past years had only crept up to 1988, several years prior to Alena's defection.

So within the bowels of Thames House, Vaux had combed through ten-year-old files and cross-reference data to finally locate the case file on Alena Hussein, previous employee of MI6's Department B3, the sub-subgroup of Mideast experts and special projects. Her 'double-cross' status was a matter of record, and since she operated out of London as a British subject, her case file had ended up under the protection of the domestic spy agency, MI5. He was allowed to sign out the unexpectedly slim file for a limited period.

***

Vaux had sat around the Acacia Avenue safe house for near-ly ten days. The routine had become predictably monotonous: breakfast at 8:00 a.m., usually bacon and eggs, toast and mar-malade, and a pot of strong Typhoo tea; lunch at midday, usually baked beans on toast or a tuna sandwich brought in from a nearby Sainsbury's; at 7:00 p.m., Mrs. Clark made some attempt at a lit-tle more sophistication, with 'gourmet' dinners heated in a con-venient microwave oven. Thus beef stroganoff, sole meunière, and spaghetti bolognese became regular menu items, along with more traditional dishes like roast beef and grilled pork chops.

In the second week, Vaux decided on a course of action; he'd had plenty of time to think things through. Reading and rereading the aide-mémoire he'd written to himself helped to resolve two questions that had obsessed him—even when he accompanied a cheerful Tripp to the Wheatsheaf, the pub around the corner. He knew he had to open up Said's safe-deposit box. He would tell Sir Nigel and Co. that the fast-moving events of recent weeks, the trauma of what seemed to be an execution-style killing of Dr. Said, a polite and cultured man whom he had grown to like, had wiped out his memory (partly true, anyway). The details of Said's surprise bequest to him in case of his death or disappear-ance had simply been smothered by the lightning sequence of tragic events that followed.

His second resolution was to dig out the inevitable files and dossiers relating to Alena's defection in 1991. He had never been consulted by anyone at either security agency about her final betrayal of British interests. But that was understandable. His assignment to Morocco to pump his friend Ahmed Kadri for the mother lode of intelligence on the Syrian economy, military readiness, locations of potential nerve gas stockpiles and nuclear plans, and so on had come soon after Alena's flight to Syria. And then, having done the Tangier job, his own decision to move to Syria to be close to her and Ahmed would hardly have persuaded any inquisitor to supplement the Alena Hussein file with any contributions from him—in terms of background information or suspicious behavior—which, in hindsight, should have registered somewhere within the walls of Department B3.

After much hesitation by Craw and no doubt lengthy discussions between Sir Nigel and his cohorts at MI5, he was finally given the green light. He could take the file out for two days, and it must be returned by 3:00 p.m. on the third day.

***

He skipped down the wide steps of Thames House and quickly got into the Daimler. Warrant Officer Tripp suddenly appeared from nowhere, covered Vaux's back, and shouted to the driver, 'Go, mister!'

Tripp, settling in to the corner of the backseat, wore a camel hair coat and a brown felt trilby. Vaux considered the drama unnecessary but thought better of making any comments that could be interpreted as flippant. Tripp was simply doing his job.

'Don't like all this at all, at bloody at all. Strictly against the rules, sir, if you don't mind me saying so.'

'I understand,' said Vaux. 'Only one more errand and we're done.'

From the Thames Embankment, the car went north toward the Aldwych and then past St. Paul's and east to Bishopsgate.

They parked the Daimler in front of the imposing building. Tripp told Vaux to stay in the car while he negotiated a parking deal. He came out of the swing doors accompanied by a

uniformed commissionaire who looked serious but efficient.
Vaux got out of the car with the briefcase that contained the
Alena Hussein file. The commissionaire led him to the manager's
office, where he was asked to wait while other clients were being
served. After about fifteen minutes, a thickset young man with
red hair and freckled face approached Vaux with outstretched
hand. The man wore a dark-blue pin-striped suit, club tie, white
shirt, and black oxford shoes. The epitome of a solid banker.

'How are you, sir? My name's Julian Marsh, assistant manager. Please come with me.' He led him into a small office
adjacent to a massive steel door that looked to Vaux like the entrance to the array of safe-deposit boxes he'd expected to find.
They sat down, and Vaux put his Justin Horner passport on the
table, along with the note written and signed by Dr. Said and a
copy of the death certificate obtained a few days ago by Anne,
who had been sworn to secrecy.

'Yes, thank you.' Marsh looked carefully at the note and
compared the writing and signature with the spidery samples of
Said's signature on a two-by-three index card he had retrieved
from their records. Then he got up and led the way to the big
steel doors. He punched six numbers into a coded electronic
lock and pushed open the heavy door. Then he led Vaux to a far
corner of the long, narrow room. There seemed to be hundreds
of shiny-fronted small safe-deposit boxes, and Vaux quickly
searched for Said's number: 9239389. He found it in the upper
reaches, on the left. Marsh was a tall man, so he didn't make use
of a small stepladder that was at hand.

He stretched up, put the key in the safe, turned twice, and
then backed away. Vaux looked at him, somewhat bewildered.

'Now you have to use your key, or the late Mr. Said's key. It
takes two keys, sir. A matter of security.'

'Oh my God,' said Vaux, cursing his oversight of the
obvious.

The two men faced each other, and Marsh, for something to do while Vaux collected his thoughts, decided to move the small stepladder to a closer position within a narrow alcove between the safe-deposit drawers.

'Dr. Said overlooked that small point. He never mentioned a key, though I suspect it must be in his belongings.'

'Yes. Well, sir, it's pretty essential. In an emergency, we could open the safe for you, but it would be better to come back once you have found the key. It's a matter of bank proto-col, you see.'

Vaux left the building, cursing under his breath. Where the hell were Said's belongings, anyway? Tripp, who waited in the vaulted marble-and-gilt lobby, took Vaux's briefcase and walked with him to the car.

'Mission accomplished?' asked Tripp, as if he had read the disappointment on Vaux's face.

'No, unfortunately.'

'Home to Hendon, then?'

'You make it sound so inviting, Tripp. No possibility of call-ing in at Gower Street?'

'Strictly out of bounds, sir.'

***

Sergeant Parry leveled his small Sig Sauer 230 at the man's chest. He had been told to stand up while Captain Stevens gave him a body search for any more concealed weapons. Stevens had pocketed the man's Beretta, having taken out the cartridg-es. Parry's arm remained steady while Stevens quickly searched the small room. The metal blinds were shut, and there was a pervasive odor of sweaty bodies and soiled clothing. Stevens then rifled through the man's canvas holdall. He fished out a passport. The man's name appeared to be Brian Stuart and his place of birth Brighton. Born twenty-six years ago in 1974. There were no other items of interest: two girlie magazines and a street map of Nice plus the usual casual clothing (khakis and jeans, a sweater, several shirts, and underpants).

'You were in England a few days ago, weren't you?' said Stevens.

'I've been here a few weeks, mister. I don't know what you're talking about.'

'Where's the air ticket?'

'I got a special price. I have to buy another one-way ticket to get back,' said Stuart. 'What the fuck is this, anyway? You the police? I don't think so. Too bloody English for the French gendarmerie, if you ask me.'

'We're not asking you, mate,' said Parry. 'Just shut the fuck up while we decide what to do with you.'

Stewart gave a nonchalant shrug and moved his leg slightly. Parry waved the gun as a warning not to try anything.

'Why are you carrying the Beretta?' asked Stevens.

'My own bloody protection, if you must know, mister. Got in with some shady types in Brighton and came here to let their anger subside, if you know what I mean.'

'No, I don't. But how did you get it through airport security?'

'I keep the Beretta here, don't I? In a safe at a friend's pad.'

There was a long silence. Parry's arm was getting tired. He nodded to Stevens.

'Ever heard the name Bob Kirby? Perhaps one of your friends?'

Stevens's face visibly paled. 'Nah, mate.'

'I'm going to call your friends now. So you'll wait here— and don't try any funny moves.'

'What fucking friends?' said Kirby.

'The gendarmes,' said Stevens.

'Oh, come on, mate. Give me a break. What are you trying to pin on me, anyway?'

'Carrying a handgun, for starters. The Sûreté Nationale aren't too keen on anyone running around town with a loaded revolver. Or didn't you know that?'

Parry moved towards the door but kept his arm high, his pistol pointed at Kirby. Stevens then skipped down the stairs to the small reception area. He asked the big blonde if he could use the phone.

***

The doorbell at 30 Acacia Avenue rang three times. Vaux and Tripp were looking at the evening news in the kitchen. Mrs. Clark was trying not to make too much noise as she prepared the evening meal.

'That'll be Anne from the office,' Vaux said casually. 'She's done an errand for me.'

'I'll go,' said Tripp.

Vaux heard their voices in the hallway.

Vaux had discussed the expected visit from B3's girl Friday, and Tripp had reluctantly agreed that Vaux would be granted some privacy. All three would go to the Wheatsheaf, and Tripp would keep his observant eyes open from a distance.

The pub was crowded and noisy. Friday-night jollity, communal joy on the payday eve of another weekend. Vaux guided Anne to a corner table, while Tripp sat at the U-shaped bar, from where, through the miasma of tobacco smoke, he could observe the couple as well as the bustling to and fro of the pub crowd. The entrance of the pub, covered by a thick red curtain, was only ten feet from his corner, and his eyes were in constant motion, almost in sync with his arm as he raised and lowered his glass of draft Bass.

Anne fished in her black handbag and produced the key.

'You're a genius,' said Vaux. 'How did you find it?'

'Dr. Said's clothing and his few possessions were stashed in our files and records room. Remember it?'

'Yes, that tiny little cubbyhole we call our own registry?'

'That's right. They were in the same suitcase as Dr. Said had at the River House. Anyway, as you know, I often work late and close the shop up at night. So it wasn't difficult to rummage through his clothing. It was so sad. I never met the man, of course, but it's just harrowing to go through the clothes and belongings of someone who's just died.'

Anne Armitage-Hallard was the youngest daughter of a rich family of tea merchants. She had gone to Roedean, the preferred private boarding school for girls of the privileged, and then to the Slade School of Fine Art in London. She was an ideal candidate for a lowly secretarial job in Britain's intelligence establishment. A rich heiresses can be trusted, her loyalty to the nation and its social system as steady and permanent as the White Cliffs of Dover. Vaux didn't know the details of her background, but by intuition, he guessed the basics. He also knew what he saw: a very beautiful fair-skinned natural blonde, tall and slim and elegant. Her nose was straight, her lips full, eyes like sapphires. Small girlish breasts. Tonight she wore a smart lame jacket, tight black ankle pants, a floral blouse, and strappy stilettos that made her look even taller.

Vaux's feasting eyes revealed his hunger. He realized how long he had been celibate, his last sex on that long-ago evening with Alena in Cairo. But, of course, it was out of the question. He'd be polite and sociable, his age providing the protection he needed to conceal the desire that was coursing through his body. He glanced at Tripp, who nodded back with a cheeky smile. After about an hour, Anne mumbled something about getting back. She had her own small apartment off Park Lane, she said, and her roommate would be expecting her. They planned to go to the Ministry of Sound.

When Vaux looked puzzled, she laughed and then explained, 'A swinging disco, Michael. You should come one night and let your hair down.'

Vaux said, 'I don't think so.'

They walked back to the house, and then Vaux hailed a passing taxi. He opened the rear door for her, and before she got in, she brushed a light kiss on his cheek. Then she asked when they would see each other again. Vaux stammered, looked at a disapproving Warrant Officer Tripp, and promised to be in touch soon.

16

He couldn't get to sleep. The evening's events kept rewinding and repeating. Alena was a long way away—physically and spiritually, or perhaps more accurately, politically. Anne's attraction for him was palpable. Gestures and smiles, that elusive, protracted look people gave each other when they were interested in pursuing where mutual attraction could lead. But then he would tell himself that he was being silly. His age (old enough to be her father) was one thing, but the challenges he now faced (a price over his head, someone out there possibly stalking him, looking to grasp an opportunity to put a bullet in his head or stab him with a poison-tipped umbrella as he walked by on a crowded sidewalk) was another thing entirely. It was all hopeless. He got up and went over to the dressing table that stood in front of the bay windows. He drew the curtains open an inch and looked out, just for the unlikely possibility of seeing a Ford Taurus parked up the street. But the yellowed, sodium-lighted scene was deserted—not a soul, only cars parked bumper-to-bumper belonging to those Acacia Avenue residents, who were now sleeping almost as closely packed together as their cars but were mercifully isolated by the thin brick walls that separated each terraced house.

He opened the drawer and took out the file.

He noted again how thin it was. It had all the ominous traces of having been rifled through to extract salient facts, perhaps incriminating facts, perhaps exonerating. He read the first pages:

Alena Hussein (AH)

(Operating cover names: Barbara Boyd, Veronica Belmont)

PROFILE:

Hussein was spotted by our friends at the Hong Kong & Shanghai Banking Corporation (HSBC) as promising materi-al. She was interviewed shortly thereafter by Sir Walter Mason, head of Department B3, and two of his deputies. Also attend-ing the preliminary interview was a representative of Sir John Blakeley, director general of MI6, Mr. John Eccles.

We were impressed by AH for several reasons: she was attractive and bright, had graduated in 1990 with a first-class honors degree from King's College (London), and was only just about to enter the workforce. She was interested in international banking and global economic trends, hence her application to join HSBC.

Our one major reservation: Although born in the UK and a British subject, her father (name: Waguih Hussein, now dec'd) was a Palestinian, born in Nabulus in 1937. His father, a civil engineer, fled Palestine with his family at the outbreak of the 1948 Arab-Israeli War, otherwise known as the Israeli War of Independence. Waguih Hussein was educated at Mill Hill School in London, graduated in medicine at University College, and went on to complete his medical courses at University College Hospital. There he met Elizabeth Barker, a nurse whom he later married.

At the outset of her series of interviews, we asked AH for her opinions on the Middle East (ME). Briefly, she made a convincing argument for current Western policies toward Israel in particular and the ME in general. She said she believed that the US, Britain, and France genuinely wanted a settlement between Israel and the Palestinians of the West Bank and Gaza, and their push for a two-state solution was the only avenue down which to proceed for a durable peace in the region. Therefore, she did not agree with the disruptive tactics of Arafat's Palestinian Liberation Organization (PLO), nor with any other of the terrorist groups that sought a solution through 'chaos and armed conflict' (her words).

We decided to engage AH in view of her potential as an agent with attributes no Anglo-Saxon could equal, her Arab background and her fluency in Arabic. (Her first tasks in the early months of hiring her were to read the major Arab dailies and give press summaries on a weekly basis—not excluding, of course, the opinion pieces as represented by a newspaper's editorials and columnists.) MI6 is chronically short of operatives fluent in Arabic, as are most Western intelligence agencies. So we naturally thought AH would be a 'feather in our B3 hat.'

In 1992, B3 launched Operation Helvetia in the wake of a report from a retired agent/talent spotter in Hertfordshire who became friendly with a former journalist. Michael Vaux, the journalist in question, had accepted a generous buyout package from his former employer and decided he wanted to live in the neighborhood where he had grown up. Our ex-agent, Arthur Davis, CMG, discovered (via chats in the local pub) that Vaux was under financial pressure due to his desire to buy a home in the area. Apparently, his buyout deal did not provide enough funds to complete the purchase of a home he seemed to want desperately to buy.

In summary, by offering him a substantial financial incentive, he agreed to hear our proposal. We had checked on his background. And the tantalizing morsel was this: he had been a college friend of Ahmed Kadri, who, at the time, according to our man in Damascus, was the chief armaments buyer for Syria. MI6 network had, in recent months, strongly indicated mounting and convincing evidence of an imminent multibillion-dollar arms deal between Russia and Syria.

Our aim: get the two men together and we could have a chance of filling in the blanks.

AH, undercover as an archivist for a think tank, met and seduced Vaux, a lonely divorcé. She was put in place to monitor Vaux—his feelings about working for MI6 and the plan to deceive an old college friend in order to garner confirmation and details of the Syrian-Russian arms deal. She was highly successful in this endeavor and was able to supplement our Vaux profile and confirm our first impressions of the man. She reported, among other character traits, that his political views were centrist (helped, no doubt, by his many years in North America and by his liberal education at Bristol University). He fell for her—and every other trick in our book!

THE DEBACLE:

Operation Helvetia was brilliantly conceived and supported 100 percent by 'C,' Sir John Blakeley, and his staff.

However, it has to be conceded that Operation Helvetia ultimately failed in its most ambitious goals. Vaux produced a blueprint of the Russian-Syrian deal, but a faked blueprint. The deal itself, we now know, was much bigger and more significant in terms of altering the balance of power in the ME.

Blame for the failure of Operation Helvetia has to be put at the feet of AH. She betrayed our plans to her Syrian friends, and despite her seeming affection for Vaux, she obviously betrayed him into the bargain. She was, in short, a mole, probably working for the Syrian secret service (GSD) from the day we hired her.

She is currently an officer at the GSD, working at HQ in Damascus and, we now hear, in line for promotion to station chief at the Syrian embassy in Cairo. This latest intelligence has not been confirmed and is not believed to be imminent.

—London, 1993

Vaux closed the file. He had read enough. He had known some classic 'cover my ass' (CMA) memorandums in his time. Most news editors were experienced hands in that fine art. But this took the biscuit for BS: 'it has to be conceded that Operation Helvetia ultimately failed in its ambitious goals' and 'brilliantly conceived'!

The final damning accusations against Alena were, of course, accurate. He rummaged through another twenty pages or so of turgid summaries of other jobs she had worked on while at Gower Street. He had read enough—and it really didn't help much.

But there was one gaping hole. And that was any cross-references to his role in the fiasco—and his admitted betrayal. The collusion between Kadri and himself to deceive MI6 and undermine the spy agency's efforts to obtain the full and comprehensive details of the arms treaty seemed to have been brushed aside, as if of no significance. Apart from a slight blow to his ego, he could only guess that 'they' had left his story for his own dedicated file, access to which he could never hope to gain.

His brain was still on overdrive. He decided to go downstairs to make a cup of tea—a cure, his mother always said, for insomnia, despite the caffeine. He didn't hear the gentle snoring usually emanating from Tripp's room as he passed the door. When he got downstairs, he saw a chink of light coming from the kitchen door. Sitting at the old wooden table was Tripp and another man he didn't recognize.

'Hello, sir,' said a surprised Tripp. 'Thought you were sleeping like a log after your enjoyable evening at the pub.'

'Couldn't sleep at all, as a matter of fact,' said Vaux, looking quizzically at the other man.

'This is Staff Sergeant Murdoch, sir. Sent to buttress the establishment, as it were.'

'What's that supposed to mean?' asked Vaux, pouring himself a cup of tea from the stained white pot that sat at the center of the table. He shook Murdoch's outstretched hand.

'Signals, sir. Message came through tonight. Two eagles have landed. Our friends are in the UK, and we've got to go on full alert.'

Vaux now sat down. He had been preoccupied by the Said business, the key, then the Alena file. He had forgotten why he was here in this threadbare safe house.

'Two eagles means two gunmen, I gather.'

'No question about that, sir,' said Tripp. 'So we're taking the usual precautions. Sergeant Murdoch's one of my regular backups. I feel a lot better with him around, I can tell you.'

Vaux looked at Murdoch. He was about thirty, stocky, and darkly handsome. 'How did you know about the signal stuff?'

'Secure phone, sir. About an hour ago.' Tripp nodded to the drawer where the red phone was housed.

Vaux went back to his room. He reopened the AH file and flipped through to CONCLUSION. Under a subsection headed AH DEFECTION—POSSIBLE THREATS AND REPURCUSSIONS, he read:

It has to be conceded that AH has very probably compromised key intelligence data. Among the areas we will have to assess are all codes / ciphers / passwords used to contact and communicate with our assets in the ME, names of same, and cover names (if applicable). The harm AH could have done to our network of agents in place and / or double agents in the area cannot be underestimated. Special attention will have to be paid to embassy and consulate staff who work for MI6 under cover of their diplomatic missions.

This is our main area of concern. However, there are other areas where we may have to take evasive action. For example, AH had access to our list of safe houses throughout London and the UK. This is not of immediate concern, but it could constitute a real failure in our security arrangements, affecting MI6 and MI5 operations.

Also, AH had access to our personnel files: lists of full-time SIS employees as well as our agents and helpers throughout the UK and the world. This includes our assets at several British

universities, as well as universities in Beirut, Damascus, Aleppo,
and Cairo and at major international commercial companies
(including, of course, HSBC) and other major banks...

Vaux closed the file. He opened his holdall and pulled out the Webley. He checked the chamber and put the revolver under his pillow. Then he fell into a heavy sleep.

17

Vaux woke to find Warrant Officer Tripp hovering over him with a cup of tea. He glanced at his old Accurist watch. It was 7:00 a.m.

'Sorry to wake you from your beauty sleep, sir. But we've got an early-morning start.'

Vaux wondered what this enigmatic statement could portend. He looked up at Tripp's clean-shaven, lined, and weathered face with an expression that invited an explanation.

'Full dress meeting at Gower Street. Top brass and all that. You're to attend, sir.'

'I suppose this has something to do with the two birds of prey?'

'Not for me to figure out, sir. But the car's coming at 8 sharp.'

'Look, you recall my wasted trip to the bank on Cheapside?'

'Yes, sir.'

'Can we use this opportunity to go back there? I've got the additional information they had asked for, you see,' said Vaux.

'We'll try and fit it into the schedule, sir.'

'Thanks.'

***

Sir Nigel Adair was already conferring with Alan Craw when Anne ushered Vaux into the sanctum. She had beckoned him with a sweet smile from the small office he shared with Chris Greene. He asked her if she had enjoyed her night at the Ministry of Sound.

'Oh, yes, but we didn't stay long. I'm not really a night owl,' she said. 'Sir Nigel is waiting for you.'

'Where's Greene?'

'He's over at Century House. There's a bit of a flap on, from what I can gather. But I'm sure you'll learn all about it from Sir Nigel,' she said.

'Ah, Vaux, my boy. Nice to see you. How's your vacation going?' asked Sir Nigel, his version of dry humor.

Vaux responded in a similar vein. 'Splendidly. Never knew Hendon could be so good for one's health.'

'Ha-ha-ha!' exclaimed Sir Nigel. He looked at Craw, whose legs stretched out so that his shoes tapped quietly on the front of Sir Nigel's battered rosewood desk. Craw raised his eyebrows, indicating that he didn't think present circumstances justified humor or false jollity. His attitude brought Sir Nigel back to reality, and he asked Craw to give Vaux the latest news.

'A flash from Greene who's just got off the phone, Vaux. The MI6–Special Forces inquiry into the killing of Dr. Said has been called off. We are to be briefed on the details later. But Greene reports that the two-man expedition to France was highly successful, even though it was later aborted. Seems one of the suspected culprits was indeed arrested and held in joint custody by the DGSE, French external security, and the local Police Nationale.

'He confessed to everything. Paris and Jerusalem had a crisis conference, and the upshot was that a furious Chirac and a conciliatory Barak had a lengthy private conversation and did some horse trading. A French agent, accused of spying by Israel two years ago and currently in a Tel Aviv jail, has been released on condition that the whole Said inquiry is dropped. Jacques Chirac then got on to the prime minister, and Blair agreed to shelve the matter.'

Vaux couldn't resist rubbing it in. 'So I was right. It was Mossad.'

'Not quite, Vaux. The Israelis neither confirm nor deny any complicity in the plot to assassinate the Syrian scientist,' said Craw, happy to crush any self-congratulatory consolation Vaux might have felt entitled to.

Sir Nigel had been looking through the sash windows, again spotted with pigeon droppings and smudged with the grime of London. He couldn't even see as far as the office opposite, a firm of busy accountants and pretty office girls. He realized that Craw had concluded his report.

'Well, now let's get down to the more immediate business before us. Vaux, I'm afraid you're going to have to end your vacation in Hendon. You will be transferred today to another location—safer, more secure, and I may add, somewhat more salubrious, eh, Craw?'

'Absolutely, sir.'

Vaux couldn't help thinking Craw was always eager and happy to take him out of circulation.

Sir Nigel resumed. 'We now know that two agents have been sent over by the GSD, and we understand, through

"Gertrude" '—Sir Nigel raised his arms and jiggled his forefingers to indicate quotation marks—'that their mission is, to put it bluntly, to wipe you off the map.'

Sir Nigel paused to garner the reaction to what he thought was a clever variation of the usual euphemisms to denote murder.

Craw took over. 'The thing is, Vaux, there's bad news and bad news. The first bad news is that they have clearly decided that you are Enemy Number One in their books for the reasons we have discussed before—your proximity to Said at the time of his death, in effect implicating you in his murder, and, of course, the fact that they assume you are once again in our employ, plus the shabby way you treated your former Syrian employers, et cetera.'

'Don't rub it in,' said Vaux.

Sir Nigel smiled in sympathy.

'The second bit of bad news is that they have arrived on our shores, but we have so far failed to detect where they are. This is a serious gap in the information available. All border points were under orders yesterday and last night to watch out for the hit men. And, of course, the manhunt continues. So we're sending you to a hyper-safe house out of London and hopefully out of danger. As you probably read in the file you took out from the registry, many of our safe houses have probably been compromised by your former lover's defection. But this place has always been off record and is maintained mainly for the big wigs of UK intelligence as well as for very senior representatives of other Western security outfits.'

'Well, that's comforting,' said Vaux, not caring if he sounded sarcastic. 'But how reliable is the current intelligence about these man hunters? If, as you say, they were expected to arrive within the last twenty-four hours, how come they haven't materialized?'

His question met with embarrassed silence. The opening was there, and he took it.

'I have perhaps a better idea. Why don't I stay in circulation and entice these buggers to their target? If I remove my cover, they'll find me, and then, with the help of our true and trusted Special Forces, they could be eliminated quickly and effectively.'

Craw said, 'Look, Vaux, never underestimate the guile and deviousness of our Arab friends. So far, they've outsmarted us, but we'll get 'em. Just as we got the now officially disowned Mossad mercenaries.'

Sir Nigel nodded vigorously in agreement.

Vaux chose to ignore Craw's remark. 'What do you say, Sir Nigel? I could be the live bait to lure these killers out into the open. It would save an awful lot of time—and expense.'

Vaux thought the awesome cost of keeping him indefinitely in a faraway sort of quarantine could swing Sir Nigel's views to his side. If his suggestion was rejected, he had no other option but to accept their plans for him. The only faint hope that remained was the potential earthshaking contents in a safe on Cheapside. Like a poker player, he would see what the cards turned up. A winning hand provided by the foresight of Dr. Nessim Said might alter or rearrange some of the dynamics that seemed to be framing his immediate future, perhaps even his very life.

Sir Nigel's verdict came fast. 'We can't accept the risk that would involve. Strange as it may seem to you, Vaux, we value your life and see no point in embarking on some violent gamble that could end up with you dead and no certain outcome for the assailants. No, it's out of the question.'

As he stood to leave, Vaux thought he'd ask one last question: 'So where am I going this time?'

'Under wraps, old boy,' said Craw as he put his arm around Vaux. He pulled him closer in an unusually warm gesture. 'But you'll like it, and it will be totally secure.'

***

Vaux stretched up to the steel safe-deposit box after Mr. Julian Marsh, assistant manager, had turned the bank's master key twice. He then turned his key two revolutions counter-clockwise, as instructed, and pulled out the long steel tray. He lifted a latch that held the lid firm, opened the lid, and looked inside the safe. He saw shiny, glittering stainless steel nothing-ness. The safe was empty.

He stood there, stunned. Marsh had walked away, pretend-ing to be checking other safes to give Vaux privacy. He closed the lid, slid the drawer back into its home, relocked it, and nod-ded to Marsh, who was now looking his way.

'Thank you,' said Vaux as he walked through the open twelve-inch-thick main steel door and mounted the staircase to the lobby.

Upstairs, Tripp was waiting for him, hands behind his back. 'Mission accomplished, sir?'

'Yes, let's go,' said Vaux.

At midnight, the official armor-plated black Daimler whose trunk was filled with Vaux's few belongings moved slowly down a dim and quiet Acacia Avenue, turned left, and headed for the M1. Vaux got himself comfortable in the backseat. Tripp was up front with the driver, and Murdoch sat on the small jump seat that faced Vaux.

'Look, Sergeant, why don't you sit back here —it's far more comfortable. I presume it's going to be a long journey.' Vaux had figured they were headed north, probably to the far reaches of Scotland or even the Hebrides.

'No, that's all right, sir. From here, I've a good view of the rear. This way, if any nosy parkers get too close, I can see what's going on. Thanks all the same.'

Instinctively, Vaux felt for the holster under his left arm. He was exhausted. Tripp was having an animated conversation with the driver, but he heard nothing through the glass partition. Lulled by the low hum of the engine and the warmth inside the car, he fell into a dreamless sleep. Even fleeting thoughts of Anne couldn't keep him awake.

18

Alena Hussein sat opposite Abdul Fatah Mamluk, deputy to the chief of Syria's intelligence agency, the General Security Directorate, in his chaotic office in an auxiliary GSD outpost close to al-Umawiyeen Square in the heart of modern Damascus. Mamluk weighed three hundred pounds, and he was a short man, about five feet six inches. He boasted a walrus moustache, and a bald patch at the back of his head accentuated his thinning black hair. Steel filing cabinets surrounded the walls of the office, most of them open, with folders that looked as if they had been selected for perusal, only to be shoved back casually to their ordered places. Newspapers, mainly Arabic, were piled on top of one another, so that several tall pillars of newsprint appeared to be supporting the low tobacco-stained ceiling. The dusty, yellowed venetian blinds behind him were half rolled up and hung unevenly.

'Would you care for some coffee?' he asked Alena.

'No, thank you. Just a mineral water,' she said. She had traveled that morning from Cairo, where she acted as a liaison officer between the Cairo station and the Damascus GSD nerve center on al-Thawra Street, facing the historic Citadel.

'Well now, Alena, we have to tie up some loose ends on this Said business. As I understand it, Said was shot outside some MI6 safe house—probably by UK operatives who were leading him by the nose and promising him asylum, provided he brought our top defense secrets with him. Is that the picture?'

'Yes, although our latest intelligence suggests there could have been collusion with our Israeli enemies.'

'Really? Those devious bastards pop up everywhere, don't they? But let's move on. Am I right in assuming that our Michael Vaux—the late, lamented Ahmed Kadri's English friend and, until recently, the Cairo columnist for the *Damascus Times*—is suspected of leading our lamb to the slaughter?'

'Unfortunately, it would seem so. He was at the house at the time. He had been staying there for several days with Dr. Said, and he had probably pumped him for every tidbit of information he could get out of him. He was good at that sort of thing. That's why London rehired him after he quit Cairo. They wanted him to be a key player in what they called Operation Ebla.'

'Why that name?'

'It's where Said was working on plans to build a nuclear facility—an enrichment plant that would produce uranium for the power industry and eventually for nuclear weapons, of course.'

'I'm getting the picture,' said Mamluk. He retrieved a big cigar from a box of Montecristo No. 3s. He lit it with a two-inch-high flame from a slim gold lighter and pushed his chair back, as though more distance between them would help her avoid the puffs of cigar smoke he now blew out the side of his mouth.

Alena waited, her hands resting on her lap. She took a sip of water from the small plastic bottle. She knew she was there to receive orders, not just for a mutual briefing session.

'So, my dear, we have to take action. Two of our best special operatives have arrived in England. They were told to eliminate this man Vaux and then make their way back—a quick, tidy operation, to remind the English that we can be just as efficient as they are at this game.'

Alena knew that this meant the deadly and ruthless al-Saiqa forces were now playing a role. She tried to read Mamluk's mind now. Where could she fit into this operation?

Mamluk said, 'But there is a problem. Vaux has gone into hiding. He's disappeared. These two men are brilliant—it took them only a few days to trace him to a safe house in North London.'

'Sir, if I may? I brought a complete list of their safe houses back with me when I quit England, remember?'

'Before my time, Lieutenant.'

Actually, she had been promoted to captain with the liaison job, but she ignored the unintended demotion. 'Sorry, continue.'

'Well, he suddenly quit. That's all we know. Left in the small hours, it seems, just when our boys had thought it safe to slip away for a few hours' sleep. A serious mistake, but it can't be helped. So now, my dear, here is the crux of why I summoned you here. We want you to go to England, find Vaux, and our two men will then finish the job.'

Alena felt a sudden bewilderment, an emptiness. She hated the thought of going back to all those familiar surroundings. It had been ten years. Oceans had passed under the bridge. She still loved Vaux. And now she was expected to play a part in his execution. Her thoughts were broken by the sound of Mamluk's gravelly voice.

'You will go back and contact Vaux. You will say that you must meet him. Are you still friends?'

'My duty outweighs my friendships,' said Alena. She was determined to show no emotion.

'Good. Excellent. So you will go—undercover, of course—and check in with our people in London. You will, I'm sure, find ways to communicate with your old lover, perhaps by contact with one of his colleagues in the security unit he works for. You'll find a way, I know it!'

'And then?'

'Oh, I thought you might have guessed. You will entice him to meet you, obviously. It will be a nice setup. Our two operatives will then move in for the kill. And our people will see to it that all three of you will be back in Damascus within twenty-four hours. At least, that's the basic plan. Any comments, my dear?'

Plenty, but not for your ears. 'Not really. You are quite sure our two officers have hit a wall in their search for Vaux?'

'Absolutely. All known safe houses have been covered by our people in London. He's simply disappeared, run for the hills.' He sniggered, as if Vaux's disappearance were an act of cowardice.

Alena stood up. She thought the interview was over, and all that remained was for her to go to the logistics people and arrange the dreaded trip.

'One last thing. Before you leave for London, we want you to question Said's wife, Rawya. We feel she knows things she hasn't chosen to tell us. We heard through our most secret sources that a plan was afoot to smuggle her out of Syria, along with her two children. We had the security police break into her apartment, and there was evidence of preparations to move. Packed bags, new clothes—everything but air tickets. Find out what you can. Woman to woman, candid talk, friendly talk, sympathy.

'I suppose it's likely that the Brits had some plan to bring her over. Maybe everything got so complicated that the most efficient thing was to kill off the would-be defector and simply take the secrets he presumably carried with him. These things have to be confirmed, Alena. I think his wife, once you have persuaded her to confide in you, could have some interesting answers. My secretary will give you her address. Tell her we are willing to pay a lifetime pension to her—if she cooperates. It would be in return for her husband's invaluable contributions to the defense of the Republic of Syria.'

Without a word, Alena got up and left.

Mamluk rested his cigar on the rim of a big round ceramic ashtray. He watched her leave and felt a frisson of desire as he observed her fine legs, the feminine sway of her hips, her long black hair. He chuckled to himself. He was her spymaster, and men in his position were entitled to tell their underlings only what they needed to know. Not the whole picture, just that part of the jigsaw they could be useful in placing within the main picture. What Mamluk had left out of the briefing was the fact that, three weeks earlier, two of his agents had indeed searched the Said family's apartment and had found clear evidence that Said had rented a safe-deposit box in a London bank. They threatened Said's wife that they would take her two children away if she didn't tell them the significance of the few details they had found on a scrap of notepaper in a small drawer of her writing desk. That was all that was needed. The one thing Said's grieving wife now prized above all else was the safety of Didi and Abal, her daughters.

London was duly informed. At a cost of $50,000, his agents at London GSD secured the cooperation of an impecunious assistant bank manager. And Said's top secret dossier was re-trieved. He smiled with satisfaction. So far, the British plot to purloin the Syrian state's most treasured secrets had totally failed. The job just had to be cleaned up to teach the Brits not to toy with the Assad regime.

***

It had been a long day. The creaky air-conditioning system in the old government building had once again failed. Even for mid-October, it was very hot, some thirty-five degrees cen-tigrade. Mamluk decided to have a cold shower at his lover's apartment in the classy Abu Roumaneh district on his way home to his wife and three small boys.

Tahiyya al-Sharqawi was a little overweight but still a classic Arab beauty, thirty and intelligent, the daughter of a former Syrian ambassador to the Court of St. James's. Her father's lifelong Anglophilia—officially undeclared—had rubbed off on his daughter, who had attended St. Swithun's, a private school for girls in Winchester. Her first adolescent crush was for an English teacher at the prestigious school, and this erotic experience helped to solidify her bonds with English society. It helped, also, that she had been born a Copt, a member of that small Christian sect that had long been tol-erated in Syria.

Tahiyya was now a senior analyst within the GSD bureau-cracy and viewed by insiders as a worthy product of Syria's sometimes-wavering determination to 'Westernize' and move to a more tolerant, less orthodox society.

Tahiyya waited for Abdul Mamluk to finish his long shower. She was in bed, and her mind was running through the list of questions sent to her via her contact at the British embassy.

'I feel so much better now, my love,' said Mamluk, emerging from the large white-marbled bathroom. 'What a day. Decisions, decisions, decisions.'

'The right ones, we hope.'

'*Insh'allah*. God willing,' said Mamluk with a tired smile.

'You have been smoking those dreadful cigars again,' said Tahiyya. 'I can smell it on your breath.'

'Sorry, my darling. I am still trying to get off them. I think perhaps I'll acquire a narghile for the office. That should help.' His thick, wet lips touched her fleshy shoulder. 'Now, come here, sweet one.'

***

When he had left for his home, she began to write down what she had learned. The key fact seemed to be that Alena Hussein was to be dispatched to England in a plan to locate the whereabouts of Michael Vaux and thus secure his elimination. It was a sheer act of revenge, as far as she could see. He had been found guilty of the murder of Dr. Nessim Said, with no facts to support the charge.

Also, of course, for some time, she had detected a deep antipathy toward this man Vaux. The higher echelons of the GSD had always considered him suspect, his friendship with Ahmed Kadri highly dubious. Some of those close to Abdul had always considered him a plant by the British to get ever closer to the Syrian government. But considering what had happened to Ahmed Kadri, perhaps Vaux would be better off with a quick bullet through his head than the long, drawn-out agonies Ahmed had had to suffer. Kadri's brutal end had not yet been communicated to her MI6 case officer, so the spymasters in London were still unaware of his cruel fate.

19

'This tops the lot,' said Sir Nigel as Craw entered his office.
'What's that, sir?'

It was a gloomy Monday morning. Heavy rain fell in all parts of London, the gutters carrying torrents of water into the bubbling culverts and the city's ancient drains. The general gloom emphasized the final end of a lingering summer. It was a challenge to find a happy face.

But Craw made an effort, all the more difficult because he was chronically hungover, having spent the previous evening with his colleague and flat mate Chris Greene and a few of Greene's old SOAS chums. It was an excuse for a going-away party. Greene had been appointed as Michael Vaux's handler, while the latter was confined to a top-security retreat 'in the middle of nowhere,' as Craw had described it.

So Craw smiled, then sipped Anne's excellent Nescafé from a stained and cracked coronation mug on which the profile of the young queen had been all but obliterated over the years by many devoted washer-uppers.

'Cheltenham passed on a top-priority message from "Gertrude". She reports that very soon none other than Alena Hussein will be visiting our fine shores. Her mission: to contact Vaux and presumably entice her former lover to meet her and discuss their wonderful future together.'

'Really, sir?' Craw was not able to detect any humor in Sir Nigel's comment.

'Oh, come on, Craw. Get with it. It may be Monday, but for heaven's sake.'

'Sorry, sir. Yes, this is serious, I realize that.'

Sir Nigel, usually a tolerant man, felt impatience well up at what seemed the impenetrability of his long-surviving deputy. He knew he had gone through an excruciating divorce, but the sooner he could find another deputy to complement the official establishment numbers, the better. Meanwhile, he would have to make do.

'If the border people and the police are as efficient at apprehending her as they have been so far in rounding up the two-man hit team, we're out of luck. Any comments?'

'Well, sir, our one consolation is that Vaux, by now, is firmly installed in his new habitat, and I don't think those two bozos have much chance at getting to him—or I should say *any* chance. The closer they get, in fact, the more likely they will expose themselves, and our team will grab them. As to Alena Hussein, she's a woman, and although no doubt traveling undercover with a false passport, she's probably very unlikely to take any radical precautions regarding her appearance. Women are vain, and she'll probably try and brazen things out, thus making an easy target for our hunters and gatherers.'

Sir Nigel said, 'I worry about that, though. You know Vaux. He's a restless kind of individual. And Greene is what I would call a sort of "party type." They could well break out and go to the local pub, and that's just the sort of opportunity those thugs would be waiting for.'

'First, I know Greene well, sir. He knows he's made some mistakes, especially when he let Vaux slip out of his sights in Geneva—'

'God almighty, Craw! That's eons ago. You do keep things filed away, don't you?'

'Good memory, that's all, sir. But as I said, I think Greene now feels largely responsible for Vaux's safety, and I really don't think we have a Prince Harry–Pointz sort of situation here.'

'Don't you mean Falstaff? It was Falstaff who led the young Henry astray, wasn't it?'

'Pointz was his mate. Falstaff was an older man.'

Sir Nigel was momentarily stunned by Craw's unexpected erudition. 'Vaux's no chicken, either. Never knew we had a Shakespearean scholar in the office. Very well, I just hope you're right. Now, what do we make of this Alena Hussein business?'

'She might want to defect—who knows? I've been running agents all my life, and I've come to realize that it's impossible to divine their real motives. Greed and avarice are common motivations. Personal aspirations of power, wanting to be close to the action, is another strong incentive. But loyalty? That's a scarce commodity among our crew of diligent spooks. Vanity and pride are two other very common attributes. Then we have the ideologues—the Philbys, the Blunts, the Macleans and Burgesses—the classic double agents who betray their country for a half-baked idea. Unfortunately, this Hussein woman belongs to this latter category.'

Sir Nigel visibly winced at the mention of the string of Soviet Russia's double agents who had worked for MI6 and betrayed Britain in the late 50s and 60s. And Blunt's exposure was even more painfully recent.

'Yes, yes, Craw. Don't go on so. Put your mind to the possible reasons for Alena's sudden journey into the snake pit. We'll get her this time—of that, I'm quite sure. Maybe she'll turn. And maybe, just maybe, she'll be able to locate Dr. Said's missing nuclear arms dossier. That would be a gift in return for which I would gladly give her forgiveness and refuge. Plus, she could offer us a mine of data and intelligence she no doubt carries in her head.'

'I have my doubts about all that, sir. She's a zealous Arab nationalist. You know the story. Her young brother was shot dead by Israeli troops in a minor scuffle on the West Bank. Plus, she's a Palestinian, for God's sake.'

'But she did use to work for us, Craw.'

'Yes, as a bloody double agent,' sighed Craw.

'There's a species known as triple agents, I believe.'

With this perhaps forlorn hope, Sir Nigel called the meeting to an end by standing up, pushing back his chair, and walking to the sash window. He peered through the teeming rain at the offices opposite. Smudged, watery figures went to and fro as if in a fish bowl. He did hope the weather would dry up for the week-end pheasant shoot.

***

But it was still raining later that day when Bert Clark, the easygoing, work-shy husband of Mrs. Clark, met Abdul Halim and his assistant, Rafik, at a dully lit fish-and-chip bar in Hendon, just down the road from the Wheatsheaf. Hamin knew that Clark's wife was called in from time to time to be housekeeper and cook for the ever-changing tenants of 30 Acacia Avenue, an address filed away some years ago at the time of the defection of one Alena Hussein, a one-time employee of their traditional foes, MI6. They knew from her long recorded debriefings that it was an official British government safe house and often wondered why the bosses at MI6 hadn't simply closed the place up after Hussein's betrayal. But any Arab knew well the intricacies of officialdom, the slow-moving wheels of bureaucracy, the reluctance to change things long established, for they were the very characteristics that plagued their own lethargic establishment and conservative state organizations. So it was attributed to a collective inertia. They understood, and it could, one day, work to their advantage.

Clark had been told long ago by a grateful recipient of some minor intelligence only a snooper could acquire that information was a commodity like any other—its possession worth a market price to any comer. So, having little else to do, he made it his business to gather information and then approach any party he thought might be interested. His clients had included wives suspecting that their husbands were cheaters, politicians bent on getting the goods on their opponents, tabloid journalists demanding a tip-off whenever celebrity targets presented themselves as perfect camera shots.

And then there were the spooks. But Hamin also knew using Clark was cost-effective. With him in tow, he didn't have to waste time organizing watches on the Hendon safe house—a costly operation since most of the guests were of no interest whatsoever to the Syrians.

'What have you got for us, Mr. Clark?' asked Hamin.

They had ordered three portions of chips and three Coca-Colas. They sat at a table in the far corner of the long room, next to the swing doors that lead to the café's storeroom.

'Well, sir, my wife's been working for a few gentlemen these past few weeks, you see. She gets hold of their names, like, when they're out of an evening. The other night,

I followed the two parties to the Wheatsheaf, where they've been going quite regularly. Well, this time an absolute knock-out of a young girl appears, doesn't she. She's talking to this man who's probably named Vaux, according to my missus, anyway. They're having a nice old chat, while the big man who looks like a cop sits apart from them, at the bar. Long story short, I follow them back to the house, and they go in, of course. But the girl says good-bye and hails a passing cab. I get my own cab almost immediately and tell the driver to follow her. She gets out somewhere in Mayfair, just off Park Lane. I get out and watch. She comes out later with a friend—another smasher—and off they go. I freeze my balls off waiting for them to return. I wanted to make sure this was where she lived, you see. And sure enough, about 1 a.m., they get out of a taxi, all laughs and playing the fool, like, and go into the building.'

'And the bottom line, as they say?'

'Well, I reckon she's sweet on this guy Vaux. And I'm pretty sure it's mutual, like. So I says to myself, if Vaux ever disappears from the 'ouse, I could find him by following the girl. See what I mean?'

'But how would you know we're interested in this man?'

Clark nodded toward Rafik. 'He showed me the picture in the paper, didn't he?'

Rafik turned to Hamin. 'That's right. I did the rounds after we discovered it was Vaux in the newspaper that day. It was an insurance policy in case we were asked to find the man.'

'Good work, Rafik. But brief me on your little projects in future, will you?'

Hamin filed Clark's information in the turbid recesses of his brain. To his relief, events overtook him. Later, communications from his GSD superiors ordered him to cease and desist any further inquiries as to Vaux's location. A third, friendly party would handle the Vaux case. Hamin was happy to let others do his work.

'*Tamam, al-hamdoulilah*,' he muttered. 'Thanks be to God.'

20

The black Sikorsky S-61 hovered over the landing strip at the heliport in Penzance. The helicopter then descended slowly, kicking up dust clouds and propelling gusts of wind that ruffled the fronds of the surrounding palm trees and agitated the neatly trimmed privet bushes. The mayor had planted the palms only six months earlier to reassert Cornwall's claim to be the English Riviera. For a few seconds, Alena Hussein was disoriented. How could she be looking out at palm trees in autumnal England? Her slight misgivings were resolved when the pilot announced their arrival in Cornwall, England, and wished his passengers a good night and an enjoyable stay.

Manaf Fouladkar stood at the base of the metal steps that had been wheeled to the aircraft. A young flight attendant opened the door, then stood aside to let Alena exit. The attendant had been told to give this passenger VIP treatment during the twenty-minute journey from St. Mary's in the Isles of Scilly to Penzance, and the flight, with six other passengers, had been delayed one hour to await her arrival on a late Lufthansa flight from Athens.

She wore a head scarf, but Fouladkar recognized her immediately. Alena slowly and elegantly descended, holding the handrail firmly as the other passengers on BMA Flight 360 assembled at the top of the stairs, impatient to get to the small customs building.

Holding her hand in both of his in a gentle grip, Fouladkar welcomed her. '*As-salaamu 'alaykum.* Good flight?'

'Not really. We were late getting into the Scillies. That's why you have been waiting a long time, no doubt.'

'Always worth it to meet you again, Alena.' He thought she looked more beautiful than when he had last seen her. Her skin was golden, her figure slimmer. Under a lightweight beige raincoat, she wore a blue linen shirt, a khaki skirt, and sensible flats.

It was a warm night, and a light drizzle put a wet sheen on the tarmac as they walked swiftly to the terminal. Alena, under the name of Patricia Watkins, passed through passport control and customs as if she were a regular traveler to these remote parts. She told the sole immigration officer that she was a director of Southern Fragrances, Ltd., which had three processing plants in Greece, and her home in St. Ives was the reason for returning by this circuitous route. Fouladkar listened in amazement, picked up her one suitcase, and guided her to a waiting clapped-out old Vauxhall Cavalier.

Rafik Shihabi jumped out of the driver's seat to open the trunk. He bowed slightly to Alena, and she smiled back. 'Only five minutes in this wreck, ma'am. Our staff car's in another location.'

Alena couldn't quite understand this, so she looked questioningly at Fouladkar.

'Just keeping a low profile, Madame Hussein.'

She blamed herself. They hadn't known she was coming in as an executive type who would have expected a luxurious limo to be waiting for her. They probably thought she was traveling incognito, as a poor student making her way home from backpacking in Europe. She hadn't the energy to make any remark, so she let it go. *Next time, check with Logistics about cover mode.*

Five minutes later, at a lay-by on the airport approach road, they drove up beside a parked black Mercedes Maybach. The driver got out and exchanged places with Rafik. As the great car purred along the A30 toward Exeter, Alena fell into a deep sleep. There was no talk between the two GSD operatives until they had a quiet, hushed debate about where best to join the M3 for London.

***

An official talent spotter who operated within the confines of academe had recruited Chris Greene. It was some ten years ago, in the last days of his student existence. He had studied economics and Arabic at the School of Oriental and African Studies (SOAS), a prestigious college within the London University complex and a by-product of Britain's colonial past. The college's academic standards were high, and Greene graduated with a good second-class degree. His father had been a colonel in the Royal Horse Guards and then an equerry to one of the queen's offspring. His father's prestigious preretirement posting was probably what had distinguished the young Greene in the eyes of the official Secret Service recruiting board.

He had begun his career as a trainee at MI5's Thames House. He was essentially a deskman, he told those few close to him who sensed he worked in a secretive and confidential capacity for some hush-hush branch of the government. He volunteered

for a vigorous six-week 'real world' course on an army base in
Aldershot where he learned the stratagems and techniques of clandestine operations and how to track down and eliminate enemy
agents who worked against the interests of the United Kingdom.

Within a year, he was transferred to MI6, the arm of the
service that dealt with the acquisition of foreign intelligence
that threatened national security, as well as the monitoring
of spy networks in sovereign nations deemed unfriendly and
friendly. Sir Walter Mason, then head of Department B3, a sub-
subsection of MI6's Middle East desk, was prowling the corridors at Century House one day, loudly complaining to all who
would lend a sympathetic ear that he was still six people short
of the staff strength he had been granted several years ago. Then
he happened upon the name of a young 'comer' named Greene
who had gained some local fame as an Arabic translator.

Here, Sir Walter thought, was a promising candidate
to help replenish his depleted staff, none of whom could
speak a word of Arabic. Chris Greene was duly transferred
to Department B3, housed in a decrepit building between a
small cottage hospital and an art school on Gower Street. His
first major assignment was as a player in the elaborate but ill-
fated Operation Helvetia. He was to be a watcher, and his task
was to observe the operation's main protagonist, one Michael
Vaux, in an effort to protect him, as Sir Walter darkly hinted,
from any 'external' influences that Vaux could be exposed to.
Greene had been told that Vaux, whose loyalty was not doubted, was the key man in the operation. But—and Sir Walter said
it was a big *but*—because the man, a former journalist, had
not undergone the rigorous training and discipline required
of those career men who manned Britain's security services,
there was a need *not* to give him the benefit of the doubt. With
a wink and a nod, Greene was put into the tender care of Alan
Craw, a veteran staffer who aspired to Sir Walter's job when, if

ever, he retired. The final implosion of Operation Helvetia was primarily due to the treachery of an in-house field agent by the name of Alena Hussein, but Greene's own performance—when in Geneva, he let Vaux slip out of his protective sights for several days—was not regarded as impeccable in the eyes of Alan Craw and Sir Walter.

But within the secrets hidden in the files and records of Department B3 and stored in the complex memories of those who worked in this specialist subsection of MI6 was a buried reality of what Greene liked to call the human factor. And it had to do with the human heart—with love and even perhaps with obsession. Greene loved Alena Hussein.

He was attracted to her on her first day at B3. He invited her for late-afternoon drinks at the pub up the road. But he had never made a breakthrough. She was aloof but gentle in her rejection, a happy and cheerful companion, but that was all. Greene's passion lingered. They seemed to become closer in Geneva, where, he later realized, she had played her double game to perfection. And then, after her putative death in a gruesome road accident, he finally had to store her memory away in his mental archives. But then, when an indifferent Alan Craw told him casually that she was alive and well in Damascus and living with Vaux, who he had always known was his rival for her heart, it seemed to make little difference. He still loved her.

So when he heard her voice on his unsecured line at his Chalk Farm flat that morning, his heart pounded, and he felt sweat trickling down his armpits. Of course he would meet her.

***

Anne brought in a coffee and, by special request, one chocolate éclair. Craw had arrived at around 10:00 a.m., late for him, after supervising his move out of Chris Greene's apartment to a more luxurious accommodation in a mansion flat on Pont Street in Knightsbridge. He had enjoyed his stay with Greene but, in the end, decided that two men living together, one nearly two decades younger than the other, had dubious connotations. He had heard the tittle-tattle about his attachment to his younger colleague, and not only was it way off base, but possibly damaging to both men's careers. The Foreign Office, let alone the SIS, had been betrayed by both gays and straights, but in the view of the Establishment, the defections of notorious practitioners of sodomy, like Burgess and Maclean, took the biscuit and had fortified these government agencies in their refusal to join the universal trend toward tolerance and acceptance of these age-old 'vices.' Craw knew all this, and so he decided to lance the boil of gossip once and for all. He would live alone, a divorcé and a candidate in the market for second spouses.

Anne told him that Sir Nigel had been asking for him.

'Urgent? Or can it wait for me to enjoy this wonderful cup of coffee?' asked Craw as he nibbled on the éclair.

'He seemed pretty agitated. I think you'd better go in now,' said Anne.

Craw quickly ate the éclair, emitted a sound of pleasure, picked up his Styrofoam cup of coffee, and headed up the passage for Sir Nigel's office.

He knocked gently.

'Come!' cried Sir Nigel.

'Morning, sir. Sorry I'm late. Moving time, back to Knightsbridge at last.'

'Oh, really, Craw? Getting back with the wife, then?'

'No, no, sir. I don't think that's in the cards anymore. No, things were rather cramped, as it were, in Greene's establishment, so I thought it was time to move and give us both some space.'

'Of course. I understand perfectly,' said Sir Nigel, suppressing a slight smile.

Craw wondered if there was some sort of patronizing innuendo in Sir Nigel's attitude. He sat down in the usual hard bentwood chair that faced him. He saw Sir Nigel straighten up, his face suddenly grim, a blue piece of paper in his hand.

'New developments in the Operation Saladin case, Craw. By the way, I've decided to call our efforts in this regard "Operation Saladin" to replace the now defunct Operation Ebla. After all, our main priority now is to retrieve that dossier we all think old Saladin stashed somewhere. And it's Saladin's dossier, hence the operational name change.

'In any event, our man in Damascus, code name "pearlyking," cabled this early this morning. Here's the decrypt.' He handed the note to Craw.

TOP PRIORITY:

Gertrude reports Said's widow has told her that Dr. Said sometimes communicated with her in their own prearranged codes. Certain phrases had specified meanings (e.g., 'I went to the theater last night' meant 'I had successful talks with the British authorities'). She confirmed to Gerty that one message (on the back of a postcard showing BIG BEN) gave her the location of a 'duplicate' file on Syria's nuclear/chemical weapons plans. Gerty reports no knowledge of the original dossier but assumes that, upon Said's death, Department B3 gave up the chase. Rawya, Said's wife, does not want to exit Syria now that Said is dead. But she STIPULATES that the only person she trusts to talk to is Vaux. Her husband apparently took a shine to our colleague when they were staying in the 'health farm' together. Action required: Gerty is ready to arrange Vaux's transit. The aborted plan for the family's exfiltration from Syria could be put into reverse, with Vaux embarking for Syria.

The sooner we have the dossier, the better. Operation Saladin can be rescued from disaster and transformed into a remarkable intelligence success.

——pearlyking

Craw read and reread the message. Vaux had done it again, seizing the initiative and falling despite himself into a situation that would bring him praise and accolades. He took his gold Cartier half-moon glasses off and placed them on Sir Nigel's desk.

'How on earth do we get Vaux to Damascus, sir? And who's this "pearlyking," anyway?'

'I thought you kept better tabs on the people who do essential work for us, Craw. He's the go-between, if you will, between Gerty and us. She's much too close to the GSD bigwigs to be constantly communicating with us, so old pearly is her case officer. He works undercover, of course. Officially, he's the first commercial officer at our embassy in Damascus. He's been with MI6 since he left Cambridge.

'He and Gerty communicate via dead letter drops, and apparently, they sometimes meet face-to-face in some beach resort in Lebanon. So far, thank God, the liaison has worked wonderfully. He's the man who cultivated this Gerty character after he learned she'd been to school in Blighty and was something of an Anglophile—like her father, a former Syrian diplomat. She also happens to be a Copt. Leave it at that. The Gerty contact is invaluable. And by the way, if you ever see "pearlyking" capitalized with a capital P, you know he's under duress and is being forced to send us intelligence as a compromised double agent. By the same token, never, ever refer to him as "Pearly King."'

Sir Nigel stroked his toothbrush moustache, then continued. 'But the fly in the ointment for us, dear Craw, is that Vaux is under immediate threat from these thugs who have been sent over to kill him. That's why he's presumably now settling into the highest security accommodation available in this country today. Greene's with him, I take it.'

'Not yet, sir. He's scheduled to leave London this coming weekend.'

Craw now decided to keep his mouth shut. He would await Sir Nigel's answers to the problems that now presented themselves. Sir Nigel looked over to the sash window. The morning light was pale, but at least it was a dry, if somewhat crisp, day. He looked back at Craw, and the two men remained silent for some time.

Beyond the door, they heard the steady stream of gentle clicks as Anne's long feminine fingers played the new computer keyboard, the replacement for the upright Imperial typewriter that had served B3 so well for forty years.

Sir Nigel had to confess his lack of originality. 'Now you understand where I got the new name from. Pearlyking had taken it upon himself to rename the operation, so I let it go. I rather like it. "Saladin" has a nice Middle Eastern ring to it, don't you think? Got to keep the men in the field happy too, you know.'

'Indeed, sir.'

Sir Nigel passed the ball to Craw. 'In light of our new goal to get Vaux over to Syria, what do you suggest we do now, Craw?'

'To get Vaux to Syria in the current circumstances would require the planning and luck that went into D-day, sir. That's my opinion.'

'I've been looking at the map, Craw. We could infiltrate through Lebanon. And I have an update from the FCO on current political and military developments. The Israeli withdrawal from south Lebanon is completed and is regarded as highly positive by Whitehall. Things should be calmer over there, which is a positive for our own plans. There's still some dispute over an obscure place in the south called Shebaa Farms, but it's of little significance, as far as I understand. In any case, Syria is north of Lebanon. And there's a very long coastline shared by both countries. That has possibilities, in my view. Plus, you should liaise with "Gertrude" through pearlyking. She knows the ropes about getting in and out of Syria, does Gerty.'

Sir Nigel took off his horn-rimmed glasses, stroked his moustache again, and looked very earnest. He said, 'The point is, C is breathing down my neck heavily.' Whenever the opportunity arose, Sir Nigel liked to use the time-honored shorthand for MI6's Director-General Sir John Blakeley. 'He wants quick results. He's as frustrated as hell that we got so close, only to lose our prize by sheer thuggery.'

Craw adopted his usual evasive attitude. 'Let me think about this, sir. I'll come up with something by 4 p.m.'

'No later,' said Sir Nigel.

21

Chixham is the unlikely name for a ten-acre spread of farm-land in the heart of Bedfordshire, about fifty-five miles northwest of London. The military-intelligence complex nestled within this rural setting has been part of the local community since World War II. It was then that Britain's security service set up one more listening station to intercept top secret communications between Britain's enemies. Little decrypting went on. The coded messages between German agents and their bosses in German intelligence were sent on to Bletchley House in Buckinghamshire, where the Ultra decoding computer deciphered the messages and helped the Allies win the war.

Wartime needs called for the construction of an airfield for Spitfires and Hurricanes, and after the war, Chixham was turned over to various US intelligence groups of arcane origin. Then, in the 1980s, the place was vacated once more, and the Army Intelligence Corps moved in. Amid the cluster of low-lying concrete buildings and Nissen huts, they installed massive saucer-shaped antennas that

intercepted microwave signals, big round radomes that housed sophisticated radar antenna , and large oblong objects that pointed
up to the heavens to spy on satellite communications.

When Michael Vaux arrived with Tripp on a cold autumn
night, he found difficulty in actually locating the main buildings. He saw some sheep grazing and heard the screeches,
squawks, and quacks of waterfowl from a nearby pond. Then
Tripp pointed to the old priory at the epicenter of the compound. It was an ancient ivy-covered Gothic pile, and the cren-
ellated portico and stained glass oriel window that faced the
water stirred Vaux's long-dormant appetite for English history.
Tripp, now apparently an expert local historian, said the priory
was founded in 1185 as a monastery. The sprawling building
now housed the officers' mess in the east wing, with the rest of
the building empty and vacant.

'Except for Rosata, the local ghost, said to have been a nun
who was locked up here for bad behavior,' Tripp said grimly.
'She takes her exercise on a nightly basis, I'm told.'

After a respectful silence, Tripp added, 'This is our destination, sir. You'll be meeting the base commanding officer there,
and he'll tell you where we are kipping for the night.'

They left the driver with Sergeant Murdoch, listening to
Radio 2 in the Daimler.

***

Alena met Greene in a pub overlooking Hampstead Heath.
In Greene's appreciative eyes, she looked stunning in blue
jeans, stilettos, and a yellow polo-neck sweater. Her hairstyle
had changed. Once long and luxurious, her hair was now short
and spiky with blonde highlights.

'Welcome home,' said Greene with a broad smile. He knew
it sounded fatuous.

'Not there yet,' said Alena with a coy smile.

Greene brought her a Campari on ice. He had a pint of Watney's.

'Where are you staying? Or shouldn't I ask?' said Greene.

'Let's not get into that,' she said. 'Let's just relax a little and perhaps talk about old times,' she said.

He found her warm, beguiling. He thought that maybe there was just a slight possibility that she would understand his feelings toward her after all the years that had passed. She seemed to know by some feminine instinct that he held no resentment—for her betrayal and defection.

'I don't have much time, Chris. I'm sure you understand. We'll have more time perhaps when things are arranged.'

'Yes, of course. What is it you want me to do for you?'

'I'll try and be as unemotional as possible about this.'

Greene's heart pounded. Perhaps she was in love with him, after all.

'I have to see Michael Vaux. It's absolutely imperative. I want him to handle my homecoming, if you will. You know we had a fling in Geneva, and you know the story about his subsequent trip to Syria to see his best friend, Ahmed. And, of course, I was there. We practically lived together—all three of us. We had something going. I can't explain it, and I don't want to analyze it. But now I'm making perhaps the most important decision of my life. I want Michael in on it and to offer me a helping hand—advice, if you like, about how I should go about this thing.'

'But you haven't said what this "thing" is,' said Greene.

'I want to come back, Chris. I want to offer my services to B3, MI6, the Mideast desk—whatever. It would be an unbelievable intelligence coup for them, and in return, I would come back to dear old England. I've always loved it here, you know. And there's Michael, of course. I want him to forgive me for not helping him more when he got into deep water with our people. But I can't turn back the clock. This is my way of saying I'm sorry. And I will be bearing gifts. I can give them a total rundown on Syrian intelligence groups, agent operations, names and locations of sleeper cells, and much more.'

Greene had always nursed a suspicion that Alena was in fact "Gertrude".

He said, 'I thought you had never left, really. Spiritually, you were still with us.'

'What on earth are you talking about, Chris?'

So his suspicions were wrong. She now planned to become a triple agent, it seemed. Why else would she risk contacting him in 'enemy territory'? He could have notified the obvious people, and she could be arrested on sight, charged with betraying England and aiding and abetting her potential enemies. He sipped his beer, looked at her quizzically.

'So why don't you contact Michael?'

'I thought you would have known the answer to that question.'

'Tell me, anyway.'

'All right. Our sources tell us he's gone underground—some perceived threat to his life or some such nonsense. If there is a threat, it's not coming from our side. Maybe Mossad has turned against him. They know he's what they call an "Arab lover."'

Greene scoffed at this suggestion. He decided to wait for her to outline what she wanted him to do. He knew that whatever she asked, he would help her.

'Go on,' he said.

'Chris, could you somehow arrange a meeting between Vaux and me? That's the only favor I ask of you. I swear I shall never let on that you helped me arrange some sort of rendezvous. It's a favor that I shall treasure for the rest of my life. And I want so much that life to be lived in London, in England.'

'It's true that he's under tight security. A meeting would be very difficult to arrange. Are you telling me that your first step has to be to talk to Vaux and then decide whether to come, sorry, in from the cold?'

'No! It's not like that. I'm a woman. You must understand I have to feel some support in these important decisions. I have made up my mind, of course. But surely, you realize that I can't just walk into old Sir Walt's office and say, "I'm back, sir. How have you been all these years?"'

'Yes, of course I understand,' said Greene. He would do what he could but didn't have the faintest idea how he'd go about it. 'Look, as it happens, I've been ordered to go up and join Vaux in the secure location they've sent him to. It's not a typical safe house, I can tell you that. But I'm due there this weekend, and I'll see if anything is possible. No promises, mind.'

'I love you!' exclaimed Alena.

But Greene knew it was only a manner of speech.

***

Vaux and his party—Warrant Officer Tripp, Staff Sergeant Murdoch, and Lieutenant Samuel Fox, seconded from military intelligence—were assigned to a small old farmer's cottage within the grounds of the military base. Two guards, young grunts in the small contingent of the base's Logistics Corps, were to act as armed guards, patrolling the vicinity of the farmhouse from dusk to dawn. A short, very thin corporal cooked meals and supervised the cleaning lady who came from the local village.

The days went by. Vaux was beginning to feel as if he were serving a lifetime sentence. Late nightcaps at the officers'

mess made sleep difficult, and he became much more intro-
spective than was his true nature. His experience with the secret service, from Day 1, had seemed a disaster. Not only had
it wrecked his plans to retire quietly in the neighborhood he
loved, but it had led to the ill-fated sidetrack that propelled his
life to Damascus and then to Cairo, where he had ended up as
a rootless journalist basking in the Arab milieu. His love for
Ahmed had ended in disaster; his old college friend was probably dead, killed at the merciless hands of Syria's state security
apparatus. He was on the run from the same thugs and, for
self-preservation, had all too easily fallen once again into the
hands of Department B3.

Yet here he was, handcuffed, in effect immobilized from
doing anything he found worthwhile. He was yet again holed
up in a safe house—even if this time it was more like a for-
tress—and he was as far away from Alena as he had ever been.
The rupture of their relationship in Cairo had been cruel and
probably irrecoverable. His future, in short, seemed bleak.
Hours in front of a television with army types—whom he
respected even if at times they acted more like protective
jailers—and frequent visits to the bibulous officers' mess became the stuff of his life. He lay, eyes wide-open, on many a
night thinking such thoughts of despair. What would be next
for him? And when the immediate danger of assassination had
evaporated, what should he do? Resign, probably—with, he
hoped, a generous gratuity from H. M. Government.

One evening, about ten days after arriving at Chixham,
Tripp told him that a Mr. Chris Greene was due the next
morning. He would be staying for the 'duration,' Tripp said,
and Vaux wondered why Sir Nigel had condemned the young
and happy warrior to such a fate. But he was looking forward to seeing his colleague, who had never been boring,
was adequately rebellious against the powers that be, and

was bright into the bargain. A stark contrast, Vaux mused, from their immediate boss, Alan Craw. Vaux thought that if Craw had been assigned to keep him company, he'd have been forced to plan a dramatic breakout.

***

Vaux looked through the small sash windows of the front parlor with the aid of his army-issued Baker 8X42 binoculars and watched the regimental theatrics as the guards stomped and about-turned at the gatehouse to change shifts. It was 8:00 a.m. Suddenly, a white MG-H two-seater sports car drew up. The driver waved some document to a sentry, and after a five-minute scrutiny and consultation with comrades in the guardhouse, the driver was waved in. Chris Greene had arrived.

'This calls for lunch in the mess, I think,' said Vaux, happy to see a new but familiar face.

Greene dumped his leather holdall in the narrow hallway, and Vaux led him into the small kitchen. Because it was Saturday, the other tenants in the farmhouse hadn't yet roused themselves.

Vaux made some Nescafé and offered a jug of creamy milk. 'Straight from the local cows,' he said. 'It's a healthy life around here. You'll see.'

Greene downed the coffee and milk quickly. 'Look, Vaux, we have to talk. Something big has come up, and you have to know about it. Where can we go that's totally secure?'

Vaux's eyes widened. 'Are you representing Sir Nigel in this?'

'No, no, no. It's for your eyes and ears only.'

'We can probably arrange an isolated table at the officers' mess,' suggested Vaux. 'We'll have lunch there.'

'I passed a nice little pub up the road. Couldn't we go there?'

'How the hell could I get out of this bloody prison? I'm told the threats are real. Who knows who's out there?'

Greene then took him to the window that faced the guard-house. He lowered his voice to a whisper. 'Vaux, Alena will be waiting in the pub. She wants desperately to see you. And she's thinking of coming back to us.'

Vaux was so shaken that he grabbed an upright chair that had been placed just in front of the window and sat down. He looked up at Greene, incredulity mixed with total shock. Greene said nothing, waiting for some verbal reaction from his colleague.

'Then, yes, we must go to the pub.' He grabbed a tissue from the pocket of his shirt and wiped his eyes. He found it difficult to breathe. He got up and headed for the narrow staircase. He locked himself in the bathroom for fifteen minutes. So she loved him, after all. The hard-nosed Alena, Arab patriot and dedicated Palestinian, had at last suc-cumbed to an affair of the heart. His love for her, subdued by force of absence and reason, had suddenly and unexpect-edly resurfaced—maybe to flower and flourish. He would have to meet her.

***

Greene loaned Vaux the MG after they had agreed his presence wasn't vital and that he should stay at home base to monitor any contacts or communications that might need a quick response. Vaux's three bodyguards followed the MG in a green Land Rover. They drove fast, down narrow and winding country lanes bordered by thick woods and the occasional green field where cattle and sheep grazed.

When they pulled up, Tripp decided to act as external lookout. He sat in the military vehicle, which was parked directly opposite the one entrance to The Cock, an old, isolated public house up the road from the Chixham compound. It was a remote spot, about half a mile from the base and about half a mile from the village in the opposite direction. Murdoch sat at the bar, and at the far end of the long room, next to the door that led to the pub's toilets, sat Lieutenant Samuel Fox.

Greene had explained to Vaux, who had turned cautious and hesitant, that the Special Forces security guys and their sidekicks had no idea what Alena looked like. He had told all of them before they left that she was Vaux's longtime girl-friend—and probable fiancée—and that his department head had sanctioned the meeting in the hope of boosting Vaux's sagging morale. A groggy, half-awake Tripp had said his morale wasn't all that high, either, and he wasn't averse to getting out of the bloody camp and having a pint.

On Greene's advice, Vaux had agreed to carry a voice recorder.

'This is state-of-the-art stuff. A body-wire transmission gizmo with built-in digital recorder,' he said as he handed Vaux the slim recording unit. It wasn't betrayal of trust, Greene had assured Vaux, just an insurance policy if things went awry, if developments took an unexpected turn and Vaux required backup to his version of the story.

'In our world, things are not always as they appear,' said Greene.

'You're becoming quite a veteran spymaster, aren't you?' Vaux replied as he put the slim audio-recorder in the breast pocket of his navy blue blazer after he checked the operating button to make sure he could press it with some skillful stealth.

***

Vaux entered the pub some ten minutes after Murdoch had perched himself at the long bar and about three minutes after Lieutenant Fox had come in like a weary traveler and chose to sit as far back from the front window as possible. From his chosen position, he had a clear view of the one-room pub, Murdoch on a tall stool at the bar, and the Land Rover through the narrow sash windows.

Warrant Officer Tripp had ordered that all men on the detail should dress in civvies and carry concealed arms. 'I'm suspicious by nature,' Tripp had said in his gruff Yorkshire voice. 'And you can't be too careful in a situation like this. It may be low-risk, but I've seen many so-called minor-risk situations explode in mayhem.'

Vaux had told his chief guardian not to be so lugubrious, but obeyed orders all the same. He also agreed to carry his Webley in a side pocket.

***

It was poignantly déjà vu. When he saw her sitting at a table by the artificial fireplace, his heart skipped a beat. He saw the vivid flashback: her, perhaps younger, but just as beautiful, sitting at a similar round table at the Pig & Whistle on Watford Lane. Their first easy conversation. Their mutual attraction. The prelude to a strong durable and clandestine love affair, eventually ruptured by political events beyond their control.

She smiled that indelible, friendly smile as he approached her. Then she stood up and they hugged each other long enough to raise a few eyebrows between Fox and Murdoch, who both took quick sidelong glances of the encounter. She looked stunning to him: the new short haircut, the white blouse that contoured her small breasts, the narrow corduroy pants, and the knee-length brown Ciao Bella leather boots to match the country excursion.

She offered to buy the drinks. But the landlord, who had been standing behind the bar assiduously wiping and shining glasses, had quickly come over and asked them what they would like.

She said, 'Cutty Sark for this gentleman, and I'll have a gin and tonic, please.'

'Where do we begin?' said Vaux. As she looked down at her drink, he quickly pressed the 'on' button of the recorder. He knew he had sounded trite but couldn't summon up a particularly original first line.

'I've missed you more than you can ever imagine, Michael. And before we go any further, I can't say how much I appreciate what Chris Greene has done for us. Where is he, by the way?'

'Sleeping. We had a few early-morning beers to celebrate his arrival in these parts.

'You never change, do you? Not that I ever want you to.'

'It's lovely to see you.'

'Darling, I don't know how long we've got. I just want you to know that I plan to come back. I want you and need you more than any career or any job. I know nobody will want to "put out more flags," but I honestly think we can do a deal.'

Vaux said nothing. He thought Alena sounded rather cold. 'Deals' and her 'need to come back'? Didn't she know she could be arrested any moment? He could even turn her in here and now. But he had no desire to betray her. He would rather take her by the hand, walk down the hedge-lined country lane to base camp, and make love to her for twenty-four hours. All of which, of course, was impossible. He broke the silence.

'Alena, you...It's you who must do the talking. You have to tell me how you plan to go about this...well, second defection. You have to tell me your strategy. Then I can see where I can possibly help.'

'Why are you here, out in the wilds, the back of beyond?' The question was sudden and even accusatory.

'Greene didn't tell you, I take it.'

'He said something about threats that have been made.'

'That's all you need to know.'

'You're sounding like a professional spook now. Please don't change, Michael.'

'I haven't changed. I'm telling you the truth.'

She looked into his eyes and then smiled.

'We're having words already,' she said sadly.

Vaux nodded to the landlord, a very thin, reedy man in his fifties who had been looking over at their table, monitoring their rate of consumption and the need for possible refills. He came over, wiped the table with a stained dishcloth, and plunked down two more drinks.

'Tell me what you want me to do, and then we can go from there,' said Vaux. He was holding her hand across the table. He thought they had got off to a tense start, and he wanted to show her how he really felt.

'All right, darling. I want to come back because I love you, and after you left Cairo, I felt I was drowning in my loneliness and despair. They posted me back to Damascus, promoted me. But it made no difference. It may sound what the Americans call corny, but we're made for each other, despite our different upbringings—'

'Not so different. You were brought up and educated here.'

'Yes, but I'm a Palestinian.'

'British by birth,' said Vaux.

'Have it your way. But having had months to ponder this while I missed you so achingly, I realized that if I were permitted to return, I could offer your people a mother lode of intelligence about Syria's secret operations, undercover agents, signals data, foreign and military policy priorities. It would be in return for my safe reception, of course. No recriminations for my earlier defection. I would be home and free. You would have netted a GSD captain willing to spill all the beans to MI6 and, in particular, Sir Walter Mason's Department B3.'

'Your intelligence is faulty. Sir Walter retired some time ago, and now we have a Sir Nigel Adair. But the organization's still the same. I'm, as usual, a semi- or part-time operative.'

'But they forgave you, your defection, didn't they?'

'I never defected, Alena. I simply decided not to go back to London from the Tangier assignment. My job was completed, and although Sir Walter was livid, no laws were broken by me, and there was no possibility of any prosecution. With you, it would be different.'

She sipped on her g&t, her eyes never wandering from his. He turned his head to look around the bar. Some civilians had come in and the place was getting busy and smoky. He quickly looked at his guardians. They both appeared determinedly nonchalant, with drinks half-finished.

'What about Ahmed? What happened?'

'Ahmed's dead, darling. State Security arrested him one night and took him to Sednaya, tried him on some phony charges, found him guilty, and shot him. He was buried within the prison's walls. I spoke to his sister, the mother of Safa, whom you probably remember from your Tangier caper.'

Vaux knew about the notorious Sednaya prison, a few miles north of Damascus. Horror stories of torture and trumped-up charges against political prisoners were rife among the expat community. Summary executions were common, and the most convenient way of dealing with anyone suspected of anti-regime sympathies.

'The bastards,' said Vaux, almost to himself. He freed his hand from hers.

She had seemed to deliver the news so coldly. And how did she know about his fling with Safa, Kadri's twenty-one-year-old niece just out of university?

'At that time, I might remind you, I thought you were dead, killed in that ghastly road accident—'

'Which, as I told you in Cairo, never happened,' she said.

'We're going round in circles. Alena, darling, I have limited time. I have to be back. Tell me what action I can take to help you. And, of course, if and when you come back, nobody, not even you, will be happier than I.'

'Broach the subject with the high-ups—Craw, perhaps, and certainly this new chief of B3. I'll get back in touch with you. All you have to say is that feelers have been put out, you have been contacted by certain people—lawyers, perhaps—and Alena Hussein is offering a treasure trove of intelligence for her safe asylum in the UK and, of course, immunity from any prosecution stemming from my earlier defection.'

The pre-lunch crowd now filled the long saloon. The landlord had recruited the help of two young men behind the bar, and Lieutenant Fox had moved up to the bar from the table. Because of the milling and jostling crowd, he hadn't been able to get a fix on Vaux and his companion from his seat in the corner.

Vaux said, 'Where are you staying?'

'A small b&b in Shefford, just up the road.'

'How will you get there?'

'I'm to phone for a local taxi from a call box at the crossroads.'

'Shall I walk with you?'

'No, darling, that won't be necessary. And you? How will you get back to the base?'

'What do you mean, "base"?'

'I told you, Greene drove me up, and we had to look for the place before he drove to Shefford for me.'

'Well, I too must be getting back, Alena.'

They embraced again, but not for long, because body contact with the pub's raucous and jostling customers prevented any intimacy.

'Don't forget to take your friends with you, Michael,' she said.

He put on an air of surprise and puzzlement. 'What are you talking about?'

'I've been in the game too long not to notice, darling. There must be three watchers in this room, and then there's the man in the Land Rover.'

Vaux didn't correct her. He smiled shyly and guided her to the door with his hand behind her back. At the exit, they kissed again.

'How shall we get in touch?' she asked.

'I'll appoint Greene as our mediator.'

'Sounds good. Bye, darling.'

She strode southward to the local Norman church of St. Michael's and Angels and then on to the crossroads where the main road to Shefford connected to the A507, which passed the Chixham intelligence base. Vaux glanced at the spectacle of Murdoch and Fox clambering into the Land Rover. He started to walk to the car. He got in, started the engine, and drove off quickly, relishing his momentary freedom. But it was barely a minute before the Land Rover caught up with him and stayed close to his tail.

In the Warden Abbey guesthouse, she met the two men who had tailed Greene's MG in a rented Audi A8 sedan, all the way from Chalk Farm to the Chixham guardhouse and then on to the b&b where a room for Alena had been booked in advance.

She only knew them by their noms de guerre: Khaldun and Baitar. They were young and lean, not yet thirty, Alena guessed, and they had that pale, white complexion many Syrians inherit through some odd hereditary quirk. Their new president, Bashir Assad, had the same pigmentation, as did his father, the former president. An advantage not overlooked by their al-Saiqa superiors was their ability to operate in Europe under this natural camouflage, not immediately exposing their Arab roots.

In her room, she gave specific instructions. Khaldun, who seemed to be the senior partner, then picked up a notepad from the mantelshelf of a small, disused fireplace. He sketched a rough plan of the Chixham base. He pointed to the guardhouse and the road that led straight past the gothic priory to a small cottage close to a duck pond. He marked the cottage with an 'X.'

They chose to speak English.

'That's where we reckon he's holed up,' said Khaldun, in a slight American accent.

'And how do you propose to effect an entry?' asked Alena, playing what she regarded as an appropriately skeptical role.

The two men looked at each other and smiled.

'Leave that to us,' Baitar said confidently.

22

At dawn the next morning, Vaux was awakened by several loud bangs on the front door of the cottage. He quickly looked at his Accurist. It was 6:30 a.m. He wondered why the duty sentries had allowed some would-be visitor to wake up the clandestine household so rudely and so early.

Earlier, a silver Aston Martin Vantage had been stopped at the guardhouse for identification. Two German shepherd guard dogs sniffed around the car as Alan Craw produced the required documents, and the sergeant, dressed in a soft navy blue beret and camouflaged fatigues, waved him into the compound. Craw passed the old priory and headed straight to the cottage. It was in total blackness, and he wondered if the duty sentries were effectively concealing themselves or—dark thought—taking a predawn snooze.

He pulled up as quietly as he knew how, switched off the headlights, and waited. He could hear the gentle gurgle of the small waterfall that fed the pond. Any moment, he expected to

see a grunt's dutiful face loom up from the ground and demand
to know his business. But nothing happened. He crunched out his
tenth Players into the overflowing ashtray—he justified smoking while driving as a necessary stimulant to keep alert—and
quietly opened the door. As he got out, he sensed a movement
behind him, and in an instant, he staggered backward as a strong
arm put a chokehold around his neck, the grip so tight that he
could only faintly stutter the answer to the man's demand.

'Name and ID, please, mate.'

With his free hand, Corporal Liam Watts passed Craw's official laissez-passer papers to Private John King for a quick perusal, and only after King had given an approving nod did Watts
release his tight hold around Craw's thin neck. Craw quickly
put his hand to his chin and slowly moved his palm down to his
prominent Adam's apple in an effort to smooth out any new
wrinkles created by what he considered excessive manhandling.

'Steady on, old chap,' said Craw.

'Just doing our job, sir,' said Corporal Watts.

Watts and King watched Craw as he stood under the
shallow porch of the cottage. Craw saw no bellpull, so he
knocked—loud enough, he thought, to wake up the slumbering
household. No lights had been put on to indicate any welcome.
But the front door opened suddenly. They heard some human
barking noises, and the door was slammed shut again. King,
a sports car aficionado, approached the Aston Martin Vantage
DB7 to look it over. Watts let out a low whistle and signaled
the resumption of their duties by slinging the C8 carbine over
his shoulder and disappearing behind the cottage.

***

Craw briefed Vaux at breakfast, a special all-English
production by the gaunt cook, a former corporal with the

Army Catering Corps. He was assisted that morning by Mrs. Parkinson, the officially vetted housekeeper from Shefford, who was called for kitchen duty only when the cottage was let out to guests.

'Make the most of it, Vaux,' Craw said as he speared another rasher of Wiltshire bacon. 'We won't be getting any good British fare for some time.'

'I guess not,' said Vaux.

'Never mind. It'll be like old times. You must be used to Mideast cuisine by now, eh?'

Vaux didn't reply. He found Craw's early-morning bonhomie hard to digest, especially in light of the nebulous assignment they were both about to take on together. He would have preferred to act alone. Craw would be an irritating companion at best, a meddlesome colleague at worst. Even gruff old Tripp would have added some dry wit to what could turn out to be another fiasco, nurtured by the ever-fertile minds of Sir Nigel Adair and Alan Craw, his deputy.

***

They boarded a solitary C-17 Globemaster military transport whose high-pitched jets ruled out any verbal communications as the two men strapped on their safety belts. They sat in individual seats that backed up to the pilot's cabin. Vaux noticed there were two pilots and a third man Craw had described as a loadmaster. He sat at the rear of the long, cavernous aircraft, headset clamped on over his blue beret, making brief comments to the ground crew and the pilots.

After a noisy, vibrating takeoff from the Chixham airfield, the loadmaster, a tall young man with rosy cheeks, came over and kneeled down to talk to the firmly strapped-in diplomats, who, he had been told, were being sent to fill sudden vacancies

at a couple of British embassies in the Middle East. He had to
shout to make himself heard. 'This is a Boeing-made military
transport aircraft. We will be flying at about 450 miles per
hour, or 720 kilometers an hour, at some 45,000 feet. Our
flight plan will take us over Paris, then south down the east
coast of the Italian boot, then east to Athens, and southeast
over Cyprus and on to Beirut, with an ETA of 9:00 p.m., local
time. The payload of this baby is 170,900 pounds, or 775,000
kilograms, so we're not, by any means, overloaded!' Craw
gave the man a warm smile. He appreciated a touch of humor
in stressed situations. Vaux had earlier observed that, apart
from himself and Craw, the plane carried just three large alu-
minum crates for appropriate cover—marked UNHCR, the
busy, often overwhelmed Mideast refugee agency. It was impossible to sleep. The noise and vibrations of the engines the
hard, spartan seats assigned to them, created a sort of purgato-
ry for Vaux. Now he wondered why and how he had again got
so entangled and enmeshed in the messy machinations of the
British Secret Service. Above all, why he had been chosen for
this latest exercise—which by past experience, would almost
certainly end in another disaster. He didn't know what it was
about the Middle East, but his love and affection for the people
and the area had always seemed doomed. It was as though,
in the final analysis, they shunned him. Perhaps the Arabs had
simply had too many unrewarding experiences with the West;
there had been historic betrayals (post-1918 and later the birth
of Israel, at which the West acted as midwife) and the steadfast
Anglo-American support of military strongmen and absolute
monarchs.

   But then there was Alena, perhaps the love of his life. Her
decision to come back was surely based on her love for him.
Those blissful days in Geneva (like wine, some of life's experiences improve with time) and later in Damascus had forged

an unassailable bond between them. She had now decided she couldn't let him slip away, out of her life. But had their relationship also been tainted? Was she so powerless to prevent the tragedy of Ahmed's final reckoning? Ahmed had been the great exception in his experience with the Arabs. They had both defied officialdom's mistrust and cynicism. They had both unconditionally embraced and revived their long-ago friendship. Now, suddenly, he had a flashback: Ahmed at the poolside in Tangier, happy and expansive in the company of his long-lost college friend; his beautiful niece Safa offering drinks from a silver tray, then challenging him to a few laps in the pool.

To shake off this sudden bout of melancholy, he tried to read. And between the complex but compelling chapters of a Javier Marias spy novel, he managed to drift away, only to feel a sharp nudge in the ribs as Craw made some remark about Operation Rescue, the plan to turn Operation Saladin from almost certain failure to ultimate success.

***

Just days earlier, Tahiyya al-Sharqawi told her lover and GSD boss, Abdul Fatah Mamluk, that she had planned one of her intermittent breaks from the general routine—a few days' rest in a health resort on the Lebanese coast. Mamluk was acquiescent. He knew her determination to shed a few pounds would only make her even more sexually alluring. And he realized that, like many Syrians, she enjoyed the decadent luxury of a Westernized beachfront resort where she could be anonymous and free from the inhibitions of Syrian society.

'How long?' Mamluk asked, feigning disapproval.

'Just five days or so, my darling. You can use the time to be kind to your wife. I get the sense that she feels rather left out of your social life these days,' said Tahiyya.

'Nonsense. She loves her nest, and she's a dutiful mother. All she wants from me is a home and the necessities for bringing up the children.'

'It will do us good to be apart for a while,' she said wistfully.

'Why? Are you getting bored with me?' asked Mamluk, who was simply following their usual predeparture script.

'Never, my dearest. You need never worry on that score.'

But a tinge of doubt entered Mamluk's thoughts. Tahiyya had never shown the sort of female subservience his colleagues expected of a clandestine lover. But perhaps that was why he loved her.

***

The Boeing C-17 Globemaster had landed in a remote corner of Beirut International Airport. Vaux and Craw, stiff and sore after a four-hour flight, clambered down the high mobile stairway to be met by a man in a shabby, ill-fitting suit who shook their hands and beckoned them to a waiting jeep.

No words were spoken. The noise of the aircraft taxiing to a distant hangar to offload the three UNHCR crates made any attempt at verbal communication impossible. The driver flashed a piece of paper to a sentry at an exit three miles or so away from the main terminal, and they were at last on a conventional highway.

The Lebanese driver offered Craw, who sat beside him, a cigarette, which he declined. Vaux accepted the proffered Camel and tried to lie back and relax in the backseat.

'My name is Jamil, sirs,' said the driver in painful English.

Craw replied, 'How do you do.'

'I am instructed to take you to a town called Juniyah. It's on the coast, about sixteen kilometers north. We'll be there shortly, sirs.'

Craw turned around to look at Vaux, who was trying to make out the scenery in the dusk that had descended soon after landing. He looked at Craw and shrugged.

Vaux knew that Craw was anxious to ask about their accommodations—always his first thought when on some dubious assignment. True to form, he heard Craw ask the driver whether their destination was a hotel or some other hostelry.

'I take you to apartment, sirs. Very nice and comfy. My mother-in-law's. She is away, and I told to put you both gentlemen up in this place. All hot and cold, fridge, and all mod cons, et cetera. You will like. No name, no pack drill, my boss says. Just for tonight.'

Craw didn't like the sound of it one bit. He turned again to Vaux with raised eyebrows.

'I've slept in worse places,' said Vaux. 'Let's give it a try.'

Craw gave a reluctant nod. 'We can't go anywhere else, anyway. Our contact wouldn't know where to find us.'

'Exactly,' said Vaux, his heavy eyes finally shutting as the jeep sped northward on the coastal road that threaded between the Mediterranean and the high wooded hills of the Lebanese littoral.

23

Vaux sat on a hard box at a rickety wooden table in a dilapidated beach hut perched near the coastal road that ran along the
small seaside town of Jablah, about forty miles south of Latakia,
Syria's main Mediterranean port. Opposite him, clad in a black
abaya, Rawya Said, wife and widow of Dr. Nessim Said, sat
on what looked like an old colonial camp chair with wooden
armrests and a canvas seat. Vaux, who wore khaki chinos and a
dark-blue shirt, peered into Rawya's deep-brown eyes, visible
through the slit in the niqab that covered her face. Her delicate
white hands shook slightly as she held several sheets of type-
written paper in front of her.

She said, 'I don't speak too good English, so I will be brief,
Mr. Horner.'

'Please take your time, madame. My French is passable, if
you would prefer to—'

'No, no. Is all right.' She looked at the papers again, shuf-
fling them as she prepared to speak. 'My beloved husband

thought very highly of you, Mr. Horner. He said in one of his brief messages that you were the sort of Englishman he found *sympatico*. He implied he hadn't met too many with this attribute. Anyway, he trusted you to be a man of honor, and that is why, in this matter, I asked for you and nobody else.'

Vaux was embarrassed by the compliment. Here he was, under a code name and having all along posed as one Justin Horner, a semiretired journalist, in all his dealings with the Syrian nuclear scientist. Once again, he was to feel the inevitable dishonor casually imposed on all players in the game of espionage.

'Please continue, madame.'

She looked up into his eyes and then beyond him through the open latticed door to the deserted beach. Her two daughters, Didi and Abal, were running around on the dry sand, playing some sort of game only they knew the rules to. Sitting on a canvas deck chair under a big parasol was Craw, their temporary guardian, in a straw panama and white tropical suit. His silk Oxford college tie testified to his refusal to bow to the local climate. It was late November, but the temperature stood at thirty degrees centigrade in the still, humid air. Craw occasionally turned his head toward the hut and then looked out to sea where fishing smacks, like the one that had brought them up the coast from Juniyah, plied the coastal waters for red snapper and sea bass.

'Well, I don't know what you were really expecting. Of course, I do not possess the papers that my husband considered his treasure trove—the information the British wanted about his work for the Syrian government. But I can tell you where you can find many of his papers. Please take a look.'

She pushed a rather tattered postcard toward Vaux. On one side a picture of towering Big Ben. On the other, a few spidery scrawls about how Said was enjoying London. In the last paragraph, he wrote:

> *Tomorrow, I shall visit the school at which my old English friend taught. It's in the lovely town of Taunton, and it is named after one of the Christian Saints.*

> *Your loving husband,*
> *Nessim*

Vaux read and reread Said's note. His immediate thought was that none of it meant much. But he knew there was more to come.

'We wrote in our own code, Mr. Horner. It means that he has somehow stashed what he called his "freedom dossier" in a school named after a saint in this English town that I know nothing about.'

'It was a fallback plan,' suggested Vaux.

'I don't understand. My English is not good, Mr. Horner. But I know that Nessim must be rejoicing in heaven for what I have done and in the knowledge that I have met his favorite Englishman, who will avenge his brutal murder by learning the deadly secrets of our country's military ambitions.'

Vaux looked down at the table, picked up the postcard. 'Your English is much better than you admit to, madame. Thank you for doing this, and thanks to your good husband for what he has done. We appreciate this, and we wish somehow to reward you for all your efforts. Can we, for instance, work on getting your girls over to the UK for their further education? The Syrian government has permitted some citizens to come to us for their higher education, you know. I even had a great friend who was a Syrian. We met up at Bristol University.'

She looked surprised. 'No, no. I think God has spoken. We do not want anything more to do with ideas like that, Mr.

Horner. In honor of my dear husband, I have decided to live out my life in Syria, and my hope is that my daughters will stay with me.'

'If that is your decision, I will respect it,' said Vaux.

They got up together, and somehow, by intuition or accident, an old man suddenly appeared in the doorway. He wore a long brown woolen djellaba and a white turban.

'This is the man who helped me to come here. We now have to return to Hamah, where I am staying with my sister. It's not so far. We should be there by this evening.'

They left. The old man called to the girls, and they quickly ran over to them. Behind the beach house, a gaunt donkey nibbled at some sparse grass on the side of the road. The slight animal was attached to a cart just big enough for four passengers and the driver. The old man lightly touched the donkey with a long whip and shouted, ' *Yallah*! Let's go!' Vaux waved good-bye and smiled in an effort to hide his affection for the ordinary, innocent people caught up in this intricate web of deceit and cunning spun by the masters and the players in his murky universe. He suppressed a sob, a cry for the innocents. Then he saw Craw, hat in hand, beckon him to the waiting taxi that would take them back to the marina.

***

Tahiyya al-Sharqawi lay on her ample stomach on a white slab of marble. Leaning over her, pummeling her Rubenesque buttocks and thick thighs, was a slim, young Syrian masseur in long white pants and bared torso. She sighed and gave out appreciative moans as his skilful hands and fists moved hard and rhythmically up and down her fleshy body.

Vaux and Craw looked on with wonder. Fifteen minutes earlier, they had disembarked from the 45 ft. motorized fishing craft that had taken them about 45 kilometers north to Jablah in Syria, relieved to get back to terra firma and 'neutral' Lebanon. The sea had been choppy, and Mohammed, the captain of the three-man crew, explained that the waters were calmer farther out from the coast, but he had been ordered to stay close to the shore.

Craw had asked why.

'The Israelis, mister. They lay claim to our outer waters. They fire bullets into the sea to warn us off.'

Craw looked at Vaux to invite comment. 'Looks like they dominate the water as well as the air in these parts,' said Vaux.

Craw was impatient to disembark, partly because he had inadvertently brushed against some fishy-smelling packing cases that contained several big snappers and piles of a local small mullet-type fish called Sultan Ibrahim. As they deftly negotiated the short gangway, Craw brushed off his suit, as if to disperse the fish odor. Then a smiling Mohammed caught them up on the quayside to present Craw with a big sea bass wrapped in newspaper. Craw looked aghast, so Vaux grabbed the gift and showed the captain his appreciation with quickly delivered thanks.

'*Chukran*, *chukran*, my friend. Our blessings be upon you.'

The old man smiled. It had, after all, been a profitable day. For a quick one-day return trip to a small coastal village in Syria, he had been paid $1,000, equal to two months' regular income that had to be shared with the two crewmen.

The two men, still dazzled by the sight of this naked lady enjoying the pleasures of what Craw later called a 'sensual Lebanese massage,' responded to a series of questions, which she delivered amid the punctuations of blows to her flesh and her verbal moans and protests at the pain she had to endure.

'Well, I'm glad everything went off all right, gentlemen. I take it you will be able to decrypt Dr. Said's clever codes?'

Craw gave a cautionary nod toward the masseur.

'Don't worry. Kamal doesn't speak or understand a word of English,' Tahiyya said dismissively. Her words were punctuated by loud cries of protest as Kamal mercilessly pummeled her thick thighs. 'Well? I asked if you had understood her instructions as to the whereabouts of you know what.'

'Oh, yes, ma'am. Everything is clear and understood,' said Craw, who seemed to Vaux to grow more obsequious with every blow and punch to the woman's body.

Craw continued. 'I'm an expert on England's private schools, you see, having sent two of my orphaned nieces to what I considered the best in the country. The school to which our Dr. Said referred is undoubtedly St. George's, a prestigious private girls' boarding school in the heart of Taunton in Somerset. I know it well.'

Vaux had been told this information in the taxi coming over to the Hotel Acropolis from their seedy apartment overlooking the rail tracks. It was the first time he'd heard anything about Craw's orphaned nieces, but he didn't doubt that Craw was correct in his decrypt. It was the sort of useless knowledge a man like Craw would accumulate through life.

When they had said their good-byes, they followed the taciturn masseur's gestures to indicate the location of the lobby bar.

'Thank God this is Lebanon. I feel like a big scotch,' said Vaux.

'You do realize, don't you, dear boy, that that was the great "Gertrude", perhaps our strongest and biggest asset in this part of the world? I promised to ship over that bloody big sea bass to the hotel chef as soon as we get back to our hovel. Thank God, only one more night in that slum.'

'Yes, I did realize that we were speaking to Gerty, as some of the old hands call her,' said Vaux.

'And that bit about hiring the donkey cart for the family rather than a taxi or hire car was classic tradecraft,' Craw said enthusiastically.

They took their drinks to a table that overlooked a big swimming pool, now empty of water.

'How do you mean?' asked Vaux.

'Well, clearly a car is often stopped for identification in Syria—after all, it's a police state. Who's going to be suspicious of a few peasants trotting to market, eh?'

Vaux got up and asked for another Cutty Sark.

24

It was a crisp mid-December day, and Sir Nigel Adair, chief of B3, the sub-subsection of MI6's Near and Middle East desk, got to work early. Today promised to be one of the most glorious in the annals of his small subgroup, whose remit had always been to exercise its unique talents in the successful completion of what MI6's director general, Sir John Blakeley, called 'special situations.' So-called because Sir John had subscribed for years to a stock market sheet that, according to the advertising copy, always 'zeroed in' on unique 'special situation stocks' whose prices promised to shoot up like a rocket once the inattentive general investing public had caught on to their attractions. He liked the phrase, and impressed upon all who worked for Sir Nigel at B3 that their duty lay not in the general routines and deskwork of intelligence, but in the fast, efficient completion of espionage coups—such as the odd defection or the deft filching of unfriendly States' secrets—that would stand out as big successes when enough time had elapsed to broadcast such victories to the skeptical politicians and the cynical public.

Anne, who was always first to appear in the cramped office suite on Gower Street, cleared Sir Nigel's desk and then put the kettle on in the small storeroom to make her standard pot of instant coffee. She wore a pale-blue sheath dress that emphasized her attractive knees and slim figure. Her hair—a golden, straw blonde—hung down to her narrow shoulders. She knew that Vaux was due for an appearance, along with Craw, her immediate boss.

The two agents arrived at about 9:30 a.m., accompanied by two men from Special Branch. Vaux was still the subject of what Sir Nigel apologetically called 'protective guardianship,' and as soon as he had been debriefed, he would be transported back to the safe confines of the Chixham intelligence base.

Vaux slipped into the storeroom after a visit to the cramped toilet and pecked Anne on the cheek. She feigned embarrassment, but a smile curled her lips. She said she was happy to see him return safe and sound. But Vaux's gesture was that of a colleague and betrayed a fondness for the girl, nothing more. He had dreamed too much of Alena's return now and the promise of a renewed romance.

Craw opened the door of the storeroom and told Vaux to get a move on. Sir Nigel was waiting.

***

Chris Greene left Chixham soon after Vaux's quick departure with Craw to Beirut. He drove his MG south on the A6 to join the M1 at Hitchin. He wanted to catch up on any mail and enjoy his Chalk Farm flat for a few days. He also knew that if Alena had been trying to contact him, she would have left some harmless messages to hint that they had to talk about her 'plan of return.' Since their conversation in the pub on Hampstead

Heath and her later meeting with Vaux, they had not been able to contact each other.

The flat smelled damp. It was a second-floor conversion of an old Victorian terrace, and he could also detect the odor of the strong Indian curry the neighbor on the ground floor seemed to be addicted to. His phone rang within five minutes of his arrival.

'Chris! Thank God.' It was Alena.

'Is this telepathy, or suspicious as I always am, have you got someone watching my flat?'

'Let's not get into that,' said Alena. She sounded lighthearted and happy to talk to him again.

Greene's heart pumped a little faster; he even felt his sex stir as blood flowed to the part of the body that responds to erotic thoughts and images—even to a voice that embodies the object of that allurement.

'We must meet, Chris,' she said. 'I want to know so much. Have you broached the subject with anyone yet?'

'I don't think we should talk now. Are you free for a late lunch?'

'Where?'

'The pub on Hampstead Heath, where we met before.'

'Time?'

'Two o'clock?'

'Done. Bye.'

***

'This is quite remarkable,' said Sir Nigel.

Earlier, he had scanned the hundred A4 typewritten pages outlining Syria's order of battle in any future war with Israel, its military shopping lists, plans to press ahead with the development of nuclear power and nuclear weapons at Ebla, and voluminous minutiae about preparations for talks with Russia about the revamping of Syria's depleted air force. The documents also revealed Syria's almost chronic dependence on Russia—a longtime ally since Soviet times—for financing these major strategic programs.

'Quite remarkable,' repeated Sir Nigel. He looked up at the two men opposite him, took off his horn-rimmed glasses, and smiled. 'Which one of you two gentlemen will tell me, very, very briefly, how all this came about in the wake of the failure of our previous efforts? Or, in other words, how we managed to transform Operation Saladin into a very notable success from the ashes of outright failure?'

In an uncharacteristically generous gesture, Craw gave the nod to Vaux. 'Let's wrap this thing up, Vaux. You're less long-winded than me,' said Craw.

'Well, sir, Alan must take full credit for locating the school where the dossier had been in safekeeping—'

'Tell me about the school, how you went about retrieving the dossier,' said Sir Nigel.

Vaux related the trip to the small Syrian fishing village, with its sandy beach and the row of derelict beach huts; the meeting with Said's widow; the cover and security organized by "Gertrude" ; and the key postcard that had given them the lead to the school in Taunton.

'Yes,' said a fascinated Sir Nigel. 'But how did you get the bloody file out of the headmistress's safe and secure hands?'

'I told her—a Ms. Patricia Ballantyne, BA, (Oxon.)—that it was in the urgent interests of queen and country that we should have immediate access,' said Vaux. 'She seemed to have been under the impression that it was Said's last will and testament. He had told her that if anything should happen to him, she should call a solicitor to handle the papers.'

'Fat lot of good that would have done, under the circumstances,' said Sir Nigel.

'I suppose his thinking was that a sharp lawyer would sense the importance of the dossier and quickly hand it over to the Security Service,' suggested Craw.

'Well, Vaux, you handled it beautifully. I congratulate you both. And I'm sorry, Craw, that we couldn't send you to Beirut on British Airways, first class.'

That was the nearest Sir Nigel came to any sardonic comment about Craw's habitual grumbling and complaints in the wake of an uncomfortable and slightly hazardous assignment.

Sir Nigel resumed. 'Of course, nothing would have been possible without the help, assistance, and planning by "Gertrude". Revealing her identity, I need hardly remind you, would be regarded as a capital crime. And I ain't joking.'

'She was marvelous,' said Craw. 'She even got my seersucker suit cleaned at her hotel overnight. It smelled to high heaven, but now it's as good as new.'

Sir Nigel had always considered Gerty an ace in the hole. It wasn't so much her position in the highest echelons of Syria's General Security Directorate. It was the feeling of sweet revenge—for the GSD's outright devilry and audacity in placing a mole otherwise known as Alena Hussein right in the center of B3's operation.

'Well then, all's well that ends well,' said Sir Nigel.

Craw got up quickly and headed for his office. He smiled at Anne, who raised her sapphire-blue eyes from the computer monitor to briefly acknowledge the friendly gesture.

Sir Nigel called Vaux back and closed his door. 'One last thing, Vaux. SIGINT traffic indicates that the hunt for you is intensifying. Make no mistake, these GSD thugs want you taken out. So don't start relaxing your guard. You'll be safe at

Chixham, but until we can chase these bastards down, you'll unfortunately have to stay there. Understood?'

***

Chris Greene was hovering in the corridor outside Sir Nigel's sanctum. As Vaux left, he nodded to him and beckoned him toward the storage room. Two sturdy Special Branch officers were waiting in the foyer to escort Vaux back to the Chixham base.

Vaux gently closed the door. 'Are you coming with me this time?' he asked.

'Yes, of course. I'll be in the convoy, two car lengths behind you in the limo. The army Land Rover will lead the way,' said Greene. 'But that's not what I want to talk to you about, Michael.'

Vaux leaned back on a metal filing cabinet. 'What's on your mind?'

'Alena, my friend. Alena. She wants some resolution to her dilemma, if you will. She's talked to you about her deal—her wish to return to the fold, with no recriminations, no legal charges, in return for a full and comprehensive debriefing on GSD's operations in the UK and in Europe. She's offering names of undercover agents, locations of safe houses, codes—the lot. I thought she spoke to you about it.'

'Of course she did. But I've been somewhat preoccupied of late.'

'Yes, of course, old boy. Just quickly, what can we do for her? Her time is limited too.'

Vaux had always known that Greene was in love with Alena, ever since those far-off days in Geneva. It was clear then, only to be confirmed when Greene had tearfully broken the news of Alena's 'elimination' in that corner pub off the Gower Street offices. So now he was playing her advocate. But he also knew that he himself was desperate to get her back, and in the wake of Operation Saladin's success, about which she knew nothing, he now realized it was time to act.

An idea flashed through his mind. It made a lot of sense, and perhaps it would give her the leverage she needed to persuade the top brass at MI6 to agree to her penitent return to a private life.

'Look, get her to give you the identity of the thugs who are apparently trying desperately to hunt me down. If she can do that—and I can't see why not—it would convince even the most skeptical of our superiors that she's genuinely sincere. She's high up enough within the GSD to have access to those names and presumably even the location of the would-be assassins.'

Greene's reaction was one of shock mingled with a distant hope. 'That's a brilliant idea, Vaux. It would call her bluff—if she is bluffing, which I don't buy at this point.'

'We shall see. I'm going to be cooped up for the foreseeable future. You will have more freedom of movement.'

'But I'm to stay with you like a long-lost friend.'

'Yes, but you're not on their hit list. You're reasonably mobile. You can have the odd pint at the odd pub. I gather she's in contact, so go to it,' said Vaux.

***

Vaux looked through the narrow sash window of his bedroom at the small cottage inside the Chixham base. It was a clear night, and he could see the gazebo-shaped guardhouse in the distance, lit up by the powerful fluorescent streetlamps that bathed the area with a yellow glow. Car headlights shimmered through the long stand of leylandii

that, along with the twelve-foot high barbed wire barrier,
shielded the compound from curious sightseers. As his gaze
swept around the base, he could also see the dim lights
through the small windows of the officers' mess that dotted
the east wing of the old priory. Once again, Alena came into
his thoughts. Could she, after all they had been through,
provide the key to his liberation from this hellhole? What a
neat resolution to the problems they both faced.

***

Just below his window, Corporal Liam Watts was enjoying
the slight high his own rolled, stringy cigarette gave him on this
quiet, cold night. He reached for his flask in the inside pocket
of his camouflaged fatigues and mumbled a toast to himself as
he took a swig of the vodka. 'Thank God,' he said, almost audibly, 'this is the last night of guard duty.' He and Private John
King were to be replaced by two (King had heard three) Special
Forces personnel. That, he told himself, was what they should
be doing. It wasn't the job of Logistics Corps wallahs to do this
sort of top security stuff.

He took another swig, but as he lowered the flask, he felt
a sudden chokehold around his neck, a stinging sensation, as
something sharp dug deeper and deeper. He gasped for breath
and tried to push away from his assailant's tight grip but he
couldn't move and the sudden dizziness came almost as a bless-
ing. Just before he blacked out, he knew he had been garroted.

The two men rolled his body close to the brick wall of
the house. Five minutes earlier, Private John King's head had
been quietly crushed from behind by a heavy metal cosh. He
never had time to wonder what had hit him. The man known as
Khaldun used his trainer-clad foot to push King's body under
a big rosebush at the side of the cottage. Khaldun looked at

Baitar and gave a thumbs-up. Their first task had been successfully completed.

They hauled a heavy backpack up from under the privet
hedge that bordered the gravel path that lead to the front door
of the cottage. They synchronized their watches; it was just
3:00 a.m.

***

Vaux had slept his habitual three hours before waking up.
He usually tried to get straight back to sleep, but after a few
days at Chixham, he'd had more rest than he needed. So he had
got up and approached the window. Nothing stirred except a
sudden squawky outcry from an indignant duck in the small
pond that glistened in the moonlight. He looked for any signs
of human activity. It had always been reassuring to see either
one of the two night sentries walking casually with their C8
carbines slung over their shoulders.

He said out loud to nobody, 'All quiet on the Western front.'

Then it happened. A loud crashing noise, splintered glass,
shouts, bursts of semiautomatic firing, and the whine of bullets
as they ricocheted between the narrow walls. Tripp's curses and
yells sounded more like the roar of a lion whose sleep had been
disturbed. Doors were banging. More loud clatter and cries.
Vaux quickly grabbed his old army Webley .38 from the drawer
of the bedside table. He broke open the gun to check if the cyl-
inder was full. There were six rounds. His first instinct was to
open his door and rush into the melee. Then he heard a light tap
and the lowered voice of Lieutenant Samuel Fox.

'Let me in, Vaux.'

Vaux opened the door. Fox slipped in. He carried a walkie-
talkie and quickly told Vaux help was on its way.

'What's happening?' asked Vaux.

'Two men broke down the front door and came in firing their AK-47s like madmen. Tripp and Sergeant Murdoch have got them pinned down in the front dining room. Luckily, Tripp was actually still up, having a coffee or something in the kitchen. So the invaders, whoever they are, didn't have the full advantage of surprise as much as they had planned.'

'This is hardly the time for a postmortem, Fox. What can we do now?'

'I'm to guide you down to the cellar.'

'What the hell for?'

'There are tunnels that lead directly to the priory. These bastards have no idea that we've an escape route. So let's go.'

'Where's Greene?'

'By a stroke of pure luck, he left late last night for a quick trip to London.'

Vaux followed Fox slowly down the staircase. Tripp, arms around an SA-80 assault rifle with a 30-round magazine, was crouched behind the wall of the dining room. The door was shut. When he saw Vaux, he gave his usual sardonic smile.

'They're well and truly pinned down, sir. Lucky I was up, otherwise they could have got to you. Now, please follow Lieutenant Fox's instructions.'

'I'm not completely useless, Tripp. Why do you want me to abandon ship?'

'Just go,' said Tripp. 'Our job's to protect you. Now, please follow Fox.'

Fox, a Browning 9mm in hand, pushed Vaux forward to the kitchen and then down the lower stairs. In the center of the dank cellar, a heavy round stone had been slid to the side to expose a large manhole. Vaux could see steps had been carved in the ancient brickwork that led down to the tunnel. Fox pushed him forward again. Vaux began his descent. After a drop of about nine feet, he came to a dark tunnel. Fox urged him on.

'It leads straight to the priory, old man. Let's go.'

***

In the besieged dining room, Khaldun and Baitar agreed that the only way to save the situation and locate and kill their target was to blast their way out of the one exit they had. The leaded windows were barred on the outside. To rush the door, all arms blazing, was risky and desperate but better than the alternative of sure death or arrest. Their companion, who had slipped into the cottage after they had axed down the door, advised them that to shoot their way out of the room and face a spray of bullets was suicide. But they ignored her cautionary advice. They rushed the door, blasting everything and everybody in sight. When Tripp saw the barrel of Khaldun's gun pointing directly at him, he knew he had only a nanosecond to react.

But then he saw the slightly-built masked gunman fire what looked like a Colt .45 directly at the man who had him in his crosshairs. Hit directly in the chest, the gunman fell to the ground and Tripp swung around to see Vaux coming from the kitchen. Vaux pumped his old Webley in a rapid volley of bullets through the gaping hole of what was left of the door as Tripp's steady fusillade riddled the two remaining terrorists from head to kneecap. Almost simultaneously, Sergeant Murdoch, kneeling beside Tripp, aimed his short-barreled C8 at the gunman he had seen kill his fellow assailant. It was an unnecessary coup de grâce, but what difference did it make? They were all legitimate terrorist targets.

25

Vaux sipped a large Cutty Sark from a crystal glass tumbler while he watched Chris Greene kneel down in front of the hotel's minibar and choose a drink. They were alone together for the first time since what Sir Nigel Adair had labeled the 'grand denouement.' Vaux still had no fixed abode, so he had been quickly transported back to the Hotel Monet in Swiss Cottage, where Department B3 had a permanent safe house on the top floor known as the Penthouse. Greene had driven over from his flat in Chalk Farm, a short journey since both districts were located in the gray confines of the north London suburbs.

Vaux nursed the feeling that he hadn't been told the full story of the bloody and brutal incident that had killed two terrorists as well as their alleged co-conspirator, Alena Hussein, and had lightly injured Staff Sergeant Murdoch. He told himself that he could be wrong, but his theory was that his previous and known romantic relationship with Alena could have persuaded

Sir Nigel and his colleagues to clam up about some of the key details of the disaster.

To them, of course, it was no disaster. It was a triumphant climax to the six-week-long pursuit of two elusive Syrian terrorists who were bent on killing Vaux. That Alena Hussein was on scene for the final shoot-out appeared to be fortuitous (again, Sir Nigel's interpretation), and it was officially acknowledged as regrettable that she wasn't still alive and thus available for the questioning and probing that could have shined more light on the devious antics of Syria's troublesome General Security Directorate and—even more important— the activities of its sister terrorist outfit, al-Saiqa.

Greene sat down in the big leather armchair. Vaux sat at the small writing desk, as if he were preparing to take notes.

'So, Michael, what can I help you with? You said you had some questions for me.' Greene feared Vaux might want to let off steam about Greene's efforts to help Alena and for his transparent adoration of the woman. But he was wrong.

'Look, I know there was a full-scale inquiry about the firefight at Chixham, and I know my name must have come up many, many times, not to mention Alena's and yours. It's just that I've been treated like an idiot—as they used to say in the army, like a mushroom kept in the dark and fed shit.'

'I can only tell you what I learned through Craw. We had a few pints the other night, and he told me a lot more, added some color, if you like.'

'I do like. For instance, why was Alena killed? Why was she even there?'

'I'm as devastated as you about what happened to her, Michael. If you want to know the truth, I had an incurable crush on that woman—but I knew I'd never get anywhere with you in the background. She truly seemed to love you, and I know that you were the reason she wanted to come back.'

Vaux emptied his glass and got up to pour a refill. 'Go on,' he said.

'As to why she was there, nobody knows. She deliberately shot the guy who was about to fire several rounds into old Tripp. Tripp confirmed that himself. Perhaps she even saved the day—his day, anyway.'

Vaux said, 'So my theory is that she was genuine in her desire to return to our side and to me. Perhaps she went along with their plans so that she could sabotage the operation, kill the assailants, and as a by-product, save me. In other words, she figured there would be no surer entry permit to get back to the UK and to the good graces of MI6 than to assassinate the assassins.'

'It's a theory I can't argue against. You're probably right. And she didn't know that you could have fled through the tunnel.'

'I couldn't do that. I was so bloody angry that all this mayhem had come about because the Syrians really believed I killed Said. I was condemned without a trial, without any attempt on their part to analyze the situation or the circumstances of the poor guy's death. I was so mad I just couldn't go through that tunnel to save my own skin. Tripp said I must have been suicidal, and he was angry as hell because I defied his orders. He got his revenge by telling me later that my bullets had smashed a few pieces of furniture and a glass cabinet, but my presence was more hindrance than help. But that's Tripp. Even so, I'm glad I did what I did, if only it was to vent my anger at the whole bloody situation.'

Greene said, 'Those tunnels were built in the sixteenth century, or at about the time the Catholics were being rounded up and their property confiscated by dear old Henry. There were several that spread out beyond the priory to inns and cottages in the nearby village as well as to the several other lodges within the priory grounds. You never knew you had that fail-safe means of escape, did you?'

'No, I didn't. But in the end, I couldn't just bolt to safety. After all, I had my old trusty Webley. I thought at least it would have been honorable to go out in a blaze of gunfire—appropriate too, considering the line of work.'

Greene smiled.

'What resolution or conclusion did Sir Nigel's quickie inquiry come to?' asked Vaux.

'We decided to inform the Syrian embassy of Alena's death. They acknowledged she was a GSD field officer but offered no explanation for her presence at Chixham. They agreed to ship her body back to Damascus, where she was viewed as a heroine, killed in the line of duty, and given a state funeral. The embassy here denied any knowledge of the two men and said they had never heard of al-Saiqa—it was a figment of our collective imaginations. They suggested the two terrorists were employed by Mossad and could be the same men who had killed Dr. Said. Of course, those charges were laughable, and it brought us to a dead end, in more senses than one.'

Vaux now broached perhaps the most emotional question left over from that bloody, violent night. 'And what about Murdoch? Did he say why he shot the person he'd seen shoot the chief assailant?'

'In his eyes, they were all terrorists, Michael. What difference did it make to him? Do you think he had time to debate the morality of killing the enemy of his enemy?'

'And, of course, he had no idea it was a woman,' said Vaux.

'Not the slightest. Bundled up in those camouflaged fatigues and masked by the army-issued balaclavas with slits for the eyes and mouth—are you kidding?'

'What about the gunmen slipping into the compound? I thought the place was as safe against infiltrators as Fort Knox.'

'They'd been in the village for some six weeks, and they apparently befriended a local baker who brought in supplies to the base every day. He gave them casual work, and they helped him on his early-morning rounds. Apparently, they hid in crates that should have contained dozens of large loaves—all three of them. The guards, of course, knew the van and let the familiar vehicle in with no formalities. His early-morning, pre-dusk deliveries were par for the course. They just waved the old guy in—no inspections, nothing.'

Vaux, his own private inquiry completed, now felt a deep emptiness. His hopes for a better life with Alena at his side, their shared memories, tales of classic spook hijinks exchanged on quiet evenings in their own home, had been dashed forever. There was a long silence. Greene poured himself another vodka and tonic.

'Christmas is coming, Michael. Why don't you spend it with me and my family in Shropshire? The old man's a decent sort, great host and all that. And Mother's a great cook. Turkey, stuffing—the lot. What do you say?'

Vaux loved Greene for that gesture. It was so human and so English. But he knew he wanted to be alone this Christmas. Too much had happened, a tragedy to be digested, the future to be considered.

***

Two weeks later, Vaux sat in the sunny glass conservatory at the River House. It was a wintry, cold day and the sun was pale, but the view was somehow warming. Sir Walter Mason, Sir Nigel's predecessor, had invited him to spend Christmas at his country estate in Dorset. There would be balls and parties, young and old, morning fox hunts, splendid feasts—a classic festive celebration that Sir Walter thought, from what he'd heard of Vaux's recent exploits, Vaux fully deserved.

But Vaux told his old chief the truth. He didn't feel sociable this year. It took time, he said, to put the immediate past behind him. Perhaps next year. Vaux knew the sort of people Sir Walter would play host to would simply be on another emotional planet. He'd pass, for this year.

But Sir Walter was a determined man. He was also fond of the ex-journalist whom, a decade ago, he had brought into the espionage game. So he insisted that Vaux leave the dreary Swiss Cottage hotel a few days before Christmas Eve and spend the holiday season at the River House, the country residence inherited by his wife, Sybil, from her late sister. They still hadn't sold it, and Mrs. Appleby came in on a daily basis to tidy up and dust. He would also see that she bring over a Christmas dinner, and he could enjoy all the solitude he needed and wanted.

Vaux was grateful. It was a lovely spot: the gurgling river at the bottom of the long garden, the ducks and swans elegantly cruising up and down, a happy collared dove cooing incessantly from the upper branches of the weeping willow at the river's edge.

   He had walked up to the nearby village to see if he could buy a morning paper. But the streets and the shops were deserted. It was Christmas Day. He looked at his watch. He still had an hour to go before Mrs. Appleby had said she would bring in his special, if solitary, lunch. And then there'd be the queen's speech at 3:00 p.m.

So he got up from the big chintz-covered armchair and walked over to an audio cassette player that had been placed on top of the ancient 14-inch screen TV. He inserted the cartridge Anne had given him at the small pre-Christmas office get-together. Duke Ellington and his band launched into their jazzy version of 'Lullaby of Birdland.' It was his and Ahmed's theme song, requested every Saturday night at the Students' Union dance. Now bathed in nostalgia, he sat down in a low rattan chair next to a mahogany side table, on which was neatly placed a pack of playing cards and the new brick-size Nokia mobile that had been put at his disposal. He shuffled the pack and proceeded to lay out parallel rows of cards for his morning session of solitaire. He reached for his packet of Camels, but then changed his mind. His New Year's resolution was to give up the fatal weed. Then the phone purred.

'Hello?'

'Oh, Mike? John Goodchild here.'

Vaux wondered what his old schoolmate could possibly want on a Christmas morning.

'Sorry to disturb you, but they gave me the number.'

Vaux was puzzled. 'Who gave you the number?'

'Look, mate, it doesn't matter. I called to tell you that your house is now empty. You can move in tomorrow. Needs a bit of TLC, but it's habitable.'

'What happened to the tenants?'

'They did a moonlight flit, didn't they. Owed six months' rent and decided to take off.'

Vaux thanked his old friend, and they both wished each other a happy Christmas. He put the heavy receiver back on the table.

So he could now go home. He took up the cards again and reshuffled. But before he had completed the task, he heard a loud bang at the solid-oak front door, then excited youngish voices. It was probably Mrs. Appleby with some of her family. He'd get the sherry out.

But at the door stood Anne Armitage-Hallard, rosy cheeked and clad in a fur-collared camel hair coat. Two young men, equally bundled up, were with her, and all three carried basket hampers and parcels.

'Merry Christmas, Michael!' said Anne. 'Please meet my brother Julian and his friend Robert. Can we come in?'

The question was rhetorical. Vaux felt a surge of gratitude. All was not lost. The human race was resilient. It was, then, after all, going to be a classic Christmas—even if on Anne's terms. He looked into her bright blue and happy eyes, and they told him all he wanted to know.

About the Author

Roger Croft is a former journalist whose reports and feature articles have appeared in numerous publications including *The Economist, Sunday Telegraph* and *Toronto Star*. He also worked in Egypt where he freelanced and wrote editorials for *The Egyptian Gazette*.

CPSIA information can be obtained at www.ICGtesting.com
Printed in the USA
LVOW01s1514120913

352192LV00014B/644/P